THE SKIFF TURNED TO FACE IN THEIR DIRECTION.

"Damn," La Forge hissed through gritted teeth, freezing in place as the tiny craft angled toward him. There was still a possibility that the pilot had not yet seen any movement or other indications of the away team's presence, but the chief engineer realized that as nothing more than wishful thinking as the skiff moved to within twenty meters. Its nose dipped toward the asteroid's surface, allowing the Dokaalan seated inside the ship's cockpit an unfettered examination of the rocky ground below him.

Even from twenty meters away, the pilot locked eyes with La Forge.

And he smiled.

"He's got us!" La Forge shouted, no longer making any effort to remain hidden as the skiff accelerated toward them. Bringing the phase pistol up, he moved the weapon's selector switch to Kill, its maximum power setting, sighted along the pistol's short barrel, and fired. . . .

Current books in this series:

Forthcoming books in this series:

STAR TREK®
A Time to Harvest

DAYTON WARD
&
KEVIN DILMORE

Based on
STAR TREK: THE NEXT GENERATION®
created by Gene Roddenberry

POCKET BOOKS
New York   London   Toronto   Sydney

An *Original* Publication of POCKET BOOKS

POCKET BOOKS, a division of Simon & Schuster, Inc.
1230 Avenue of the Americas, New York, NY 10020

STAR TREK is a Registered Trademark of
A VIACOM COMPANY Paramount Pictures.

This book is published by Pocket Books, a division of
Simon & Schuster, Inc., under exclusive license from
Paramount Pictures.

ISBN: 0-7434-8298-0

First Pocket Books printing May 2004

10 9 8 7 6 5 4 3 2 1

POCKET and colophon are registered trademarks of
Simon & Schuster, Inc.

Manufactured in the United States of America

For information regarding special discounts for bulk purchases,
please contact Simon & Schuster Special Sales at 1-800-456-6798
or business@simonandschuster.com

ACKNOWLEDGMENTS

Hmmmm.

It seems we thanked a whole bunch of people on the acknowledgments page of *A Time to Sow*. However, once that book was laid to rest, it dawned on us that we had committed a most critical error the first time around.

Yep, you guessed it. We forgot to mention our wives.

Whoops.

You're probably saying to yourself, "Yeah, but their wives are, like, adults. They probably couldn't care less if their names aren't mentioned in a *Star Trek* book. I think Dayton and Kevin are making a big deal out of nothing."

Think again, Naïve Reader.

So, without any further delay, we'd like to take this opportunity to thank **MICHI** and **MICHELLE,** both of whom display endless patience as their goofball husbands continue in their quest to be the oldest students never to graduate from Romper Room.

And in our own best interests, we're not thanking anyone else. Ever.

Except—and here's where you should picture that poor guy at the award shows who has to talk over the music because his colleague sucked up all the allotted air time—Kevin gives his sincere thanks to Rosy King and the staff of the Paola (Kansas) Free Library and to Gloria and Chuck Gray and the staff of the Paola McDonald's franchise for allowing him to use their respective establishments as satellite office space for the writing of portions of this novel.

Okay, that's it.

No, we really mean it this time.

Really.

Push the button, Frank.

Prologue

Translated from the personal journal of Hjatyn:

As I WRITE THIS, I wonder whether generations to come will read what I have recorded here and think they have somehow mistaken one old man's journal for a work of fiction.

On many nights while sitting alone in my library and reviewing what I have written in these pages, I marvel at the events I chronicled along with the thoughts and feelings I experienced as those extraordinary events unfolded. The fact that all of it is true, free from embellishment and requiring no such aggrandizement on my part, is what makes our story all the more astonishing.

There can be no doubting that our journey has been a remarkable one. Watching the destruction of our homeworld, Dokaal, and struggling for generations to forge an existence out here, within the artificial environs of the various mining outposts among the asteroid field, it seemed impossible that we would ever be able to achieve anything beyond simple survival. Still, we are here, having thrived splendidly despite the challenges facing us and in fact having become dissatisfied with simply living. Despite all we have accomplished, one vital thing keeps our lives from being complete: We still lack a genuine home. But in true Dokaalan fashion we have set out to make one.

The remaking of the planet Ijuuka in Dokaal's image can be described only as the singular technological feat in our history. Transforming its poisonous atmosphere into one capable of sustaining our people has required the employment of scientific and engineering principles never before imagined, not to mention the invention of the technologies, equipment, and skills necessary to complete the task. It is a project of mammoth complexity and duration, and watching our brightest minds devise and implement each stage of the project has been awe-inspiring. Though I never shared the deep spirituality of my late wife, Beeliq, I have found myself thanking Dokaa on more than one occasion for the blessings she seems to have given this mammoth effort. My only regret, one I have harbored since the transformation project began, was that I would not live long enough to see it completed.

That belief changed with the arrival of the magnificent alien vessel, the *Enterprise,* its crew representing a vast community of people from hundreds of planets not at all dissimilar to ours. Incredibly, they have come in response to a call for help issued generations ago.

As one of a shrinking number of Dokaalan alive at the time disaster struck our home planet, I remember the speech First Minister Zahanzei gave to the people where he outlined a plan to dispatch unmanned craft into space, each carrying an appeal for help. Everyone I talked to at the time considered it an outlandish scheme born of desperation and panic, with no actual chance of success. While I had always been of a mind to believe that there could be life on other planets far beyond the confines of Dokaal, I held no illusions that three tiny vessels would be able to cross the immense void of space and be found by such people, or that those same people would have the ability to help us. Still, a small part of me prayed for the first minister's plan to be successful, right up until the moment I watched my homeworld disintegrate before my eyes.

And yet, here we are, long after Zahanzei's death, with the answer to everything he prayed for all but handed to us. I wonder what he would say today if he could be here to meet those who have traveled so far in answer to his plea. My appreciation for the true size of our universe only grew as I listened to the *Enterprise* captain's account of how long it took to travel here from his home planet, despite his ship's ability to travel many times faster than the speed of light. It also goes a long way toward explaining why such a large gap of time passed between the launching of our three unmanned ships and the discovery of the first one, to say nothing of the interval that lapsed before the second probe was encountered.

Several members of the council expressed natural suspicion as to the aliens' true motives. It is apparent even from a cursory inspection of their vessel that they possess the technology and weaponry to conquer us with minimal effort, and I will admit that I had my own reservations about our guests at first. Their dark uniforms are intimidating, reminiscent of those worn by the military forces of a rival nation on Dokaal.

It is there that the similarities begin and end, however. That much was evident from the moment the ship arrived here and its crew set to work attempting to rescue mining workers and their families from a damaged outpost. Even though some people were lost in the effort, it was evident that the *Enterprise* crew's actions saved countless others. Their medical staff worked tirelessly to treat the wounded while others provided all manner of support to displaced victims until our own ships could arrive from the central habitat. In short, they are an extraordinary group of people.

Captain Picard in particular is an impressive man. While he is somewhat diminutive in stature compared with the average Dokaalan, watching him during his interactions both with me and my staff and with members of his own crew, there is no denying that he is a confident leader. His crew follows him of their own free will, not simply because they are bound by an oath or contract. Even from my two brief meetings with him I am drawn by a desire to trust this man.

It is also evident that the captain is a practiced diplomat. He has offered to help my people in a number of ways, most notably to move us to a planet where we might make a new home for ourselves. Instead of being offended at my polite refusal of his most generous offer, Picard expressed admiration at our desire to complete our formidable task of remaking Ijuuka ourselves. Honoring the millions lost with the destruction of Dokaal by completing the reformation ourselves and using the materials, tools, and skills at our disposal is a pledge our people have taken very seriously, after all.

Still wishing to help, Captain Picard already has directed specialists aboard his ship to examine our techniques and look for areas where we might improve what we are doing. He has posed the idea that his crew might be able to provide suggestions for accelerating the project's completion while still leaving the work to us. It is a notion I find most agreeable, especially since, if it is successful, I will actually get the opportunity to walk beneath a real sky and with real soil and grass under my feet, alongside nearly everyone currently laboring to make our people's collective dream a reality.

Beyond that, I am also intrigued and excited at the idea of learning more about Picard's interstellar community, his United Federation of Planets. It sounds like a wondrous ideal, with each member world adding its individual technological and artistic gifts to the greater cooperative. Perhaps one day, after we have established our new world, we will be invited to join that Federation.

The very possibility warms my heart, for I truly believe that accomplishing such a goal would be an even greater testament to Dokaalan society and the legacy we seek to honor each day.

Chapter One

ALONE IN HER OFFICE, Fleet Admiral Alynna Nechayev
relaxed in her favorite overstuffed chair and held her
mug of coffee close to her nose, allowing its aroma to
warm and tickle her nostrils. The chair was positioned so
that she could look out over San Francisco Bay, watching as the first feeble rays of sunlight began to highlight
the Golden Gate Bridge through the dense morning fog.

The coffee, along with the splendid view, was her private pleasure, one of few she allowed herself while ensconced in the surroundings of Starfleet Headquarters.
The combination of Colombian beans and Klingon *rak-
tajino* was a blend introduced to her by friend and colleague William Ross, and it had quickly become a
favored component of her morning ritual. After all, reading status reports and intelligence briefings before sun-
rise went a lot easier over a good cup of coffee.

On this day, however, Nechayev was also able to take
satisfaction from another quarter. The padd resting in her

lap and containing the latest status report from Jean-Luc Picard, sent from the Dokaalan sector and the site of the *Enterprise*'s current mission, had already proven to be the highlight of the scores of reports she was required to review. She had no doubt the report would cause much discussion during the various meetings she would be required to attend today.

The sound of her door chime interrupted her reverie. "Come," she called out, spinning her chair around in time to see her office doors parting to allow Admiral Ross himself to enter.

"Good morning, Alynna," Ross said as he stepped into the room. With his immaculately tailored Starfleet uniform, close-cut dark black hair liberally peppered with gray, and blue eyes that seemed powerful enough to bore through tritanium, the admiral presented the epitome of a Starfleet flag officer. That description went far beyond simple appearances, of course, as Nechayev knew all too well. Ross had overseen much of Starfleet's operations during the Dominion War, establishing himself as a dynamic leader and imaginative tactical commander. It could be well argued that a significant portion of the Federation's success during the war was directly attributable to William Ross.

"Hello, Bill," Nechayev replied as she rose from her chair. Crossing the room toward the replicator set into the wall to the left of her desk, she asked, "Coffee?"

Ross nodded. "Absolutely," he said as he took a chair opposite hers by the window. Holding up the padd he had brought with him, he added, "The morning briefs make for interesting reading, don't they?"

"You could say that," she replied as she moved back across the room, offering to Ross one of the two coffee mugs she carried. Settling into her own seat, she looked through the window and saw that the hills surrounding the bay were becoming visible as sunlight began to peek over the eastern horizon, signaling the start of a new day. "I'm sure the day's meetings will be just as enjoyable." She took a sip from her second mug of the morning, savoring the rich brew and knowing that her private time to truly enjoy the enticing beverage had passed. It was no more than fuel now, providing what she hoped would be enough energy to push through the numerous reports, briefings, and meetings that were part and parcel of the day-to-day life of a high-ranking Starfleet staff officer.

"Some of these new directives are a little troubling," Ross said, glancing down at his padd. "Can you believe all this? Proposals for augmenting security patrols along the Klingon and Romulan borders as well as the Bajoran sector, long-term plans for retrofitting all Starfleet vessels with heavier armaments regardless of their current mission, permanent assignment of ground-combat units to line ships." Looking up, he shook his head. "I've even heard rumors of some new kind of elite classified unit being developed to test starship and starbase security using the tactics of known enemies. That's a bit extreme, don't you think?"

"I hadn't heard that one yet," Nechayev replied, thinking to herself as she spoke the words that, on the surface, the idea did indeed seem a bit over the top. Upon further reflection, however, the admiral realized there might well be some merit in the concept worth pursuing.

Shrugging after a moment, she added, "Still, we've learned some hard lessons over the years. Mr. Azernal seems hell-bent to see that we learn from them and that we don't get caught with our pants down ever again."

In addition to his notable political skills, Koll Azernal, chief of staff to the Federation President, had garnered like many of his fellow Zakdorn a reputation as a renowned and cunning military strategist. More so than people like Ross, Benjamin Sisko, and even Nechayev herself, Azernal's tactical prowess had contributed significantly to the Federation's winning of the Dominion War. Now, in the wake of that success, Azernal was using his formidable talents along with his newfound popularity to push forward policies designed to ensure the Federation's continued protection.

His speech to the Federation Council a month previously had left no doubt as to his feelings on the matter. Citing the invasions by the Borg and the Dominion in recent years as well as other interstellar emergencies along the way, Azernal had shown no mercy in recounting how these incidents had exposed and exploited numerous weaknesses in Starfleet's ability to defend the borders and people of the Federation. In his view, drastic changes were required, and it was an opinion that appeared to be gaining support.

"You have to admit he has a point," Nechayev continued. "Maybe it *is* time we reexamined our approach to defense. We've been taking it on the chin for a long time, Bill. Some of what Azernal is proposing makes sense, when you think about it."

Sipping his coffee, Ross replied, "I'm not going to argue that we can always do better when it comes to defense." He held up his padd for emphasis. "But some of this smacks of 'too much too fast.' Even Starfleet Academy's having to jump through hoops. Admiral Brand's staff worked two nights straight putting together a proposal for expanding the Academy's combat strategies and tactics curriculum, and introducing it earlier in the cadets' training cycle. Azernal wants to increase class sizes at Command School, too, so we can put more junior officers through before they take their first assignment."

Her attention partly focused on the world beyond her window, Nechayev said, "None of that is out of line. In fact, some of it's been on the table for discussion for quite a while now." Light flickered beyond the window that formed the back wall of the office and a crack of thunder reverberated through its thick glass. She turned to see that the approaching dawn had revealed a distant squall line of gray clouds converging on the bay. Rain was about to christen the new day, it seemed. She hoped the imminent storm was not an omen that might signal a change in her mood.

Nechayev knew that getting Admiral Brand to recommend changes to the Academy's military training curriculum would not have been difficult. The Academy superintendent had proposed greater emphasis on such subjects almost from the first day she had assumed that posting and soon after the initial discovery of the Borg and the awesome threat they represented.

"There may be such a thing as going too far," Ross countered, rising from his chair and crossing to the replicator. "Azernal's paying a lot of attention to military initiatives, but what about other areas? We still have a lot of problems to solve, after all."

He had a point, Nechayev conceded. More than a year after the end of the Dominion War, rebuilding efforts were still under way on many member worlds and would require much in the way of time and resources to complete. If those concerns were ignored, the Federation risked alienating valuable allies at a time they were most needed. While Nechayev appreciated the need for a strong defense and had always advocated what she believed to be reasonable measures to assure that security, she had not joined Starfleet merely to wage war. Were the policy changes proposed by Koll Azernal too drastic?

"I imagine the Federation Council will make sure he doesn't go too far," she said. "President Zife has assured the Federation that his first priority is rebuilding and reconstruction efforts. I'm sure that when he submits his plan to the council, all the issues, civilian and military, will be addressed accordingly."

"I hope you're right," Ross said as he retrieved another cup of coffee from the replicator and moved back toward his chair. "For the first time in a while, we're at a point where we can concentrate on something besides war. I joined Starfleet to explore, after all."

As he passed her, Nechayev caught the scent of his coffee, its pleasing aroma touching off a grumbling in her stomach and reminding her that she had not yet eaten breakfast. A glance to the wall chronometer told her that she had fifteen minutes to see to that particular issue before the demands of her daily schedule began in earnest.

Ignoring her stomach for the moment, she instead said, "I take it you've reviewed Picard's report?"

Ross nodded as he sipped his coffee. "First thing." Shrugging, he added, "I needed a pick-me-up after the stuff I've been going over the last few days. His report is remarkable, to say the least."

"That there are survivors is what's remarkable," Nechayev replied, "but considering their predicament, that they're thriving the way they are is incredible."

Rather than finding the decimated remnants of a planet that had once been home to a prosperous civilization, Jean-Luc Picard and the *Enterprise* had instead found survivors of the catastrophe that had destroyed the home planet of the Dokaalan more than two centuries earlier. Having accomplished rudimentary spaceflight, the Dokaalan had established a network of mining colonies in the immense asteroid field that drifted in orbit between the fifth and sixth planets of their solar system. The colonies had provided a rich source of minerals and raw materials, extracted from the asteroids and transferred back to the homeworld.

It was that technological achievement which had also allowed thousands of Dokaalan to seek shelter among the mining colonies as their world fell victim to months of increasing tectonic stresses, uncontrollable forces that ultimately tore the planet apart. Millions of Dokaalan were lost in the disaster, leaving behind a scant fraction of the population to fend for themselves in the brutal environs of space and the asteroid field. Those people and their descendants had gone on to fashion a new way of life, one based at first on sheer survival and later augmented by fierce determination and the desire to honor those who had lost their lives so long ago.

"Their level of technology is on a par with Earth's at the time of our first permanent settlements on the moon," Ross said. "Their space vessels possess a rough equivalent to impulse drive, which at least make interplanetary journeys possible within reasonable amounts of time, but their warp-drive efforts have been almost nonexistent save for the rudimentary engines used to power the trio of unmanned probes they sent with their call for help."

Still, it was enough, she conceded. Primitive though the Dokaalan's efforts at faster-than-light travel might have been, they were still sufficient to circumvent any dissenting opinions voiced by some members of Starfleet and the Federation Council that interacting with these people was a violation of the Prime Directive. Per that very strict principle, such contact was reserved for those species who demonstrated the ability to travel at warp speeds and had therefore unlocked the potential to hurl themselves into the midst of an interstellar community they were in all likelihood ill prepared to face. So far as Nechayev was concerned, the Dokaalan certainly qualified in that regard, having met the directive's criteria in their own unique way.

"I'd like to go back two hundred years," she said, "and tell our predecessors what a mistake they made by not sending a ship out to investigate when they found that first probe."

Ross chuckled at that. "I wouldn't be too hard on them, Alynna. Times were different back then, after all."

"True enough," Nechayev conceded. "What did they have? One or two long-range ships that could travel at warp five? That, and the Vulcans second-guessing everything Starfleet did." Shaking her head, she added, "It was definitely a different time." *But an exciting one,* she amended silently.

"As for the Dokaalan, this terraforming project of theirs has a lot of people talking," Ross continued, retrieving his padd and scrolling to that portion of Picard's report. "Terraform Command is already jumping all over themselves to get a ship out there just from the information in the *Enterprise* chief engineer's preliminary report." Shaking his head, he added, "I wonder if they're excited about the possibility of learning about a new terraforming method, or just scared that someone else out there has the know-how to try it."

A rhythmic tapping sound from the window caught Nechayev's ear and she looked up to see the first raindrops smacking against the glass. The storm was definitely on the move, she decided.

"I don't think we have anything to worry about in that regard," she said. "According to Picard's report, the Dokaalan are motivated solely by survival and a desire to make a real home for themselves. Besides, it'll take generations before that planet of theirs is ready."

The rain smacking against the window was growing more insistent now, and even from her vantage point high above the ground she could see trees far below swaying as the wind picked up, and idly wondered if the weather-modification network would be required to make adjustments for the coming storm's intensity.

Interesting thought, she mused, *considering the topic of conversation.*

Placing his coffee cup on a table positioned between their chairs, Ross said, "He also said that they've declined offers not only to be relocated to another suitable planet, but even for us to assist them in their current efforts. Still, I've already spoken to Captain Scott and he tells me that as soon as we give the word he can send the *Musgrave* and its S.C.E. detachment to the Dokaalan system. They'll act as an advance team until a full contingent from Terraform Command can get out there."

Nechayev nodded at that. The Starfleet Corps of Engineers might not be the best long-term solution if the Dokaalan changed their minds and accepted the offer of Federation assistance, but she knew that Captain Montgomery Scott's department of versatile engineering and technical specialists was more than capable of filling in until a properly trained group of terraforming experts could be dispatched to the Dokaalan sector. In addition to providing assistance as quickly as possible, the presence of the *Musgrave* would be able to showcase Starfleet's vast array of talents and proficiency.

"The tough part will be convincing the Dokaalan to accept our help," she said.

"From everything Picard's included in his reports," Ross replied, "the Dokaalan are a proud and peaceful people." Nodding in approval, he added, "Still, if anyone can convince them of our desire to help them in any way we can, it's him. I trust his judgment."

It was refreshing to hear someone else say that, Nechayev realized, especially when that someone was Ross. In the weeks since the incident with the Ontailians, it almost seemed as though no one in the halls of power at Starfleet Command was willing to voice their support of Jean-Luc Picard. This despite the fact that at least a few of those same people knew the truth behind the incident and why he had taken the blame for it. Even Ross himself had offered the notion in the aftermath of that incident that perhaps the time had come for Picard to retire. He had later retracted that statement, and his comment now further illustrated his restored faith in the *Enterprise* captain.

In the admiral's defense, he originally had good reason for his original thinking. Indeed, at the outset of the affair she too had been among those with strong feelings that Picard had finally reached the point in his distinguished career where it was time to step down, at least from active starship command. Her thinking had changed after learning the details of the incident, of course, and in the days afterward she had found herself in the unfamiliar position of being Picard's ally, even his protector.

Her relationship with the renowned captain had been a strained one at times, though as the years passed she had come to appreciate the man's talents, experience, and wisdom. To this day she remembered their exchange over Picard's decision not to deploy an invasive computer program into the Borg Collective that might have destroyed the Federation's most feared enemy in one bold maneuver. To him, the attack would have been one of genocide, killing uncounted millions of individuals who were in fact helpless victims forcibly assimilated by the Borg. It was an unconscionable action in his eyes, one he had steadfastly refused to undertake.

While Nechayev still fervently believed that Picard had acted incorrectly from a military standpoint, she had come to respect what had motivated him to make that decision. For Picard, the Federation's laws and guiding principles were more than mere words. He lived his life and carried out his duties in strict adherence to those ideals. It was a position that had run him afoul of his superiors on numerous occasions, including the situation with the Ontailians and the demon ship.

Of course, none of that had prevented Picard from being caught up in the larger machinations of interstellar politics. The proverbial powder keg that was the Ontailian governmental situation was still so delicate that their secession from the Federation was a constant threat. In order to prevent Ontailian leaders from losing the trust of their people in the aftermath of the embarrassing demonship incident and perhaps causing enough internal strife that they were forced to renounce their Federation membership, Picard had instead taken responsibility for the affair. His willingness, in Nechayev's eyes at least, had done much to prove not only his loyalty to the Federation but also his absolute competence to command.

I'm sorry to be counted among those who doubted you, Captain, she thought, hoping one day that circumstances would allow her to offer that apology in person.

Listening to the melodic rhythm of the raindrops pelting her office window for a few moments, she said, "I trust him, too, though I wonder what some of his detractors will make of his report." She held up her own padd. "The trouble he ran into during that rescue mission is going to raise some eyebrows. Twenty-seven deaths, including two of his own crew." Shaking her head, she added, "It has to be weighing on him pretty heavily, I'd think, and while I know it wasn't his fault, somebody might use that as just another reason to second-guess Starfleet's decision to give him back command of the *Enterprise.*"

Ross shook his head. "They'd be picking at nits. He saved nearly four hundred victims during that rescue operation. While it's tragic that anyone was lost, it wasn't because Picard was negligent and I'd be happy to take on anyone who said otherwise."

"Something tells me that when push came to shove, you'd have plenty of company," Nechayev replied, smiling at the image their comments evoked. Rising to her feet, she added, "And with that in mind, I suppose we should be heading to the morning briefings."

Hanging his head in fine melodramatic fashion, Ross let go a heavy sigh of mock surrender. "All right, if we have to."

Nechayev chuckled as she moved to her desk to retrieve another padd, the one with her day's agenda as well as the reports she would brief other staff officers on during the morning's meeting session. It was then that her stomach provided her with another rude reminder.

Breakfast. She sighed in amused resignation. *Too late now.* Hopefully, it was not another omen for the type of day waiting for her.

Those hopes were buoyed, however, by the thought of the agitation Jean-Luc Picard's report would invoke in those people she would face on this day, specifically the ones who had voiced doubt as to the *Enterprise* captain's abilities and competence to continue as commander of the starship bearing perhaps the most storied name in Federation or even Earth history.

Good work, Picard. Damn good work. His initial report had held such promise, his simple milk-run mission having blossomed into a heartening first-contact situation and a chance to demonstrate all of those qualities that so personified why the United Federation of Planets was founded in the first place.

Alynna Nechayev wished she could be out there with Picard and the *Enterprise.* As she stepped with Ross into a turbolift on their way to their morning's worth of dreary, boring meetings, a lone question occupied her mind.

"I wonder how things are going out there?"

Chapter Two

WILL RIKER'S STOMACH LURCHED as the *Enterprise* moved around yet another large asteroid, rolling to port and allowing the massive hunk of rock to slip past.

"Sorry about that, sir," Lieutenant Kell Perim called over her shoulder from where she sat at the conn. Her fingers moved with the grace of a concert pianist's as she entered commands to her console, which were in turn translated into instructions for the ship to maneuver through the Dokaalan asteroid field. "This last stretch is going to be a little rough."

Riker almost laughed out loud at the lieutenant's comment. The Trill officer had worked at the same pace since leaving the Dokaalan central habitat for the now-crippled Mining Station Twelve. Riker wondered when she might tire—and whether that might happen before they reached their destination. For the third time in an hour, he felt compelled, pulled almost as if by tractor beam, to take the helm and fly the ship himself, but knew better than to act on that impulse. His place was the one he currently occupied—the center seat, in command of this mission, and trusting the people around him to do their jobs.

"Now you tell me." He tried to let a bit of his natural joviality lace his words, just enough to reassure Perim of his confidence in her skillful navigation through the asteroid field. Like everyone else on the ship and particularly those with a prime vantage point on the bridge, he knew that any travel through the seemingly endless expanse of tumbling asteroids drifting between them and hundreds of injured—most likely dying—Dokaalan was fraught with hazards at even the slowest speeds.

That danger was magnified as the *Enterprise* pushed forward as fast as Perim dared, responding with all due haste to a call for help sent from one of the Dokaalan mining outposts. Captain Picard had been with First Minister Hjatyn and other members of the Dokaalan leadership caste when the call came, and had dispatched the ship to respond to the outpost's plea as quickly as possible while he, Dr. Crusher, and Counselor Troi caught up to them in their shuttlecraft.

Now the lives of more than eight hundred people were hanging on the ability of Commander Riker to move the *Enterprise* through this asteroid field, and complicating the matter even more was the information that Picard had shared with him: that the explosion at the mining outpost might have been a deliberate act of sabotage. Was someone, some group of Dokaalan, trying to instill terror in the rest of the community? Were they extremists pursuing some as yet unknown agenda and hoping to extract a measure of conciliation from the

Dokaalan leadership? If so, how far were they willing to go for their cause? Was the *Enterprise* in danger?

That this was the second such rescue mission they had mounted since arriving in the system was also a point not lost on Riker. The first instance had embodied its share of obstacles, but the *Enterprise* crew had successfully rescued all but a small number of Dokaalan miners from their damaged outpost. A sour taste still filled the first officer's mouth at the thought of those they had failed to save, a feeling that had not lessened no matter how much he had tried to dwell on the hundreds of victims that had been rescued.

We'll just have to do better this time, won't we?

Further complicating things for Riker was a short-handed command staff to aid him through the rough spots. As well as Dr. Crusher not being on board to oversee the chaotic triage operation that was sure to come once the ship reached the outpost, Geordi La Forge was still off the ship, examining the Dokaalan's terraforming operation on Ijuuka, and Data had, for reasons unknown, fallen victim to some sort of as yet unexplained breakdown. Engineering had been attempting to diagnose the cause of the android's incapacitation, but that effort was now sidelined as they worked to prepare the ship for the upcoming strain on its systems and resources.

Additionally, and though he would not admit it to anyone else, Will Riker also missed the comforting presence of Deanna Troi. Not only did she provide him with his own emotional anchor, but her empathic abilities were an unmatched gauge for the mental well-being of the crew. At a time like this, such insight would be invaluable.

Well, he reminded himself, *you don't have it, so you're just going to have to get by.*

"I'm picking up fluctuations in the inertial dampers," Perim said, not taking her eyes from her console. "I think the background radiation must be affecting them somehow."

Not for the first time, Riker quietly cursed the asteroid field and its troublesome varieties of ambient radiation, which had plagued the *Enterprise* since it arrived here. Several of the ship's systems—transporters, tractor beams, sensors, and now the inertial dampers, to name but a few—had been disrupted by the constant assault of the potentially deadly radiation permeating the region.

Commander La Forge and the engineering staff had been able to tune the vessel's deflector shields to screen out the harmful rays, but the continuous need to keep the shields activated was beginning to take its toll on systems all over the ship. The shields also required repeated recalibrating in order to deal with varying levels of radiation as the *Enterprise* moved through the asteroid field.

Just another day in the Dokaalan system, Riker mused, sighing heavily.

"Commander Riker," said a new voice from the engineering station at the rear of the bridge, "I think I've found a way to isolate the problem, sir."

Swiveling the command chair around, Riker met the gaze of a wide-eyed young man, tan-skinned with closely cropped black hair and wearing a lieutenant's pips on the gold collar of this Starfleet uniform. The *Enterprise* first officer did not immediately recognize the young engineer, who obviously had been assigned to the bridge as part of the rotation schedule Riker himself had implemented during their voyage here. It was obvious by the man's expression that he was both eager and nervous, no doubt brought about by a combination of their current situation and his being unfamiliar with bridge duty and having to work in such close proximity to members of the ship's command staff.

Riker also abruptly realized that he would only inflict more anxiety on the young engineer if he could not, in the next few nanoseconds, remember the man's name.

"Yes, Lieutenant . . . Pauls, isn't it?" The engineer's features appeared to relax somewhat, telling Riker that he had at least gotten the man's name right. Making sure his words were carried by a mentoring tone that would help continue to put the lieutenant at ease, he asked, "What have you found?"

Rising from his seat and stepping closer to the command well, Pauls said, "We could retune the shields to another frequency, sir, but we're already straining the shield generators as it is, and tuning them to different frequencies every time they're compromised isn't helping. We're running the risk of the shields failing altogether, sir."

Commander La Forge and the *Enterprise* engineering staff had determined earlier that if the ship's deflector shields could be adjusted to the proper frequencies, they would be able to filter out the asteroid field's ambient radiation and protect not only the people aboard but also those systems that had seen their performance degraded or compromised altogether. It was only with this strategy that such systems as the replicators, the forcefield generators, and even the containment fields used in sickbay, engineering, and other sensitive areas were functioning at all. The plan had not been enough to return use of the ship's transporters or tractor-beam emitters, and the engineers had just as quickly set to work figuring out solutions for those problems, as well. At last report, there had been some success with the tractor beam systems but the transporters remained offline.

"Since we need the shields," Riker said as he stood up and moved to the bridge's upper deck, "it sounds like the only option is to sacrifice some of the other systems we've tuned them to protect. Is that what you're telling me, Lieutenant?"

It was simple enough. If the shields failed, the hull of the *Enterprise* would be a sitting duck out here, exposed not only to the asteroid field's radiation but to the debris that made up the field itself. A hull breach resulting from collision with an asteroid would be dangerous in its own right, but without emergency forcefields and other failsafe measures, even a small rupture of the ship's hull could prove catastrophic.

From the expression on his face, Pauls knew all of this, too. Swallowing an apparent lump in his throat before replying, he said, "Yes, sir. So long as we keep trying to protect everything, it's like spreading the cheese too thin across the cracker . . . uh, so to speak, sir."

Riker nodded as he mulled over the engineer's report. "So you're saying that with some adjustments, we can pick which part of your 'cracker' we want to cover, right?"

The lieutenant smiled at the turn of phrase. "Absolutely, sir."

"Okay, then," the first officer said, patting the younger man on the shoulder. "I need a list of suggestions for which systems to forgo, and I need it in about two minutes."

"Aye, sir," Pauls replied without hesitation. If he was intimidated by the order, he gave no sign of it as he set back to work.

Good man, Riker thought. *Geordi's been teaching his people pretty damned well.* If the ship's chief engineer could not be here to assist in their current situation, it comforted the commander to know that La Forge had ensured that anyone on his staff could substitute in a pinch.

"Commander," called Lieutenant Christine Vale from the tactical station, "sensors are beginning to penetrate the radiation, and I'm picking up the outpost. I think I can get us a visual."

"It's about time," Riker said as he moved toward Vale's station on the bridge's starboard side. "Let's see it." Reaching the tactical console, he turned his attention once more to the main viewer, which was still plagued by static despite the best efforts of the engineering staff.

In the center of the screen was a large asteroid, and even from their current distance Riker could make out discoloration on its surface. Gray metal contrasted with dark brown and black rock, and the symmetrical lines and curves of artificial constructs stood out against the asteroid's jagged, rocky contours.

"Can you magnify that?" he asked.

Vale shook her head. "That's as clear as I can make it. The picture will improve the closer we get, though. We should be there in about three minutes."

Unhappy with the report but knowing there was nothing he could do about it, Riker allowed his gaze to drop to the tactical station and the array of display monitors Vale had activated in order to keep track of her various tasks. The *Enterprise*'s security chief had been overseeing the ship's external sensors throughout the journey through the asteroid field, while at the same time monitoring communications with the stricken mining outpost as well as those areas of the ship that were currently preparing for the pending rescue operation. It was but the latest example of Vale's ability to handle multiple demands simultaneously, and in the two years since she had joined the crew Riker had learned to appreciate her versatility as well as her initiative to tackle problems without waiting for instructions.

"Life signs?" he asked.

"Indeterminate, sir," the security chief replied, "and power readings are minimal, as well. We've been transmitting on their last known frequency for an hour with no response."

The deck suddenly moved beneath Riker's feet, and he automatically reached for the railing in front of him as he felt the ship pitching to starboard. On the main viewer, the asteroids seemed to tilt and move to the left as Perim executed yet another evasive maneuver.

"Inertial dampening is definitely being affected," he said as the deck leveled out again. "Lieutenant Pauls, I need those recommendations of yours."

Still at the engineering console, Pauls entered a series of commands to his workstation before turning in his seat. "I've got a new shield configuration ready, sir. It should give us the best overall protection from the radiation while compromising the least number of necessary systems. We'll have to lose replicators and holoemission systems throughout the ship, which might be an issue for the medical staff if they're employing the EMH."

Moving back to the center seat, Riker nodded. "With

Dr. Crusher off the ship, you can count on that, Lieutenant." Until the *Enterprise*'s chief medical officer returned, Dr. Tropp and the rest of her staff would be relying heavily on the abilities of the Emergency Medical Hologram.

Pointing to the display monitor, he said, "See if you can reinforce protection in sickbay and the triage areas in case they need to move the EMH back and forth, but go with everything else you've figured out. We'll adapt from there."

"Aye, sir," Pauls replied. "This won't take lo . . ."

"Commander!" Vale suddenly called out. "I'm detecting a metallic object in our path. Approximately fifty meters in diameter. I'm not picking up any power sources or weapons."

As he leaned forward in the command chair, Riker's brow furrowed in confusion. "What the hell is it?"

"On screen now, sir," Vale replied as she tapped commands to her console. The image on the main viewer shifted to show a gray object that was roughly rectangular in shape and with what Riker could clearly see was jagged metal trailing from one end, slowly tumbling as it drifted in space.

"Part of the outpost," Riker said, standing up and moving toward the forward bridge stations. "Blown away by the explosion?"

At tactical, Vale said, "Most likely, sir." A beeping sound from her console made her lean closer to examine the readings, and when she looked up again, her face had twisted into a mask of horror. "I'm picking up biological material from inside the structure, sir, but no life signs."

Silence engulfed the bridge in the wake of the security chief's report, with nothing but normal background sounds filling the air as all eyes turned to the viewer. Riker followed the tumbling path of the module, trying to imagine the horrifying ride that the metal enclosure, once a safe haven from the void, must have offered to those trapped inside. Had they died quickly from explosive decompression in the seconds after the explosion and their separation from the outpost, or had they somehow survived that ghastly experience only to slowly suffocate as what little oxygen and heat trapped with them drained away?

The very thought of dying like that sent a chill down Riker's spine. How many more of them had suffered the same fate?

A moment later and as if reading his mind, Vale reported, "Commander, I'm starting to pick up similar readings all round us. It looks like more debris scattered by the explosion, sir." She shook her head. "Must have been one hell of a blast," she added in a quieter voice, echoing Riker's rising fears.

Is there going to be anyone left to save?

Gripping the arms of the command chair and hoping no one noticed how white his knuckles had become as he fought to keep emotion from his voice, Riker asked Perim, "How long before we reach the outpost?"

"Less than a minute, sir." Entering a new command string to her console, Perim added, "On screen now."

The picture on the main viewer changed once again to that of the asteroid that was home to Mining Station Twelve. Now that the *Enterprise* was much closer, the image was clearer and Riker could see the damage the explosion had caused. A gaping black maw had consumed much of the outpost itself, beginning at almost the center of the artificial structure and blossoming outward in all directions. Jagged metal, rock, and other materials he could not identify were forming an expanding cloud of debris around the asteroid itself. To Riker it looked as though someone had fired a missile or quantum torpedo at the heart of the facility as part of an orbital bombardment.

"Dear God," Pauls said from behind him, his voice a tortured whisper that Riker barely heard. "All of those people."

"I'm detecting life signs in some of the outer areas," Vale said, still poring over her sensor readings. "Less than a hundred, sir. I'm picking up massive structural failure throughout the complex. Their main power reactor is gone, but I'm picking up auxiliary power sources in several locations." A moment later she added, "There's one large concentration of life-forms in one of the bigger modules on the outpost's perimeter. Probably a habitat section."

Moving toward the conn, Riker said, "Perim, move us into position near that location. Vale, launch all rescue shuttles and feed them the coordinates for the other areas where you're picking up life signs." The plan had always been to use both the *Enterprise* and her small fleet of shuttlecraft, with the starship herself moving close to the mining facility as Picard had done during their first rescue mission here. It was a tactic that had saved nearly everyone on that outpost, and Riker was hoping for the same amount of luck, if not more, this time around.

As he gave the orders, he felt the energy surge through his body at the idea that they could still accomplish something here. *We're not beaten just yet. Not by a long shot.*

"Mr. Pauls," he said, his attention still riveted to the

main viewer, "stand by to initiate a forcefield to cover the docking port once we're in position. We might need the tractor-beam, too." He knew that the tractor beam system was working now, but not at full capacity, thanks to the damnable radiation field.

Take what you can get, he reminded himself.

It took him an extra second to realize that Pauls had not responded to the order. Frowning, he turned to look back toward the engineering station. "Lieutenant?"

The younger man was staring at the viewer, and Riker could see that he was obviously transfixed by the scene of destruction dominating it. "All those people . . . we're too late . . . they just . . ."

"Mr. Pauls!" Riker snapped, his voice echoing around the bridge.

It was enough to rattle the engineer, who blinked rapidly several times before looking away from the viewer. "Sir?"

"I need a forcefield ready to protect the docking port, Lieutenant," Riker said, his voice steady but firm and his eyes locking with the other man's. He resisted the urge to ask if the engineer was up to the task. After all, that question would be answered in the next seconds.

Finally, Pauls nodded. "Aye, sir. I'm on it now," he said before turning back to his station.

Allowing a small sigh of relief, Riker took a brief moment to ensure that no one else needed any extra attention before making his way to the rear of the bridge. Pauls, visibly shaken by what they had all just seen, kept his blanched face toward his console as Riker approached and placed a calming hand on the other man's shoulder.

"Lieutenant, are you okay?"

Focusing on his task, Pauls answered, "Yes, sir. I'm sorry for what just happened. I don't know what to say, sir. I just froze."

"You're not the first," Riker said, "and you won't be the last." It was very likely that the lieutenant, as a junior engineer who had been aboard the ship less than a year, had rarely if ever been in a position where life and death were exchanging places as harshly as they were at this moment. "At least you recognized what happened. You'll be better prepared the next time."

"Does it get easier, sir?" Pauls asked.

Shaking his head, Riker replied, "The circumstances don't, but the way you handle them does. That doesn't mean you stop caring, it just means that you learn when to save those feelings for a more appropriate time, like after we're finished here. Can you do that?"

Pauls actually sat up a bit straighter in his chair as he looked up to meet Riker's gaze. "Yes, sir. I think I can."

His faith in the young officer reaffirmed, Riker patted his shoulder again, smiling before turning back toward the center of the bridge and taking in the scenes of determined activity all around him.

"Okay, people, we've got a lot of work to do, so let's get to it."

And let's hope we can still do some good here.

Chapter Three

"IF I NEVER SEE another asteroid field as long as I live, it will still be too soon."

Alone in the cockpit of the shuttlecraft *Jefferies,* Jean-Luc Picard hoped his voice, and his lapse in bearing, did not carry back to the small vessel's sparse passenger area where Dr. Beverly Crusher and Counselor Deanna Troi were taking a brief rest from coordinating their own aspects of the *Enterprise*'s current rescue mission. They had resisted at first but he had pulled rank, gently ordering them to take advantage of the lull their current journey was imposing upon them. After all, once they got to their destination, he knew that rest would be a rare and valuable commodity.

So, for now, he sat alone, helpless to do anything except watch the asteroids.

Yes, he decided. *Too soon indeed.*

Despite everything he and his crew had found in the three days since the *Enterprise*'s arrival in the Dokaalan sector, Jean-Luc Picard had definitely begun to tire of this region of space. Its dense collection of massive planetary debris and the troublesome radiation had done its best to hamper nearly all of the technology that might be used to make their mission here any easier. Additionally, the asteroid field prohibited all but the most cautious means of travel, a particular burden now, as he piloted the *Jefferies* in pursuit of the *Enterprise*. This, on the heels of the Ontaillian mission, with the constant maneuvering through the ship debris in the boneyard, was more than enough to make Picard nostalgic for more open space.

Refusing to admit that he might be suffering from the initial symptoms of spacesickness, he tried to ignore the telltale twinges of nausea induced by the continual bobbing and weaving of the shuttle. Despite his best efforts, though, there was no denying the slight yet unmistakable rocking of his body as he was lightly and continuously buffeted by course alterations for which even state-of-the-art inertial dampers and gyroscopic systems could not fully compensate.

I haven't thrown up since I was a cadet, he sternly reminded himself even as his stomach heaved yet again, *and I'm not about to take that up again today.*

The relative silence of the shuttlecraft's interior offered a minor sedative for his queasiness, just as it had a brief respite for Troi and Crusher, particularly the physician, who had been in constant communication with the *Enterprise* since its arrival at the scene of its second rescue mission in the Dokaalan system. In addition to the triage operations taking place under the guidance of Dr. Tropp, Lieutenant Vale and her security force were once again scrambling to provide temporary billeting for those survivors of the explosion on Mining Station Twelve who were being evacuated to the ship. The situation required the coordinated effort of a large portion of the starship's crew, and Counselor Troi, for one, was doing her best to help Vale shepherd that endeavor.

Crusher in particular was refusing to take a spectator's seat in the work being performed by the *Enterprise*'s medical staff. She had spent the time since the shuttlecraft's departure from the Dokaalan central habitat reviewing reports from Dr. Tropp and Nurse Alyssa Ogawa on all aspects of the triage operation. Picard had at first assumed that the doctor was acting out of some need to assuage some measure of guilt at not being on the ship and leading the effort in person, but he had just as quickly discarded the notion. Even more so than the captain himself, Beverly Crusher was supremely confident in the ability of her medical staff to handle this crisis.

He could understand her anxiety, of course, just as tensions were almost certainly running high for every member of his crew. The events that had transpired since the *Enterprise*'s arrival in the Dokaalan system had provided their share of emotional ups and downs, after all. Picard himself had been briefly overcome by a welcome sense of awe and fulfillment brought about by the discovery of how survivors of the planet Dokaal's destruction and their descendants had labored to eke out an existence in this asteroid field. That joy quickly leaked away, however, when disaster struck one of the Dokaalan's frail mining outposts. The *Enterprise* had rushed to offer aid, with the entire crew furiously working to rescue hundreds of the outpost's survivors. In return, they had received a harsh lesson in the reality of the Dokaalan way of life, including the dangers with which it was fraught.

And we're in for another lesson now, the captain thought, *one I fear that may be even harder to accept than the first.*

Staring out the shuttlecraft's forward viewing port, he let his eyes search through the drifting maze of tumbling rock until they detected an object that was most decidedly out of place within the asteroid field. The *Enterprise,* still nearly a quarter of an hour away at the shuttle's present speed, had reached the outpost, and survivors were already being evacuated to the starship from the damaged facility. Riker's reports had given Picard an idea of the mission's objectives and scope, but the captain knew that the nuances and necessities of the actual operation would be lost upon him until he actually laid eyes on the outpost—or what was left of it. The enormity of the task facing his crew and the likelihood that even their best efforts might prove only fractionally successful weighed heavily on him, and he knew it was a feeling that would only intensify once he stepped back aboard his ship.

What he really needed to do, he decided, was to use this last leg of the trip to collect himself, and he knew just what would help.

"Tea. Earl Grey. Hot."

Picard straightened in his chair at the sound of the voice uttering those familiar words, momentarily startled that it was not his own. "Beverly?"

"And a mug of hot chocolate, too," Crusher added from the rear of the *Jefferies*'s passenger area. Turning in his seat, Picard watched as the doctor retrieved the pair of beverages from the shuttle's small replicator before moving toward the cockpit, handing one of the cups to Deanna Troi as she walked past. As she drew closer to him, the captain caught the first scent of the tea's distinctive aroma, and he nodded in thanks as Crusher offered the cup to him.

Sipping tentatively from the tea in the hope that it might quell his still-unsettled stomach, Picard asked, "Just what the doctor ordered, I presume?"

"You looked like you could use a pick-me-up," Crusher replied as she settled into the copilot's seat. "How soon until we reach the *Enterprise?*"

"Just over ten minutes," Picard replied, cradling his teacup in his hands. "I take it your staff is up to the challenge once again?"

Nodding, the doctor replied, "We have a big head start this time, thanks to the medical database we compiled after the first evacuation." She relaxed into the copilot's seat, allowing her attention to wander beyond the confines of the *Jefferies*'s cockpit for a moment before saying anything else. "When we were at their main colony, I tried to scan some of their own databases with my tricorder, but their computer system is a lot slower than ours." Shaking her head, she added, "Data would be able to create a reliable interface in no time."

Data.

Picard did not relish the thought of going into any technically challenging operation, let alone a deep-space rescue mission, knowing that he would be without the skills of his android second officer. According to Riker's last report, Data remained inoperative in the *Enterprise*'s engineering section. The cause of his sudden breakdown remained unknown, a fact that greatly troubled Picard.

Having been a starship captain for more than forty years, he had never been one to label any one member of his crew as indispensable. Such a mind-set almost always carried the risk of failure at a critical moment should such an individual become unavailable. He had always demanded that his officers cross-train within each other's fields of expertise, thereby ensuring that anyone could assume another's duties during times of crisis.

Despite that philosophy, there was no denying that Lieutenant Commander Data was a unique and irreplaceable member of his crew, to say nothing of being one of his most trusted friends. Picard was gravely concerned that whatever had happened to Data might be a permanent condition, and was even further troubled by his own apparent powerlessness to do anything about it.

"Oh my God."

Blinking in surprise at the words, the captain realized it was Counselor Troi who had uttered them. She had come forward from the shuttlecraft's passenger area and was now kneeling between the cockpit's two seats, her expression one of unabashed shock as she stared through the forward viewport.

"Look at that," Crusher said as Picard directed his own gaze to what they were seeing. In the distance, still several minutes away, were the mining outpost and the asteroid upon which it had been constructed. The *Enterprise* was angled perpendicular to the shuttle's approach perspective, appearing to be standing upright on its warp nacelles. Even from this angle Picard could see that the starship was anchored to the outpost, no doubt having linked up with one of the facility's external docking ports. The telltale blue glow of the vessel's tractor beam was also visible, acting as a tether to keep the ship connected to the asteroid. Several shuttlecraft swarmed about the scene, one disappearing into the *Enterprise*'s main shuttlebay while another emerged and moved away on a course toward the stricken outpost—or what remained of it.

Tapping the communications panel on the console before him, Picard said, "Shuttlecraft *Jefferies* to *Enterprise*. We are on final approach and are requesting docking instructions."

It was a moment before the hail was answered, and when it was, Picard noted that the quality of the communications channel was poor even this close to the *Enterprise*. Static laced the transmission as Will Riker said, *"Glad to hear your voice, Captain. As you can probably see, we've got a bit of a traffic jam working outside at the moment. We're using both shuttlebays for the evacuation operation, but as soon as there's an opening we'll get you on board, sir."*

Continuing to survey the scene before them, Picard said, "Understood, Number One. You're in charge."

Crusher leaned forward in her seat, seeming as though she might press her face against the shuttlecraft's canopy in order to get a better view of the situation. "It looks like they're more dependent on shuttles to transfer evacuees this time," she said. "That should keep the flow of incoming casualties manageable, but they've got to move quickly."

"Judging from the damage to the outpost," Picard said as he reviewed the cockpit console's sensor displays, "the shuttles appear to be the best option. I'm sure they're doing everything they can, Beverly."

The rubble and wreckage that was much of what remained of the Dokaalan mining outpost was now clearly visible. At the center of the damage was an immense dark circle, so black that to Picard it looked almost like the maw of some giant predator. A shimmering haze of rock bits and metallic flotsam drifted about the asteroid, debris freed from the outpost and hurled into space by what could only have been an explosion of immense destructive force.

"One thing's certain," Crusher said, her voice quiet. "We won't be able to save nearly as many people as we did last time."

Picard could not argue that point, not as he studied the scene of destruction before him. The damage was obviously worst at the center of where the explosion had originated, but it was evident that secondary detonations had wreaked havoc on the rest of the facility. How many people had died in the initial moments of the attack? How many more had suffered in darkness and cold when power failed, their section of the outpost cut off as the facility succumbed to the mounting damage inflicted upon it?

Attacked? Inflicted?

The words echoed in Picard's mind as he realized he was beginning to draw conclusions without having any facts to support them. Despite what Hjatyn and Security Minister Nidan had told him, there was no way to be sure that this incident was caused by deliberate sabotage. He would have Lieutenant Vale conduct a proper investigation, he decided, but not until they had done all they could for anyone who could be saved from the wrecked outpost, no matter how long that effort took.

There will be no rushing for the fast solutions, he silently decreed. *Not this time.*

While the first rescue operation ultimately resulted in hundreds of lives being saved, Picard himself remained haunted by one decision he had pursued. When an emergency situation developed, causing twenty-seven people to be thrown into open space, he had gambled on the ability of a hampered transporter system to pull those victims to safety.

It was a wager he had lost, and despite the helpful discussions he had engaged in with Counselor Troi in the aftermath of that first mission, he knew it was also a decision that would weigh on his conscience for much time to come.

"Do you think Hjatyn was right?" Troi asked, her words refocusing Picard on the matter at hand. "Could all of this have been intentional?"

Shaking his head, Picard replied, "It certainly looks too extensive to be the result of some sort of industrial accident."

"But why, Jean-Luc?" Crusher asked. "Could it really be someone trying to frighten the people into supporting the terraforming project?"

It was a question that had been gnawing at Picard since Hjatyn had first broached the subject. According to the elderly leader, the idea of transforming Ijuuka into a planet suitable for sustaining the Dokaalan civilization was one that was not accepted by everyone in the beleaguered community. Many felt that the effort, which had required the development of entirely new technologies and construction concepts, was an unwise use of their already limited resources.

Some of the more extreme opponents of the bold plan had even gone so far as to accuse the Dokaalan leaders of committing deliberate acts of aggression, such as the reactor explosion on the first mining outpost the *Enter-*

prise had visited, in the hope of engendering fear among the fragile colonies and coercing support for the Ijuuka endeavor. No evidence had been provided to support such alarming accusations—at least, not yet—but that did not seem to stop the more zealous challengers of the terraforming concept from shouting their beliefs to all who would listen.

"Could we be responsible?" Crusher suddenly asked, drawing a surprised look from both Troi and Picard. "I mean, if these are deliberate acts, could they be some sort of response to our arrival?"

Shaking his head, Picard said, "I don't see how. Hjatyn himself said that incidents similar to this one had occurred long before we got here, though those had been classified as accidents. If the explosion on the first mining outpost was deliberate, it was done before the Dokaalan knew of our existence."

"Maybe we aren't the cause of these particular incidents," Troi said, "but I can see where our presence might serve to aggravate the situation, especially if we find a way to help them with their terraforming efforts. Regardless of what conclusions they may reach, they are all faced with the immediate reality that their lives will never be the same."

Watching a pair of shuttlecraft rising from the surface of the mining outpost and heading toward the *Enterprise*'s aft shuttlebay, Picard pondered the words of his two friends. There could be no debating the fact that life for the Dokaalan from this point onward had become impossible to predict thanks to the arrival of the starship. There was simply no way for him or his crew to anticipate what the response might be to that change.

Hjatyn and his leadership had, to this point at least, rejected any offer to make their terraforming dreams come to fruition with the aid of Federation technology. Despite their decline of Picard's offer, the captain harbored hope that the Dokaalan might reconsider their stand once they had a glimpse of the possibilities such a technology exchange might offer. It was still possible that they might alter their position and embrace the wonders of a galaxy outside their tiny civilization. Even if they did not, Counselor Troi was right: The Dokaalan people would be forever changed by their encounter with him and his crew.

His thoughts were interrupted by the shuttle's communications system blaring to life. "Enterprise *to shuttlecraft* Jefferies," said Riker's static-tinged voice. *"We're ready to receive you in the main shuttlebay, but don't expect much of a welcoming committee."*

Activating the com system, Picard said, "Understood, Number One. I'm initiating docking maneuvers now. *Jefferies* out." Keying the commands necessary to return the shuttlecraft to his control, he said to his companions, "Regardless of the ramifications, these people have asked for our help and it's our duty to render that aid. We'll have plenty of time to wrestle with the fallout later."

But if there are those who view us as a threat, he thought as he maneuvered the shuttlecraft into position for docking, *how much longer can this grace period last?*

Chapter Four

"KEEP MOVING!"

The shouted words echoed inside Geordi La Forge's helmet, almost drowning out the curses he hissed through gritted teeth at every step he took, each oath condemning the limited mobility offered by his environmental suit.

While the standard extravehicular work garment might be ideal for working on the exterior of a starship's hull or for walking around in the poisonous atmosphere of an alien planet, when it came to running for one's life, the SEWG left a lot to be desired. Sweat ran freely down La Forge's body, his continued exertion having already overworked the cooling feature of his suit's comfort controls.

Glancing over his left shoulder, La Forge saw Faeyahr, the Dokaalan miner who had volunteered to be their tour guide earlier in the day. "How are you doing, Faeyahr?"

The large Dokaalan nodded through the oversized metal sphere that was the helmet of his own, less-advanced environmental suit. "I am fine, Commander." The bulky contraption he wore looked to have been pieced together from parts of several other such garments, with a heavy respirator tank carried on the wearer's back to provide life-support.

Despite Faeyahr's reply, La Forge could see through the Dokaalan's helmet faceplate and noted the strain on the miner's face. The extended effort of being on the run was beginning to weigh on him, but there was nothing to be done about that now. They had no choice but to keep moving toward a place of concealment.

Trying not to become hypnotized by the echoes of his own breathing inside his helmet and the muffled sounds of rock continually scraping against the underside of his boots, the chief engineer asked the third member of their party, "How far, Taurik?"

Slightly behind La Forge and to his right, Lieutenant Taurik replied, "Two hundred point seven meters straight ahead, Commander." The Vulcan was running with his tricorder in one hand, his left arm held out away from his body in an attempt to keep his balance as he hobbled and jumped over the asteroid's broken terrain. "I still do not see our pursuers, but you can be sure they are coming."

"I'm not betting against it," La Forge said as he kept his attention focused on the ground in front of him, watching for holes, cracks, or other potential dangers to his footing as he ran. Even in the asteroid's low gravity and through the insulation of his suit's boots, he felt the scarred and pitted face of the unyielding rock, drifting free and exposed to the hazards of open space for uncounted millennia. It almost reminded him of the vast coral reefs lining the beaches of one of Risa's more isolated resorts in that planet's southern hemisphere. The reefs were exposed during low tide there and he had spent several afternoons during one memorable shore leave bounding across them in order to reach the deeper water.

What I wouldn't give to be there right now.

The day had started out simply enough, with La Forge and Taurik being taken on a guided inspection tour of the Dokaalan's extensive terraforming operation. The *Enterprise* engineers, accompanied by Faeyahr, had traveled to Ijuuka, the onetime planetary neighbor of Dokaal, to get a firsthand look at the network of massive processing stations erected at carefully selected points all over that inhospitable world. Already in place and operational for decades, the factories had been working steadfastly to convert the planet's poisonous atmosphere into one capable of sustaining life, a task that would continue for years to come. The result of the momentous project would allow the Dokaalan to leave their makeshift homes in the asteroid field and live on the surface of a real planet, an experience many of the colonists had never before enjoyed.

Ahead of him, La Forge saw what had to be the area that Taurik thought might provide them with some protection. From more than one hundred meters away, to the chief engineer it looked like nothing more than a crack in the side of a rolling hill rising up from the surface of the asteroid. "Is that it?" he said, pointing to it.

"Yes, sir," Taurik replied. "According to my scans, it is a fissure that extends below the surface of the asteroid. It is three point one meters high and two point six meters wide at the opening, but begins to contract at a point below ground."

"Sounds like a tight fit," La Forge translated. Using

his ocular implants, he increased the magnification of the image the artificial eyes were feeding his brain, viewing the fissure in more detail than human eyes could ever allow. It did indeed look to be a confined space, but would it still be large enough to accommodate the three of them as well as their bulky suits?

Then he remembered Faeyahr's more primitive excursion suit. Unlike the engineers' suits and their built-in atmospheric regeneration systems, Faeyahr would have only the contents of the tank to sustain him out here. "Faeyahr," La Forge said, "how much air do you have left?"

Looking down at the gauge set into his suit's left forearm, the Dokaalan replied, "At this rate of consumption, perhaps another hour, Commander."

The options available to the away team, limited to begin with, were now rapidly dwindling. Even if they could avoid capture, or worse, at the hands of their pursuers, would Faeyahr's suit hold out long enough for the *Enterprise* to find them?

Not with the luck we've been having.

At the second terraforming station they had visited, Taurik had detected anomalies in the software used to oversee the atmospheric processing machinery's operation. The differences were subtle but definitely deviations from the normal operating parameters in use at the other facilities on Ijuuka.

While that itself had been enough to give La Forge pause, it was Taurik's later discovery of a small, isolated device attached to one of the storage tanks used by the processing plant to introduce carefully blended chemical compounds into the planet's atmosphere. The device had an outer casing composed of rodinium, an element not found in this region of space. An alien party had obviously constructed it.

Who those people were or why they had performed such an action remained a mystery, but the away team's discovery that something odd was taking place in the processing facility was enough to worry someone, and that someone had sent out search parties to either capture or eliminate the *Enterprise* engineers before they could return to their ship and report their findings.

La Forge, Taurik, and Faeyahr had managed to escape the planet in their shuttlecraft, but were unable to avoid being chased by a group of five Dokaalan mining skiffs. Smaller and more maneuverable among the asteroids than the shuttle and operated by pilots more familiar with the hazards of navigating an asteroid field than either *Enterprise* officer, the skiffs had taken little time to overtake their quarry. Unable to shake their pursuers, La Forge had opted for a radical tactic and executed his version of the Kolvoord Starburst, releasing and igniting some of the shuttle's drive plasma when one of the chasing ships got close.

The maneuver had damaged at least one of the skiffs and given the others reason to back off their pursuit, but it had also cost La Forge control of the shuttlecraft and sent it on a collision course with a mammoth asteroid. Both he and Taurik had fought the sluggish craft's maneuvering systems all the way down, managing to wrestle just enough control to keep their landing from being a fatal one. That all three of them had been able to walk away from the crash was nothing short of a miracle, La Forge decided.

For what that's worth, he amended silently as he took stock of their bleak surroundings yet again.

Continuing to run, the engineer was beginning to feel a steady ache in his chest and the protests of his legs, shoulders, and back, all of this accompanied by the sounds of his increasingly labored breathing. The prolonged exertion was beginning to take its toll on him, as well. In contrast, Taurik had sounded just as he would if providing a routine status report in main engineering. It would be nice, La Forge decided, to have some of that renowned Vulcan stamina right about now.

"Commander!" Taurik called out, and La Forge instinctively stopped, taking an extra few steps in the reduced gravity to bring his momentum under control. He turned to see the junior engineer standing motionless as well, facing away from him and holding his tricorder up so he could see its display through his helmet's protective faceplate. "I'm picking up the approach of three small vessels. They appear to be engaged in search operations rather than on an intercept course."

"They must not have seen our landing," Faeyahr offered, his words coming between ragged breaths as he gulped air, nearly exhausted from the prolonged running.

Looking back the way they had come, La Forge saw their crash site several hundred meters away and, far beyond that, a trio of small specks moving against the black of space. Flying low over the asteroid's surface, they were moving at an almost leisurely pace, but it was obvious they were heading in this direction. Still, it would be only seconds before someone in one of the skiffs saw the remains of the shuttlecraft *Ballard* highlighted against the asteroid's dark, rocky terrain.

Hide! His mind screamed the word at him. *Now!* They could not stay out here in the open like this. La Forge turned to examine their surroundings, looking for any-thing that could serve as a place of concealment. The only thing that appeared remotely promising was a de-pression to his right, less than two meters deep and barely qualifying as a ditch or hole.

"Good enough," he muttered aloud as he moved closer to the depression. "Come on!" he called out to the oth-ers, waiting until Taurik and Faeyahr joined him. The trio lowered themselves as far as they could go into the shallow hole. From ground level he was sure they were invisible, but what about from above?

Peering out over the edge of the hole's rocky parapet, La Forge risked a look back toward the shuttlecraft crash site. The three skiffs were hovering over the wrecked vessel, their pilots no doubt communicating among themselves. Were they discussing whether anyone on board the shuttle could have survived the impact?

He had his answer when the three ships broke away from the crash site and moved off in different directions. Now flying only meters above the asteroid's surface, there was no mistaking their intentions.

"They're fanning out to look for us," La Forge said as he watched one of the skiffs turning to head in their gen-eral direction.

His hand automatically reached for the ancient Starfleet first-generation phase pistol he had tucked into the large cargo pocket on his suit's right leg. The pistol was one of two such weapons he and Taurik had liber-ated from a pair of security officers who had attempted to take them into custody at the processing plant on Ijuuka. How the Dokaalan had come to possess the pis-tols, or the Klingon disruptors and other advanced weaponry that Taurik had detected as belonging to other races, was yet another in a growing list of questions requiring answers.

Would the weapon he had acquired even work out here, bombarded by the peculiar radiation that had affected a multitude of systems aboard the *Enterprise* such as phasers, tractor beams, and even the transporter? He had no idea, and there was no way to test the phase pistol without giving away their position.

Not that it matters, he thought, remembering the phase pistol's ineffectiveness when he had fired it at a pursuing Dokaalan security officer back on Ijuuka. Still, he knew he would get a second opportunity with the weapon soon enough, sighing in resignation as he watched the mining skiff moving closer. Though the craft still was not on a direct course for their location, its large cockpit window would afford the pilot a wide view of the surrounding landscape. Even if he did not see any signs of life on the surface, if the Dokaalan at the controls of the craft was any kind of tactician he would soon see the depression currently occupied by the away team and investigate it as a potential hiding place.

The skiff turned to face in their direction.

"Damn," La Forge hissed through gritted teeth, freezing in place as the tiny craft angled toward him. There was still a possibility that the pilot had not yet seen any movement or other indications of the away team's presence, but the chief engineer realized that as nothing more than wishful thinking as the skiff moved to within twenty meters. Its nose dipped toward the asteroid's surface, allowing the Dokaalan seated inside the ship's cockpit an unfettered examination of the rocky ground below him.

Even from twenty meters away, the pilot locked eyes with La Forge.

And he smiled.

"He's got us!" La Forge shouted, no longer making any effort to remain hidden as the skiff accelerated toward them. Bringing the phase pistol up, he moved the weapon's selector switch to Kill, its maximum power setting, sighted along the pistol's short barrel, and fired. Orange energy lanced forward to strike the diminutive workship on the metal plating just below its cockpit. La Forge saw the small craft shudder from the impact of the attack and observed the dark scar inflicted by the phase pistol's beam and he fired again. This time the skiff banked to its right, moving off to take up a hovering stance nearly one hundred meters from the away team's position, presumably what the craft's pilot guessed to be a safe distance from small-arms fire.

"That answers that," he said as he inspected his weapon's energy level, observing that it still retained nearly three-quarters of its power cell's charge. "Somebody's modified these things to work even with the radiation." When they returned to the *Enterprise,* La Forge was sure he would be able to disassemble the phase pistol and figure out what had been done to it that allowed its operation despite the constant interference from the asteroid field's omnipresent background radiation. He should then be able to use that information to modify the ship's own weapons.

If we get back, he amended silently.

"Commander," Taurik called out, holding up his tricorder. "The other two ships are heading in this direction. Obviously the pilot of the first ship alerted his friends to our location."

"Sure," La Forge replied. "Now that they've got us they can hem us in." Craning his neck, he looked for signs of the other two skiffs but saw nothing. He knew they would be adjusting their respective approaches so as to come in from different angles and catch the away team on three different sides, cutting off possible lines of retreat. If he and his companions did not move now, they would be trapped out here in the open and at the mercy of their pursuers.

"We need to get to the fissure before his companions arrive," Faeyahr said. He pointed to La Forge's left, and the chief engineer saw the opening in the side of the rise beckoning to them. With his ocular implants, La Forge computed the distance to be just more than fifty-two meters between their current location and the relative safety of the small crevice, a long way to travel over uneven, exposed terrain.

"I think you're right," La Forge said. "Okay, let's move." Pushing off from the bottom of the depression, he allowed his body to sail free of the low-lying area in the reduced gravity. His feet had not yet touched the rough, broken rock before he started off at a run once more, trying to keep an eye on the ground ahead of him and the lone skiff that had moved to a supposedly safe distance.

La Forge did not think he could hit the small craft with his first shot while on the move, but he aimed the weapon in that direction anyway. If nothing else, the action might make the pilot think twice before trying to come any closer. He was not surprised when the tactic did not work, and the skiff began to head toward them once again.

It was Taurik who fired this time, waiting until the skiff moved close enough that its Dokaalan pilot was clearly visible through the cockpit canopy before directing his own phase pistol at the onrushing ship. The weapon struck the craft's underbelly and the Vulcan kept his finger depressed on the pistol's firing stud, continuing to deliver the intense energy beam to the skiff's underside even as it flew past them.

"Nice shooting," La Forge offered as something exploded on the small ship's belly and it began to wobble wildly under the force of the impact, its pilot obviously struggling to maintain control. "Looks like you got something sensitive hitting it underneath like that."

"It would appear so," Taurik replied. Both engineers and Faeyahr watched as the skiff maneuvered toward a touchdown several hundred meters away, landing heavily but not badly and sending rock debris hurling upward into the airless void.

"Now's our chance!" La Forge shouted, picking up his pace. "We can make it if we hurry. Let's go!"

Any hope of escape was dashed, however, as the other two skiffs appeared from behind the rise, flying side by side mere meters above the asteroid's surface and heading straight for the away team. With nowhere to go, the engineers and Faeyahr stopped running as the two craft settled to the ground between them and their goal. A moment later, a hatch opened on the side of each skiff and the pilots emerged, dressed in environmental suits similar to Faeyahr's and carrying what to La Forge appeared to be some type of disruptor rifles.

"Those are pulse weapons," Faeyahr said in a quiet voice, "used by our Security Ministry only in the most extreme of situations. They are quite lethal."

As the Dokaalan drew closer, La Forge saw them raise

their rifle barrels to aim them at the away team. "Star-fleet officers," a voice sounded in La Forge's helmet. "Drop your weapons and you will not be harmed."

"Do not listen to them!" Faeyahr shouted. "You saw how the others acted at the processing station."

"If they are lying," Taurik said, "we will be defense-less if we surrender our weapons."

La Forge countered, "If they'd wanted to kill us, they'd have done it by now."

"I am obliged to point out that it is still a distinct pos-sibility, Commander."

The Dokaalan had closed the distance separating them, the muzzles of their weapons looking like two giant maws to La Forge. "I will ask you once more," the man on the engineer's right said, "drop your weapons."

Casting a last look at Taurik, La Forge let the phase pistol drop from his hand, the weapon falling slowly to the ground. The Vulcan followed suit, after which they both turned their attention back to their captors.

"What is it you want?" La Forge asked. The faceplates of both Dokaalan's helmets were tinted in such a manner that he was unable to get a clear look at their faces, a fact that unnerved him.

"You must come with us," the Dokaalan responded. "Minister Nidan has an urgent need to meet with you as soon as possible."

Stepping forward, Faeyahr said, "That is what your companions said at the processing facility. You cannot simply abduct these people without notifying their com-manding officer. They are our friends, after all."

Without saying another word, the Dokaalan who had spoken angled his rifle barrel so that it aimed directly at

Faeyahr's chest and fired. An angry blue ball of energy flashed from the weapon and slammed into Faeyahr, driving him back several meters in the reduced gravity before he crumpled to the ground.

"No!" La Forge cried as he and Taurik bounded to where their friend had landed. Turning Faeyahr onto his back, he saw the massive scorched hole in his chest. The fixed expression on the Dokaalan's face left no doubt that he was dead.

"Why did you do that?" he said to Faeyahr's killer, each word laced with anger. "You murdered him for no reason!"

Now aiming his weapon at La Forge, the Dokaalan said, "He was of no further use to us. You are, but we will kill you if you attempt to resist any further."

Raising his hands in surrender as their captors stepped forward, La Forge cast a worried look to Taurik, who returned the gaze with his own typically Vulcan stoic expression.

Chapter Five

ALARMS, CALLS FOR HELP, and the sounds of people in pain echoed throughout the cargo bay, but Beverly Crusher ignored all of it.

As it had been with four previous patients with equally severe injuries, her attention was focused on the unconscious female Dokaalan before her. The woman's pale blue skin was mottled with white patches from the extreme frostbite she had endured. Like so many others, she had been subjected to the vacuum of space when an emergency hatch had failed inside the mining outpost. While she had survived the exposure, the freezing temperatures had taken their toll on nearly all of the patients now being treated in cargo bay four.

Crusher's hands moved with the assurance of hard-won experience, administering drugs or manipulating a piece of medical equipment, her every movement tracked by the increasingly frequent sounding of emergency alarms on her patient's diagnostic bed.

She was competing in a race she knew she could not win, but neither could she quit.

Fight, dammit. Fight!

Her plea went unanswered, however, as the Dokaalan woman drew a final ragged breath and a shiver racked her frail body before she became still. Warning tones on the diagnostic bed confirmed what Crusher's eyes had already told her, and she reached up to the monitor panel to silence the alarm.

Her patient was dead.

Crusher gripped the side of the bed and took a self-steadying deep breath before looking up to Susan Lomax, the young nurse who had been assisting her. "Susan, please move her to . . ." She could not bring herself to say "black area," the section of cargo bay four that had been designated for patients the *Enterprise* medical staff were unable to save.

Lomax nodded in understanding. "I'll take care of it, Doctor," she said as she drew a sheet over the now still form of the Dokaalan woman.

Releasing a frustrated sigh, Crusher said, "Their bodies just aren't strong enough to handle the extreme cold brought on by decompression. I wish there were more we could do."

She turned from the diagnostic bed to survey the scene around her. The cargo bay was serving its second turn as a makeshift hospital since the *Enterprise*'s arrival here. However, whereas the bay had been the scene of great success during that first rescue operation, things were turning out quite differently this time around. The explosion that had all but destroyed Mining Station Twelve had done most of its dastardly work before the starship had even arrived. Crusher and her medical staff had been denied the chance to help the overwhelming majority of the nearly eight hundred colonists living on the outpost, and had instead been left with treating a small fraction of fortunate survivors.

Do what you can, she reminded herself as she regained her bearing. *You still have patients that need you.*

"Dr. Crusher!"

Turning at the sound of the summons, she saw Dr. Tropp assisting another Dokaalan patient, this one a very young female who looked to be in an advanced stage of pregnancy, to a nearby unoccupied bed. She moved to help them, leaving the intensive-care area and going into the cargo bay's postoperative ward.

And nearly fell flat on her face.

Feeling the tug of the gravity shift beneath her feet at the last second, Crusher was able to put her hands out and prevent a nasty fall, but she still fell to her knees, grunting in momentary pain as her left kneecap forcefully struck the deck.

"Oh my goodness," the Denobulan physician blurted, offering his free hand to Crusher while maintaining his grip on the Dokaalan woman. "Doctor, are you all right?"

"I'm fine," Crusher spat in disgust as she pushed off the deck and back to her feet, already shaking off the fleeting pain in her left knee. "I just forgot where I was." The fall was her own damned fault, she knew, having forgotten about the shift in gravity between the two sections of the triage area. The emergency treatment area had been configured for one-sixth Earth gravity to better accommodate the Dokaalan, while the post-op ward had been configured for normal gravity. The beds themselves were outfitted with antigravity generators to assist in keeping the Dokaalan patients comfortable while still allowing the *Enterprise* medical staff to move about normally.

As she regained her feet and gently took hold of the Dokaalan woman's other arm, Crusher noted how the patient was having trouble breathing. "Don't worry," she said, hoping to lend some assurance to the woman before she started to hyperventilate in panic. "We're going to take care of you."

Helping Tropp move the woman into the bed, Crusher checked the bed's gravity control and ensured that it was set properly for the woman. The Dokaalan even seemed to calm a bit as she allowed herself to relax within the grasp of the bed's lighter gravity. Looking up at Crusher, the woman's face was a mask of anguish as she struggled to speak.

"I am coming to bear," she said, her voice a strained whisper.

Smiling reassuringly, Crusher reached out to pat the woman's arm. "I know. We're going to examine you and make sure your child is unharmed." Eyeing the diagnostic panel above the Dokaalan's head, she said to Tropp, "It looks like her lungs have some damage, though I won't know if it's due to the cold or some kind of chemical exposure without further examination."

"I tried to administer a tri-ox compound to help her breathe, but she refused," the Denobulan replied. "In fact, I had just stopped her from trying to leave the cargo bay when I called for your assistance."

Crusher nodded. "She's just worried for her baby." Turning back to the Dokaalan woman, she said, "Lie back and relax. We're going to give you something to help you breathe easier. You'll feel much better in a minute."

Her eyes wide with fear, the Dokaalan replied, "I will soon come to bear. Please do not hurt my child."

Holding up a hypospray so that the woman could see it, Crusher said in a soothing voice, "Listen to me. Your lungs have been damaged and you're beginning to suffer from oxygen deprivation. This is a medicine that will let you breathe without straining your lungs. I promise you it is perfectly safe and will not harm your child."

During the previous rescue operation, she and the rest of her staff had compiled as much information on Dokaalan physiology as possible. It had been a necessity in order to provide useful medical care for the hundreds of Dokaalan patients they had treated. Thankfully, many of the medicines that had been created to treat the wide variety of humanoid species that composed the United Federation of Planets had proven compatible with the Dokaalan. Fortunately for Dr. Crusher's current patient, that list included tri-ox.

The woman's anxiety seemed to ebb and she finally nodded assent. She relaxed almost immediately as Crusher administered the medicine, her breathing growing less labored with each breath. Along with Tropp, Crusher waited for the tri-ox compound to take full effect, and after a moment the woman looked up and smiled.

"I do feel much better," she said. "Thank you."

Crusher and Tropp spent the next several minutes assessing their patient's condition, administering a sedative and preparing her for surgery to repair the woman's damaged lungs. Diagnostic scans confirmed the chief medical officer's initial suspicion regarding the Dokaalan's condition, with her lungs having suffered massive damage.

"She'll be fine now, though," Crusher said as a pair of her nurses completed the preparations. Patting the resting patient's arm one last time, she stepped away from the bed with Tropp close behind.

"Dr. Crusher," the Denobulan said in a quiet voice as they moved toward the triage ward's small control center, "how could you be certain that the tri-ox would not harm her child?"

Pausing a moment before replying, Crusher allowed a relieved sigh to escape her lips. "I wasn't." This particular situation had not been among the extensive Dokaalan medical database her staff had compiled. "But without treatment she would have eventually asphyxiated. Given the circumstances, I figured it was worth the risk."

Tropp replied, "Unorthodox, but I can find no fault with your reasoning." Shaking his head, the doctor rubbed the bridge of his nose, a sure sign he was beginning to feel the initial signs of fatigue. "I have made my share of choices such as that today, even more so than last time."

Sighing, Crusher glanced down at a padd that had been prepared for her by Nurse Ogawa. "We've treated eighty-five people, out of a population of eight hundred." She knew that the rescue operation was proceeding much more slowly than the first one, with the *Enterprise* forced to hunt and peck for survivors amid the ruins of what had been Mining Station Twelve. Other than a group of thirty-six Dokaalan who had been gathered in one section of the facility, the rest of the evacuees had been retrieved in groups of five or less. Many had been alone when they were found, with members of the *Enterprise* crew having to travel back and forth to the outpost via shuttlecraft on retrieval missions.

She held up the padd. "According to this report, most of those areas still capable of sustaining life-support have been searched for survivors. It looks as though most of the hard choices have already been made." Shaking her head, she added in a quieter voice, "We were just too late getting here."

Enough of that, she chastised herself. *Tend to the patients you do have.*

With that mental rebuke to fuel her, Crusher dropped the padd into her pocket and went back to work.

"Lieutenant Diix, I'm registering a power fluctuation in the port forward deflector shield generator."

In the *Enterprise*'s main engineering section, Kalsha heard the report from Ensign Veldon as she worked at her station. The Benzite sounded agitated, he decided, but that would be understandable. All around him, the chamber that housed the heart of the starship's propulsion system was a hive of frenetic activity. The engineers were endeavoring to carry out their responsibilities under demanding circumstances, with much of their equipment compromised by the asteroids' radiation field. Further, the lack of certain key members of the ship's senior staff, most notably Commanders La Forge and Data, was undoubtedly adding to their stress levels.

The tension and the continuing activity taking place

here were causing several of the human engineers to perspire. Already sensitive to the distasteful odor they normally emitted, Kalsha now found it almost unbearable to stand in proximity to some of the engineers. Likewise, it was difficult to maintain his composure when circumstances required him to be close to one or more of the humans.

Veldon was looking to him for direction, he realized. That made sense, of course. Thanks to his mimicking shroud, Kalsha still sported the outward appearance of Diix, the Andorian lieutenant he had been forced to kill in order to keep his presence here a secret. The shroud, a garment worn by many in his line of work while on undercover assignment and capable of presenting the appearance of nearly any humanoid form, was one of his most preferred accessories. Its integrated network of sensors and holographic emitters was working perfectly, allowing him to interact with the *Enterprise* crew without risk of detection, just as the technology had allowed many of his people to assume the form of various Dokaalan citizens throughout the mining colonies in this system.

One thing it could not do, however, was repeat whatever someone said to him when he allowed his attention to wander.

What had the Benzite said? Something about one of the deflector shields fluctuating. Thankfully, Kalsha had dealt with this twice since the beginning of the rescue operation, as problems with power distribution were beginning to assert themselves on many of the shipboard systems affected by the asteroid field's omnipresent background radiation. The course of action was simple.

"Route power from all nonessential systems in that section," he said, his voice sounding exactly like that of Lieutenant Diix.

Veldon continued to look at him askance for several seconds. What was wrong? "Ensign?" he prompted.

As if worried about the reaction her next words might evoke, the Benzite cleared her throat before saying, "Uh, sir, we have already done that. The power deviations are unchanged."

It was an effort for Kalsha to maintain his composure as he heard the ensign's reply. Had he allowed his attention to drift, even slightly? Such carelessness would likely draw the scrutiny of the other engineers if he did not quickly cover his mistake. Looking over at the master situation monitor, Kalsha took in the current status of the various shipboard systems and the rerouting of power distribution that had taken place since the beginning of the rescue operation and saw that Veldon was right. Nonessential systems in that part of the ship had been already deactivated in deference to more important concerns, but more power was still needed.

"Cut environmental control in that section by fifty percent until further notice," he said. "That should be sufficient for now."

At the station next to Veldon, Ensign Leisner turned in his seat. "Sir, with all due respect, you might want to check with Commander Riker before we do that."

Not an unreasonable observation, Kalsha conceded. A reduction in temperature in that area of the vessel would not go unnoticed, but it could not be helped. Due to the instability of the ship's forcefield generators and other containment systems, Commander La Forge had cautioned the command staff about the risk of engaging warp power while still within the asteroid field, even to channel the massive energies generated by the *Enterprise*'s main engines for other uses. Therefore, the ship's impulse drive had been called into service to provide much of the power requirements for the current operation.

With that in mind as well as other factors currently playing into their present situation, routing power in the manner he had instructed was, for the moment at least, the most effective way to channel energy needed to keep the deflector shields stable.

"Duly noted, Ensign," he said. "I will take responsibility for the action and notify Commander Riker, but make the necessary arrangements now, please. Time is of the essence."

Leisner nodded, apparently satisfied with that clarification. "Aye, sir," he said before he and Veldon turned back to their stations, leaving Kalsha to look on in satisfaction. The engineers had heeded his instructions and turned to their duties without a hint of uncertainty or distrust. He decided that they were simply too focused on the more important concerns of the ongoing rescue activities to notice anything untoward.

Interesting, he thought. *You seem to be getting quite caught up in all of this.*

It was perhaps unavoidable, given the identity he had assumed. He had been content to remain in the form of Lieutenant Andrea Tyler, one of the *Enterprise*'s several junior engineers, whose appearance Kalsha had taken soon after boarding the Federation vessel. After using his mimicking shroud to disguise himself as a Dokaalan and blend in with a group of Dokaalan receiving a guided tour of the massive ship, he had managed to slip away from his companions while searching for an appropriate *Enterprise* crew member to replace.

He had found Lieutenant Tyler working alone to replace some kind of power coupling. After determining that the human woman was an engineer, someone who could access the ship's more sensitive areas without raising suspicion, he had used the shroud to duplicate her appearance in every detail. It had been his intention to complete his mission quickly and leave before someone noticed the discrepancy of the woman apparently being in two places at once, but that plan had been hindered by two problems.

The first obstacle had come in the form of the *Enterprise*'s main computer. Though Kalsha had acquired more than a passing knowledge of covertly accessing even the most secure computer systems, working his way into the starship's vast storehouse of information without being detected had proven to be quite the challenge. It had not taken him long to realize that more time than he had allotted for the task was required.

Things had become more complicated while he was working in the office of the ship's chief engineer and Lieutenant Diix entered. Since Kalsha had appeared to him as Lieutenant Tyler, the Andorian had naturally inquired about the woman's presence when she was supposed to be working elsewhere on the ship. Tyler was, of course, and Kalsha had concluded that in order for him to continue working aboard the *Enterprise* in stealth, Diix had to be eliminated.

It was an action I took with great reluctance, Ando-

rian, Kalsha silently offered. There had been no other option, of course, given the parameters of his mission. He had always strived to reserve the taking of life for the most extreme of situations, and part of him still questioned whether or not the murder of the Andorian had truly been necessary. Still, he had carried out the action with great remorse, unlike many of his contemporaries and even his superiors who had callously killed those Dokaalan targeted for replacement.

As it turned out, assuming Diix's appearance had given him justification to spend more time in main engineering as he pursued his primary goal: finding a way to disable the *Enterprise*'s android crew member, Lieutenant Commander Data.

Kalsha's superiors had decided that the android posed the greatest threat to their activities here in the Dokaalan system. Though Kalsha himself did not fully understand the reasons behind this deduction, such comprehension was not required for him to carry out his assignment. After working with deliberation to access that part of the ship's computer containing the most sensitive information, which included Data's technical schematics, he had found the means to disable the android.

So he thought.

His efforts to render Data inoperative had proven only partially successful, with the very real possibility that the other engineers might be able to diagnose and resolve its incapacitation. That in turn could lead them, with the android's help, to investigate and identify the cause of its shutdown. Kalsha could stop that, of course, but another covert attempt to permanently damage or even destroy the android was too dangerous at this point. It would only prove that Data had been deliberately sabotaged, leading the *Enterprise* captain to begin looking far more closely at the activities taking place in the Dokaalan system than he had already.

I cannot allow that, Kalsha reminded himself, *no matter the cost.*

"Lieutenant Diix?"

It was yet another of the engineers, a Bajoran lieutenant whose name Kalsha could not remember. She was moving toward him, a padd in her hand and a worried expression clouding her features.

"What is it?" Even as he spoke the words, he was still unable to recall the female's name as she turned the padd so that he could see its face.

Pointing to the device's main display, she said, "We're registering a minor flux in the antimatter containment system, sir. It's not serious, but it is outside the norm."

The report caused Kalsha to look to the massive cylinder dominating the center of the engineering room. Despite the extra safeguards put into place by Commander La Forge to limit the ship's primary source of power while the *Enterprise* traveled within the Dokaalan asteroid field, the warp core still pulsed with energy.

"When did it start?" he asked.

"The computer detected the first indications about three minutes ago, sir," the Bajoran replied. "Looking at this along with the other status reports we're getting from around the ship, it looks like all the rerouting we've done so far is starting to take its toll."

Kalsha nodded, knowing that the lieutenant was right.

It made sense that the extra strain being incurred by those systems directly involved with the rescue operation would have effects on other areas of the vessel.

Wait. . . .

Regarding the warp core once more, Kalsha realized that the answer to his troubles might very well have been delivered into his lap. The core's elaborate network of containment features, designed to shield antimatter from normal matter except during those carefully controlled intervals where the two substances were allowed to mix, was beginning to show signs of strain or even potential failure. If left unchecked, the situation could conceivably become dangerous as the *Enterprise* continued to render whatever assistance to the Dokaalan Commander Riker was currently overseeing.

Would it be serious enough to cause them to halt the recovery activities? What if the situation escalated to the point that it could no longer be controlled? The containment field would collapse, unleashing the fury of a warp-core explosion that would consume the mighty starship.

That could not be allowed, of course, not while the ship was still a useful tool to the larger mission.

"Engage the backup systems," he said after a moment. "It is overkill, but it does not require us to route power from elsewhere."

The Bajoran nodded. "Aye, sir." She tapped commands into her padd as she returned to her station, leaving Kalsha alone in the center of engineering.

He stared at the enticing target that was the warp core, listening as he did so to the flurry of activity taking place around him. With other duties occupying most of the other engineers, it was feasible for him to commit a single act of sabotage that would solve all of his problems. It would not be easy, of course. Circumventing the antimatter containment system's multiple backup and protective safeguard processes would take time, but Kalsha was sure he could do it, and in such a manner that no one would be able to react in time to stop it.

While it was true that the *Enterprise* was needed for the next phase of the larger mission, there was a definite risk in attempting to make use of the ship and its vast resources without the knowledge of its crew, and it was well within Kalsha's purview to destroy the vessel before that time if he felt it necessary.

Naturally, blowing up the ship would likely require him to sacrifice himself, as well, but that also was not a troubling proposition for him. While he was not reckless or prone to rash action, Kalsha had long ago accepted that he might die while on assignment. It was simply another aspect of his chosen profession to be acknowledged as eventual fact, rarely dwelled upon and never feared.

Murder this vessel's entire crew? Along with any Dokaalan they might have rescued? No matter the possible gain, causing so many deaths was incomprehensible to Kalsha while other options remained to complete his assignment.

"Lieutenant Diix?" Ensign Veldon called out to him from across the room, returning his attention to the situation at hand. "Commander Riker is requesting a status report."

Kalsha nodded. "Very well," he said, returning to the persona of the Andorian engineer. "I will see to it." As he moved to the master situation monitor to compose the report, he caught site of Data's immobile form, still housed in his diagnostic alcove. He still needed to find a way to permanently incapacitate the android so that the plan could proceed forward, but there was nothing to be done about that for now.

Patience, he reminded himself. His chance would come soon enough. Of that he was certain.

Chapter Six

"THE *KEUKA* HAS JUST LANDED in the aft shuttlebay, Captain," Riker said as Picard exited his ready room and stepped onto the bridge. "They managed to rescue three more, but all are in critical condition. Dr. Crusher promises a full report as soon as possible."

Picard took the proffered padd from his first officer as he moved to his command chair, reviewing the status report it contained as he took his seat. He knew that the *Keuka*, along with two other shuttles, had been sent to one of the last areas of Mining Station Twelve where life signs had been detected. While hoping the report would contain better news, the captain already had resigned himself to the fact that the *Enterprise*'s rescue efforts were nearly done here, and that the results of their work were less than uplifting.

Studying the computer terminal next to his own chair, Riker said, "If Dr. Crusher pulls these last three through, we'll have rescued a total of one hundred and four from the outpost." Shaking his head, he added, "Most of those who survived the explosion were trapped in areas where life-support and environmental control were cut off. They never stood a chance."

Listening to the commander's report, Picard let his eyes linger on the scene of destruction playing out on the main viewscreen. With the *Enterprise* no longer tethered to it by tractor beams or emergency umbilical conduits, empty space had reclaimed its dominion over the large, rough-hewn asteroid and the devastated mining station it harbored. Home to more than eight hundred Dokaalan mere hours before, the mining outpost was now little more than a lifeless hulk.

Those who had perished in the initial explosion were the fortunate ones, the captain decided. Better to have died instantly than suffer the aftermath, huddling in the dark as the air and the heat were slowly, inexorably drained away from the remnants of the colony.

"One hundred four," he said after a moment, his voice barely a whisper as he lightly tapped the back of the padd against his open palm. "Damn."

"Considering the damage and the conditions the survivors faced," Riker said, "we were fortunate to save that many. I suppose that's something."

"Is it?" Though he did not raise his voice, Picard knew his response was sharper than he intended even as the words left his mouth. Pausing a moment to collect himself, he said, "I'm sorry, Number One. That wasn't an indictment of the crew's efforts, or yours."

Nodding, Riker replied, "I know, sir. If it helps, I'm feeling the same frustration."

"My frustration," the captain said, "is stemming from

a growing concern that these incidents are not accidents. Once, perhaps, but twice? I think not."

"Do you think we should inform Minister Hjatyn of our progress?" Riker asked.

Picard frowned as he considered the question, tugging on the lower edge of his uniform tunic as he did so. After a moment he said, "Not just yet. I want to give Lieutenant Vale and her team a chance to see what they can find over there." Looking over to the junior security officer currently staffing the tactical station, he said, "Ensign Forst, let's see what your boss has to say, shall we?"

"Aye, sir," Forst said as he entered the proper commands to his console. "Channel open, Captain."

"Vale here," came the voice of the *Enterprise*'s security chief a moment later. Much to Picard's irritation, the communications channel still harbored noticeable background static as the effects of the asteroid's radiation field continued to vex the ship's sensor arrays and subspace receivers. The lieutenant's words managed to cut through the interference. *"We're still making our way through the colony's main power center, sir. There's really not much here to check, though."*

"I understand, Lieutenant," Picard replied. "Have you been able to find anything at all?"

Vale replied, *"Nothing yet, Captain. We're still trying to get into the area of the outpost hit hardest by the explosion."* The security chief had led twenty of her people down to the outpost, investigating the interior of the ruined facility in the hope of finding any remaining stragglers who might still be alive as well as beginning her preliminary investigation into possible causes for the explosion. *"Just one second, sir,"* she said a moment later. *"I'll let you see for yourself."*

A moment later, the image on the main viewer shifted from that of the destroyed mining colony to what Picard barely recognized as a ruined corridor, the transmission originating from Vale's helmet transceiver. The only source of illumination was a beam of light stabbing through the surrounding darkness, generated by the security chief's exterior helmet lamp.

The beam bounced and bobbled as Vale moved forward, scanning back and forth to reveal debris littering the passageway. Watching the transmission, Picard gave silent thanks that the corridor seemed to be free of bodies. In the near darkness, he saw an opening in the bulkhead in front of the lieutenant. The large metal hatch that had once sealed the portal now hung by a single hinge, partially blocking entry into the next chamber.

"If our information is accurate," Vale said, *"this hatch leads to a service elevator that descends to the outpost's fuel storage depot. According to our initial scans, the explosion likely originated there."*

"Be careful, Lieutenant," Picard cautioned, out of habit as much as a genuine concern for the away team's safety. The security chief was not prone to taking foolhardy risks with herself or her people, but she was operating under less than ideal circumstances on this occasion. "We can't yank you back if things go wrong."

"Understood, sir," Vale said as she stepped up to the hatch. *"Careful is my middle name."*

"I don't remember seeing that in her record," Riker said, a small smile playing at his lips as he attempted to lighten the somber mood enshrouding the bridge.

Picard watched as two members of Vale's away team, dressed as she was in environmental suits, moved into the range of her visual feed. One of the security officers grasped at the handle of the twisted, blown-out hatch and appeared to tug without budging the sizable metal door. The second crewman then joined in the effort but to no avail.

"It's warped and jammed into the doorframe, Lieutenant," one of them said.

"Stand back," Vale said in reply. A few seconds later, an orange phaser beam struck the hatch, engulfing it in a bright aura of energy that momentarily overloaded the feed from her helmet transceiver. When the interference cleared, Picard could see that the mangled hatch was gone. *"We're proceeding down to the next level, Captain. I figure we'll need at least an hour to get to the fuel depot and conduct a decent tricorder sweep."*

"Proceed at your discretion, Lieutenant," Picard replied. "Keep us informed of your progress."

"Aye, sir," the security chief said. *"Vale out."*

As the connection severed and the image of the mining outpost returned to the main viewer, Riker shook his head. "You think they'll find anything?"

Shrugging, the captain replied, "I honestly don't know what to think." As he spoke the words, he realized he was hoping Vale would not find evidence that the explosion that had destroyed the mining outpost was the result of an intentional act. Given all that had already happened since the *Enterprise*'s arrival in the Dokaalan system, the prospect of having to search for one or more saboteurs was one that filled Picard's heart with dread.

"Engineering to bridge."

The urgency of the voice startled the captain for a brief moment. Looking up to activate the bridge's intercom system, he called out, "Picard here. Go ahead." As he did so, he looked to Riker, the knit of his brow conveying the obvious question.

The first officer was already consulting his own console and shaking his head. "No alerts or warnings."

"This is Lieutenant Diix, sir," the disembodied voice said. *"Commander Riker left orders to report if there was any change in Commander Data's condition."*

His eyes widening in surprise and even a brief glimmer of hope, Picard replied, "Has he reactivated himself?"

"Not exactly, sir," the lieutenant said. *"It appears that he is attempting to do so, however."* There was no mistaking the nervousness in the young officer's voice. No doubt Diix's anxiety existed on several levels, not the least of which was, in all likelihood, communicating directly to the ship's captain. *"It is possible that this is but the first step in a long process. I will continue to monitor the situation and contact you accordingly, sir."*

"No," the captain countered. If Data was returning to any sort of useful functionality, Picard wanted to be there in the event the android was able to shed some light on what had happened to him. "We're on our way there now."

"Sir," Diix said, *"there is no way to tell how long this might take. If there is another change I can . . ."*

"Thank you, Lieutenant," Picard said, cutting off the engineer's response, "but I prefer to see this for myself."

The omnipresent hum of the warp core greeted Picard and Riker as they entered the engineering section. At first glance, the captain thought the massive chamber to be populated with but a skeleton crew. Only a few of the workstations–those that he recognized as overseeing the ship's most critical systems—were attended, but even the engineers at those consoles seemed to be dividing their attention between their work and looking over their shoulders toward the rear of the room.

"Must be a party," Riker said, unable to suppress a tired grin.

"Indeed," Picard replied as he inspected the various display monitors and status panels with a practiced eye. From what he could see, all shipboard systems were operating normally, or as normally as could be expected given the hampering effects of the Dokaalan asteroid field.

Continuing on past the main engineering floor, Picard and Riker found the rest of the engineering staff gathered around the alcove still housing Data's immobile form. One of the junior officers, Ensign Veldon, was the first to notice their arrival.

"Captain Picard," she said as her companions immediately turned at his approach. She indicated Data with a nod. "There has been no change since our last report, sir."

Stepping toward the diagnostic alcove as the engineers made a path for him and Riker, Picard realized he was looking at Data for the first time since his mysterious shutdown hours earlier. The multiple demands brought about by the rescue operation had dominated the captain's attention since then, but that did not stop him from feeling a pang of guilt over not having gotten down here to see his friend before now.

Studying the android, who stood motionless in the alcove and with a length of optical cabling connecting a diagnostic monitor to a connector port normally concealed by the hair on the left side of his head, Picard was reminded that only in this state did Data actually appear to be anything other than a living being.

He had seen the android deactivated or incapacitated several times, most of them against Data's own volition, and on each of those occasions the captain had found himself wondering if his friend might, upon reactivation, lose some part of himself, some intangible quality that went into making him the genuinely unique individual that he was. On an intellectual level, Picard knew that such worries were unnecessary. There could be no arguing the nature of Data's artificial construction or of the vast storehouse of information that prevented him from forgetting any fact to which he was exposed.

Still, the captain had always believed there was more to Data than tripolymer alloys, positronic relays, and extensive software processes working in concert to merely mimic a humanoid life-form. He had never required proof to support that position, even when it was provided in the form of a historic legal precedent handed down by Starfleet's Judge Advocate General more than a decade ago. That had only served to inform everyone else as to what Picard and the *Enterprise* crew had already known: Lieutenant Commander Data truly was more than the sum of his parts.

"Lieutenant Diix," Riker said, indicating the Andorian who was still in charge of the engineering section until Geordi La Forge returned. "What have you got?"

Moving closer to Picard and the first officer, Diix replied, "Commander Data reactivated himself almost five minutes ago, sir. He was functional for only a few moments before going inert again, but the cycle has repeated itself four times since I contacted you."

"Has he said anything yet?" Picard asked.

Diix shook his head. "He has spoken, sir, but nothing intelligible. Much of it sounded as though he was talking at a greatly accelerated rate. From what I have learned by reviewing Commander La Forge's maintenance logs, my best guess is that Mr. Data is running a series of startup diagnostics before bringing himself fully back online."

"Have you found anything to explain what happened to him?" Riker asked.

"Not yet, sir," the Andorian said. "We do know that the positronic pathways which form his neural net have suffered a massive cascading failure. According to his own diagnostics, he has spent a large portion of the past several hours reconstructing those pathways and isolating those that are not immediately reparable. A complete reconstruction of his neural net will be necessary at some point, but it is our assessment that such action should wait until Commander La Forge's return, sir. Mr. Data concurs, but he is continuing to do what he can in order to return to some form of functionality as quickly as possible."

"Some form of functionality?" Picard echoed. "Are you saying that his performance will be compromised?" The words were difficult to force out of his mouth, he realized, as he began to imagine the true extent of Data's "injury." It seemed that the damage the android had suffered was even worse than that inflicted upon him during the *Enterprise*'s first encounter with the demon ship. The problems Data had encountered then seemed to pale in comparison to what Data was dealing with now.

Nodding, Diix replied, "Almost certainly, sir. Based on

our own diagnostic scans, he will be unable to move under his own power, with command of his motor skills significantly degraded. He will still be able to communicate, but he will have to remain here until repairs are completed."

"Don't worry, Captain," another engineer, Ensign Leisner, said. "It's not as bad as it sounds. A lot of it is simply us waiting for Commander La Forge and Lieutenant Taurik to get back. They're the ones who do most of Data's maintenance work, and I'd be lying if I said the rest of us weren't a little nervous. We don't want to hurt him." As if realizing that his comment did not sound right, the ensign immediately appended, "Well, not hurt . . . sir, you know what I mean."

Picard considered the younger man's words, appreciating his honesty. He was fully aware that Commander La Forge was very protective when it came to the responsibility of looking after his friend, but that did nothing for him now. With the chief engineer off the ship, Data was essentially on his own to repair himself, and by his own admission those efforts would not be enough.

Another thing about Leisner the captain had noted was that the ensign seemed almost surprised by Diix's pronouncement of Data's condition. Was there some sort of disagreement over the android's diagnosis among the engineering staff? Picard supposed that too might be caused by their anxiety over figuring out how best to work this particular problem.

Before he could make mention of his observations, Picard's attention was drawn to sounds coming from behind Diix and Leisner. "What is that?" he asked as everyone turned toward the diagnostic alcove in time to see that Data had opened his eyes and was staring at them intently.

"Data?" Riker asked, moving closer. The android's head turned in response to the first officer and he blinked rapidly for several seconds. His left cheek twitched and Picard saw the corners of his mouth moving as if trying to form words.

"I . . . I . . . I-I-I-I" was all he said before the rest of his speech disintegrated into an indecipherable flood of gibberish, sounding to Picard almost like a high-speed stream of computer data.

"This is the same as the last time, sir," Diix said as Data continued his attempts to verbalize. It continued for several seconds before the android's head suddenly snapped once to the left before straightening out until he was looking straight out from his alcove.

"I am superior, sir, in many ways," he suddenly said. "But I would gladly give it up to be human."

Confused, Picard looked to the Andorian engineer. "What is that?"

Diix shook his head. "I do not know, sir."

Silent for a moment, Data merely blinked before his head twitched to the right. "*Felis catus* is your taxonomic nomenclature."

" 'Ode to Spot'?" Riker said, and Picard saw that the first officer was sharing his own bewilderment. "I haven't heard him recite that poem in years. What's wrong with him?"

Data's response was to say, "Our function is to contribute in a positive way to the world in which we live."

Checking the diagnostic monitor still connected to the android, Diix shook his head. "I am not registering a fault, sir. Whatever is happening, Data is doing it deliberately."

"In the event of water landing, I have been designed to serve as a flotation device." The engineers around him chuckled at that one and even Picard found himself put somewhat at ease by the remark.

"I recognize some of this as things he's said before," he offered.

"Same here," Riker added. "It's almost like he's reliving old memories somehow."

Still studying the monitor, which Picard knew provided a real-time representation of the computer activity currently taking place inside Data's positronic brain, Diix said, "That is essentially correct, sir. According to these readings, Commander Data is initiating a restart of his modified neural net."

"Lieutenant Diix," Data said, "I wonder if I might . . ."

The Andorian nodded in apparent understanding. "If I recall correctly, that was the last thing he said before shutting down."

A moment later, Data stopped blinking and his features became still. "Reset complete." Turning his head, his golden eyes fixed on Picard. "Captain?"

"Welcome back, Commander," Picard offered, unable to keep a small smile from revealing itself. "Are you all right?"

Data replied, "I have reconfigured my neural net in order to contain the damaged areas. My ability to access my internal data storage is compromised, but not severely. At present, I am continuing to devote part of my attention to repair efforts, but I will require Commander La Forge's assistance to complete that process."

"Geordi's not here, Data," Riker said. "He's not back from inspecting the terraforming operations on Ijuuka yet."

His head cocking slightly to his left, Data replied, "I have just finished synchronizing my internal chronometer to ship's time, and unless there has been a change in his itinerary, he should have returned to the *Enterprise* three point four hours ago."

"We know, Data," Picard said. "There have been a few developments while you were out of commission. We're trying to contact him, but the radiation field won't allow communications between here and the planet." In truth, the captain was not comfortable with the current situation and had already expressed his concerns to First Minister Hjatyn and the Dokaalan leadership, but there was little he could do until definitive word about La Forge's location and situation was obtained. "Data, can you continue your repairs without him?"

"Yes, sir," the android said. "I will endeavor to proceed as quickly as possible, but my efforts will be somewhat limited. I am also attempting to ascertain the cause for my incapacitation, but it will take some time."

"Do you think it was the radiation?" Diix asked.

"I do not know," Data replied. Unable to move except for small motions with his head, he did indeed resemble an automaton, a caricature of a living being rather than the masterfully crafted homage to the man who had created him, Dr. Noonien Soong. "I am still processing information, but I do believe it to have been an outside influence of some kind."

Something in the way Data said that made Picard frown. "Outside influence? Are you suggesting you may have been deliberately tampered with in some fashion?"

"I am unable to hypothesize one way or another at the present time, Captain."

Picard said nothing, but given what he and the *Enterprise* crew had encountered already—the odd reports that Commander La Forge had submitted, Counselor Troi's comments, and most especially the apparently intentional attack on the mining outpost—he was unprepared to rule anything out just now.

"Let's just say I'm keeping my options open for now, Commander," he finally said. "Continue your repair efforts as best you can." Turning to Diix, he added, "See to it that he has whatever resources he requires, Lieutenant, and keep Mr. Riker updated on your progress."

The Andorian nodded. "Aye, sir."

Leaving Diix and the rest of the engineering staff to their work, Picard led Riker toward the room's exit, waiting until he was in the corridor and out of earshot before stopping. He paused an additional moment until a crew member walked past and disappeared around a corner in the passageway to say anything.

"Number One, I want Lieutenant Vale to quietly begin augmenting the security level throughout the ship. If Data was the victim of some form of sabotage, there's a chance his attacker may still be on board."

"You think one of the Dokaalan might have pulled something?" Riker asked. "Would their current technology level even give them the ability to try anything like that?"

His first officer had a point, Picard decided, but it did little to assuage the nagging feeling at the back of his own mind. Shaking his head, he replied, "I don't know, but my instincts and Counselor Troi's observations of our hosts tell me that there's more happening here than meets the eye." He knew that Lieutenant Vale and her people were still examining the remains of the Dokaalan mining outpost, looking for any evidence of foul play,

and he wanted to wait for the security chief's report before undertaking any drastic action.

Still, doing nothing only invited potential disaster, a
lesson he had learned at no small cost long ago. "Until I
find out what *is* going on with these people, I want to be
prepared for anything."

Chapter Seven

FINALLY, CARGO BAY FOUR was at peace.

More or less, Beverly Crusher amended silently as a soft alert tone from a nearby diagnostic bed wailed for attention. Moving to one of the patients currently occupying the area of the cargo bay designated critical-care, she reached for the patient monitor and silenced the alarm. A quick check with her tricorder's medical scanner confirmed the bed's diagnostic readings that its patient, an older Dokaalan male, was starting to become feverish.

Retrieving a hypospray from the pocket of her smock, Crusher set it to administer a mild antibiotic, thankful once again for the storehouse of Dokaalan medical knowledge she now had at her disposal. In moments the bed's diagnostic scanner recorded the introduction of the drug into the patient's bloodstream and its immediate effects.

"At least this time your fever's a normal reaction," she said to no one in particular. This group of survivors from

Mining Station Twelve had only been aboard ship a few hours. That was far too soon for her to be seeing the first indications of the more mysterious, and serious, ailment that seemed to affect any Dokaalan who remained on the *Enterprise* for a longer period of time.

Nine point six hours, Crusher reminded herself, *according to my best estimate.*

She and her medical staff had so far been unable even to discern why the Dokaalan began to suffer their acute, withdrawal-like symptoms nearly ten hours after boarding the starship. Crusher was sure it had something to do with the omnipresent radiation field surrounding the asteroids and the Dokaalan colonies, but so far she had been unable to substantiate her theory.

Shaking her head, she stopped that line of thinking. There would be plenty of time to return to that other, much larger problem once she and her staff were finished here.

While nearly all of the Dokaalan survivors requiring medical treatment were recovering without incident, a handful of patients still resided in the critical-care section, recuperating from the lingering effects of hypothermia as a result of exposure to the vacuum of space. Elsewhere in the large chamber, dozens of convalescing Dokaalan occupied patient beds and cots, while others had gathered about the cargo bay in groups of twos and threes, seeking out-of-the-way places to engage in what she hoped was therapeutic conversation as they tried to make sense of the last few hours.

Still others had congregated in a temporary dining facility, which came complete with portable food replicators. *Enterprise* engineers had programmed the devices to create meals suited to the Dokaalan palate, but much of it seemed savory enough that the occasional wandering aroma served to remind Crusher that she could not remember when she had last eaten.

Walking among the various gatherings of Dokaalan were Deanna Troi and a few members of the medical staff whom she had trained to act as crisis counselors, doing what they could to help those beginning to show signs of post-traumatic stress. Crusher watched as Troi approached two patients, one of whom appeared to have been weeping, and placed a comforting hand on the distraught male's shoulder. It was a simple gesture, one the doctor hoped would provide even a small measure of comfort. After all, there could be no denying that these people deserved so much more.

"Dr. Crusher?"

The voice calling her name from behind her startled her, and she turned to see Kell Perim favoring her right leg and limping her way into the cargo bay. "Kell?" she asked as she crossed the room to the Trill officer. "What happened?"

Perim offered a weak smile as she hobbled toward one of the empty diagnostic beds. "I'm sorry. I know you're busy and don't have time for this sort of nonsense."

Moving to help the lieutenant to lie down on the bed, Crusher said, "You caught me at the right time. Besides, I warned you about the discomfort."

"I haven't had much time for the exercises you showed me," Perim replied, wincing as she straightened her right leg and massaged the side of her knee. "And since Data's been out of commission, I've been pulling longer hours on my shifts. Now it's stiff no matter what I do."

Shaking her head, Crusher said, "You have to take time for yourself if you want to keep the knee, Kell." She picked up a tricorder from the bedside table and activated its medical scanner, waving it in a circular motion over the lieutenant's leg. "We really should replace it altogether, but I'm not going to be able to do it until things settle down around here." Indicating the cargo bay with a nod of her head, she added, "As you can see, we're pretty booked up at the moment."

"I figured as much," Perim replied. "Maybe I should have just listened to you the first time."

They had discussed the replacement procedure a few weeks earlier, while the *Enterprise* was still traveling out here from Federation space. Perim had been reluctant, likening the unwanted surgical procedure in some ways to her decision to decline accepting a Trill symbiont into her body. That she had opted against what many of her people regarded as a singular honor had placed her at odds with her friends and family.

For reasons she had only partially shared with Crusher, Perim had equated the notion of becoming a symbiont's host and forsaking a life of free will to being fitted with an artificial joint instead of working to restore her body to full and natural health. To recant that position now and be willing to accept the idea of a replacement knee meant either that she had reconciled some of the fears she harbored or that the pain in her knee was excruciating enough to force her in a direction she did not necessarily want to go.

"Don't worry," Crusher said. "No scolding from me. Let's see if another round of regeneration therapy can work as a stopgap for a day or two."

Perim chuckled. "At this point, I'd consider amputation as a stopgap."

As she turned to retrieve a portable regenerator emit-ter from a nearby worktable, Crusher noticed Dr. Tropp heading in her direction. "Doctor," she offered in greeting as the Denobulan approached.

"Hello, Dr. Crusher," he replied before nodding to Perim. "And to you, Lieutenant." Carrying a padd in his hand, Tropp offered the device to Crusher. "I am continuing my research on the asteroid field radiation effects on the Dokaalan. I believe I have isolated the particular varieties that are causing the trouble, and I am now analyzing tissue samples offered by Dokaalan patients to study its reaction to the radiation bands I have selected."

Finished aligning the portable regenerator over Perim's knee, Crusher activated the device, watching as the Trill's leg was bathed in a soft blue glow. That done, she accepted the proffered padd.

"Excellent," she said as she perused the information Tropp had compiled. "It's too bad we don't have genetic samples from the last three hundred years to use as a comparison. That might show how their bodies adapted to their new environment."

Tropp said, "I daresay it was not without some radical outside influence, possibly even at the genetic level. I have begun researching some of the Dokaalan doctors' older medical records in order to gain some insight into the drugs that were once prescribed for all of the colonists as counteragents to the radiation. Perhaps the answer, or at least a clue, lies there."

"I agree," Crusher replied, stroking her chin thoughtfully as she continued to read Tropp's report. "That seems like the next best place to start looking." Shaking her head, she added, "We can't figure out how to reverse the problem if we can't find where it started."

"Why would you want to reverse it?"

Perim's question startled Crusher, and she offered a puzzled expression to the Trill. "Why? The Dokaalan are apparently unable to survive outside the asteroid field, and they may not be able to survive within it for much longer. If we can combat that, they'll have the option to live anywhere they want."

The soft tones of the regeneration beam filled the air for a moment before Perim said, "Maybe that's not what they want."

"What?" Both Crusher and Tropp answered in unison, their looks of confusion and even shock practically mirrors of one another.

"From everything they've told us," the lieutenant continued, "the Dokaalan don't want our help with their terraforming efforts. Why are you assuming they want our help fixing what you believe to be a medical 'problem' but in fact might not be an issue so far as they're concerned?"

"Lieutenant," Tropp said, "despite their reluctance to accept our ability to help them with the technology at our disposal, the Dokaalan might respond differently in a matter of life or death."

"Have you asked them?"

Silence hung in the air again at Perim's words, as all three officers simply looked at one another. Apparently satisfied that she had the doctors' attention, she continued, "Just because life here doesn't appeal to us has no bearing at all on whether it looks great to them. It had to look a lot more inviting than the alternatives they had when all of their problems started, after all. If what you're saying is true, then they made some drastic choices, most likely just to survive at first. For all we know now, that decision could be rooted in the culture they've created out here."

"There are many factors to consider," Crusher said, hoping to sound sympathetic to Perim's concerns, "and yours are as valid as any of them."

"I'm not a doctor, and it's probably none of my business," the Trill replied in a softer voice, "but I do know what it's like to be pushed into believing that having your own body forever changed is a good and exciting thing. Maybe it's not, and just because you *can* do something does not always mean that you *should.*"

As Tropp regarded both her and Perim with an expression that conveyed his fascination over the current discussion, Crusher took the opportunity to study the dozens of Dokaalan faces filling the cargo bay. While some remained sad and downtrodden, she noted that others were smiling, a few even laughing with their fellows in the wake of the devastating events that had consumed them mere hours earlier. She found herself no more able to connect with a reason as to why a Dokaalan might be able to laugh today than she could understand Perim's resistance to the idea of severing these people's apparent connection to the very thing that had helped them survive out here for all these years.

Both concepts, she realized, were rooted in recognizing the Dokaalan spirit of survival and independence. It was a passion that she, and everyone aboard the *Enterprise* for that matter, might do well to consider as they continued to interact with this proud people.

"Not at all, Kell," Crusher finally said after a moment, a small smile curling the corners of her mouth. "It's a good reminder. I might just have to keep you around."

Indicating the knee that was still being subjected to the restorative effects of the regenerator, Perim returned the smile. "Well, as it happens, I'm free for a little while."

Seated within the relative quiet of his quarters, Picard once again turned from his view of the asteroids still drifting past the *Enterprise* to regard the twin bowls of soup now cooling before him on his dining table, which he had set for two. The mingling aromas of the soups, a watery brownish broth in the bowl at his place setting and a thicker, orange-tinted stock in the bowl opposite his, had whetted his appetite almost to the point of impatience.

Swallowing, he raised his voice in the otherwise empty room. "Picard to Dr. Cru . . ."

His command to the ship's intercom was interrupted by the muted tone of his door chime. Smiling to himself, he quietly shook his head. "Come," he said, and the doors opened to admit Dr. Crusher. *Well timed as always,* he mused.

"I'm sorry, Jean-Luc," she said, her tone masking none of her apparent frustration. "I got caught up with a patient, and . . ." She stopped to sniff the air, her expression warming in recognition. "Is that vegetable soup for me?"

"As if I had a choice?" Picard let the facetious question hang in the air as Crusher took the seat opposite his. "When you hinted, and very strongly I might add, that you wanted dinner together, I assumed it meant more than a chicken sandwich and coffee." The rather ordinary yet tasty soup had long been one of the doctor's favored choices as a first course during many of the evening meals they shared.

Reaching for a spoon set before her, the doctor tasted

her soup. "It's a little cold," she said, recanting her words almost as quickly as she saw the mock anger on Picard's face. "Okay! Okay, that's my fault. I'll take it and like it."

Picard nodded in triumph, taking up his own spoon and welcoming the first sip of the French onion soup he had selected for himself. "I think our entree will be a bit more to your liking," he said. They ate in silence for a few moments before he asked, "How are things in the cargo bay?"

"As well as can be expected," Crusher replied. "We'll have to transport them to the central habitat as soon as we get there, before they start to present the symptoms we saw earlier, but otherwise, everything appears to be under control."

"Excellent," the captain said. "I was hoping for a quiet evening. I can't remember the last time we had an uninterrupted conversation."

Pausing with her spoon raised partway to her mouth, Crusher appeared to ponder his statement for a moment before offering, "Stardate 49423.6?"

"Perhaps not *that* long, thank you," Picard said. Reaching out for the bottle of wine he had opened just prior to her arrival, he poured two glasses and offered one to her. "Have a drink. That's an order."

They raised their glasses in salute before turning their attention to the main course. He decided that the wine—not Chateau Picard but instead a label he had acquired from a vineyard on Cestus III—was a good choice as a companion to the meal, even if he had not been able to perfectly replicate the distinctive taste of Aldebaran sea bass.

In the end, it was not the meal itself that made the

evening, of course. Whether they talked about ship's business, engaged in idle chatter, or simply sat in comfortable silence occasionally punctuated by unforced conversation, Picard had long ago come to enjoy and even anticipate the opportunities to share this quiet time with Beverly Crusher, particularly when it came at the end of a long day.

"So," he said after a few minutes, "have you had any progress attempting to diagnose the Dokaalan's mystery illness?"

Shaking her head as she sipped her wine, Crusher said, "Tropp is doing some tests, and I've got some new thoughts on the matter, myself."

"It seems obvious that the radiation field would afflict the Dokaalan in some manner, given the havoc it's wrought on the ship's systems," Picard said, "but I wouldn't have expected them to have acquired a physical dependence on it."

Crusher replied, "It's certainly a possibility. I'm following a hunch that may seem more like detective work than medical research, but sometimes the two are the same. Eliminate the impossible and whatever remains . . ."

"However improbable, must be the truth," Picard finished, the familiar quote eliciting a small grin. "I'm hardly a newcomer to the concept, you know."

"Then you know that considering my data files on Dokaalan physiology are only three days old, I still have a lot of what's impossible to rule out before I can concentrate on what's just improbable. A lot of what we're doing is nothing more than guesswork at this point." Shaking her head, she added, "I can't wait for Data to get back to full capacity. He'd be able to make short work of sorting through the Dokaalan medical databases and getting them transferred to the *Enterprise* computer."

The captain nodded. "He has his hands full at the moment. Even Data has limits, it seems." The android was dividing his time between his own repair efforts and devising a means to aid the Dokaalan's terraforming project, neither of which was proving to be an easy task. Picard had considered diverting Data's energies toward helping Dr. Crusher, but in the end he had decided she and her medical staff were progressing quite well without him. Besides, he reminded himself, the Dokaalan's peculiar medical condition, if indeed that was what it was, had been here for quite some time now and would not be going anywhere for the foreseeable future.

Leaning forward in her chair, Crusher fixed him with a hard gaze. "Here's another question for you. Let's say we discover that the Dokaalan's dependence on the radiation is reversible, something that can be changed through medicine or gene therapy or whatever. Should we tell them?"

Pondering the question as he took another bite of his meal, Picard nodded after a moment. "I think such information would provide them a new option as to how to lead their lives, be it here or elsewhere, beyond the boundaries of this system. We would have to outline any potential risks, as well, but in general I believe we should inform them of our findings, yes."

"But is that truly serving my patients' will?" Crusher asked. "If my goal is first and foremost to do no harm, is this crossing the line?"

Picard frowned at the notion. "Crossing the line? I don't understand."

"The radiation dependence," the doctor said, "if that's what it is, is a natural barrier that I'd be helping them to clear through unnatural means. Even if we can find a way to do it that doesn't kill them, what does that mean for their society if everyone suddenly has the ability to leave whenever they want? Not everyone would be interested in leaving, but if enough of them did leave, wouldn't that hurt the efforts of those who are committed to terraforming Ijuuka?"

They were interesting questions, Picard had to admit. "I never took you for a Prime Directive scholar," he said, his tone slightly teasing. "The simple fact is that they called out to us for help, and we're in a position to offer that assistance. How much of that aid they accept or discard is still entirely up to them. What you're proposing is really just another decision that they would be required to make."

"But it's still our power and technology that makes such a decision possible," the doctor countered. "This isn't like curing polio or the Canopus plague. Instead of helping this society, I might be offering the means to destroy it."

Not for the first time, Picard was in awe of Crusher's unwavering devotion to her calling as a healer and physician. He admired her willingness to lose herself in her objectivity, putting her own desires to further scientific and medicinal research aside in favor of the long-term benefits for those under her care. Never one to make snap decisions, she now had embroiled herself in an ethical conundrum that neither of them was likely to resolve easily.

"Beverly," Picard replied, "this isn't the first time we've been in a position where there were no easy answers, nor is it the first time we've been faced with an ethical dilemma about how best to render aid to another society. You've always found the way that best serves those we're trying to help." With a small smile, he added, "Even if the Prime Directive did take the occasional beating."

The small joke seemed to have no effect on Crusher. Pausing a moment to take a sip of her wine, she shook her head. "I swear, Jean-Luc, it seems like these kinds of problems get harder and harder to deal with. There are times when I just don't know which way to go."

In his most mentoring voice, he offered, "My advice to you, Doctor, is to continue your research and see where it leads you," he said. "There's no sense agonizing over possible ramifications until you know what it is you're dealing with."

"More likely," Crusher countered, "I'll fret over this for the next few days, and then the Dokaalan will say they want nothing to do with anything that we have to offer." Shaking her head, she offered a tired smile. "So, tell me again why we're doing this?"

Raising his wine glass one more time, Picard replied, "Because it's the right thing to do."

Chapter Eight

"ACCORDING TO OUR FINDINGS, the explosion originated in the outpost's main fuel storage depot," Christine Vale said as she stood before the observation lounge's main viewscreen. On the viewer was a technical schematic of Mining Station Twelve, with one area near the perimeter of the facility highlighted conspicuously in red.

"This started a chain reaction?" Picard asked, seated in his customary place at the far end of the lounge, which had once again had its artificial gravity adjusted in order to accommodate First Minister Hjatyn and a small delegation of Dokaalan council members.

Vale nodded. "Yes, sir." Tapping the screen with one finger, the security chief began to trace a path through the computer-generated visualization of the outpost's interior. "Fire swept through the conduits used to channel fuel to the main landing bay's trio of refueling reservoirs that in turn caused three secondary detonations. At least one of those was responsible for rupturing the bay's outer hatch. The combined force of the explosions and the decompression in the landing bay caused several inner hatches to fail as well as inflicting widespread structural damage in the surrounding sections of the outpost."

"Without any kind of emergency forcefields to contain the hull breaches," Riker said from where he sat to Picard's right, "the explosions decimated that area of the outpost. Entire modules were destroyed, and others were blown clear of the asteroid. Some of the Dokaalan were able to seal off portions of the facility to sustain what atmosphere they had left, but by the time we arrived on scene, most of the damage had already been done." Turning until he faced Hjatyn, who was sitting across the table from him, the first officer added in a more subdued voice, "Of those we rescued, six died while receiving medical treatment, leaving ninety-eight survivors, sir. I'm sorry we weren't able to do more."

The elder Dokaalan leader held up a withered, pale blue hand. "You did all that you could, Commander Riker. You acted without hesitation, once again placing your vessel and your people at risk on our behalf." Hjatyn smiled as he spoke, his weathered countenance and penetrating maroon eyes reflecting a hard-won wisdom that Picard had seen in other leaders who earned their positions through hard work and years spent laboring to earn the trust and loyalty of those they guided. "The circumstances of what happened were beyond your control, and the Dokaalan people are forever grateful for your efforts."

Not for the first time, Picard marveled at the genial nature with which Hjatyn and other Dokaalan treated his crew, even now in the aftermath of having lost nearly seven hundred of his own people. Was that because of what the captain and Counselor Troi had discussed during their journey in the shuttlecraft? Did the Dokaalan, any of them, regard the *Enterprise* as some sort of divine chariot, bringing forth godlike beings with the power to offer assistance or destruction on a whim? Were they concerned that their lives had been irrevocably altered by the appearance of these alien visitors, perhaps for the worse?

No, the captain decided. The more he thought about it, the idea made no sense. From his observations, a large segment of the Dokaalan seemed to be a spiritual people, but unlike other cultures he had encountered they were not slaves to their religion. This was a civilization that Fate had dealt a particularly harsh blow, and rather than caving in to the adversity heaped upon them they had instead fought it, keeping it at bay if not conquering it.

He also held no doubts that they had faced more than their share of tragedy, and while he did not believe they were callous or unemotional about such loss, they had more than likely learned to accept it as just one of the harsh realities they faced.

Sitting to Riker's right, Counselor Troi said, "Dr. Crusher and her staff treated thirty-four of the evacuees for various injuries, only a few of which required surgery. Due to the complications she experienced with her previous Dokaalan patients, she is requesting they be transferred to a Dokaalan facility as soon as possible."

The *Enterprise* medical team's continuing inability to discover a cause for the maladies apparently suffered by any Dokaalan who remained aboard ship for extended periods of time was troubling to say the least. Dr. Crusher had reassured Hjatyn and his staff that brief visits to the *Enterprise* did not seem to invoke any negative effects. Despite that, Picard had naturally worried over causing undue harm to any of their hosts, offering to hold the gathering in the chambers of the Zahanzei Council back at the Dokaalan's mammoth central habitat. Hjatyn had displayed no fear regarding the potential risk to his own health, politely resisting the captain's suggestion while citing again his enthusiasm for any opportunity to visit the starship. With that in mind, Picard had found himself hard pressed to further argue the point.

As for the strange ailment itself, all Dr. Crusher and her people had been able to figure out to this point was that the Dokaalan were adversely affected only when removed from their natural environs. The obvious answer was that it had something to do with the asteroid field's omnipresent background radiation, but the doctor had not yet been able to prove her hypothesis.

Nodding at Troi's report, Picard said, "Commander Riker and Lieutenant Vale will see to the transfer once we're finished here." Turning his attention back to Vale, the captain asked, "Lieutenant, have you been able to discern a cause for the explosion?"

Still standing next to the lounge's viewscreen, the security chief replied, "Due to the widespread damage, we weren't able to gather much in the way of physical evidence, sir. If it was the work of saboteurs, the explosion covered their tracks pretty well, I'm afraid."

"Past incidents have shown a similar pattern," said Security Minister Nidan said from where he sat on Hjatyn's left. "Bringing the perpetrators to justice has always been a foremost priority, but they have proven to be a most elusive enemy."

After thanking Vale for her report and dismissing her so that she could begin the process of transferring the Dokaalan evacuees off the ship, Picard shook his head at what he had heard. The answers the security chief had provided were not what he had wanted to hear, but that was not Vale's fault. Suspicions about sabotage being responsible for the accident had begun with the first reports of trouble on Mining Station Twelve, and it was a notion that had plagued the captain throughout the ensuing rescue operation. It was but the latest in a string of disturbing reports and theories that had surfaced since the *Enterprise*'s arrival here, beginning with the incident at the other mining outpost days earlier.

Commander La Forge had speculated that the malfunctioning power reactor, which had caused that situation and required the evacuation of four hundred Dokaalan to the starship, might well have been the result of deliberate tampering. It was a suspicion that gained credence once Picard met with Hjatyn and other members of his leadership cadre and they informed the captain of the tensions running through the Dokaalan people over the issue of terraforming Ijuuka.

A large segment of the population believed the venture to be a risky gamble of vital resources that could be better utilized maintaining the colony facilities sprinkled throughout the asteroid field. There were those who even believed that the accident at the mining outpost as well as others that had occurred in recent years were deliberate acts of terrorism, designed to coerce the people into pledging support for the terraforming effort.

First Minister Hjatyn, naturally, had scoffed at such claims, and Picard himself thought the accusations smacked of so much conspiracy theory. The only wrinkle in his belief seemed to be Counselor Troi, who had expressed concern that the Dokaalan leaders might not be telling the complete truth in their dealings with the *Enterprise* crew. At first she had rationalized what her Betazoid senses were telling her as simple hesitation on the part of Hjatyn and his people, justified anxiety in the face of first contact with an alien species who displayed technology and abilities far superior to their own.

Then there was what had happened to Data, of course.

Was it really something more?

Not two days earlier, Picard would have been prepared to argue against the idea. Now, however, he was no longer so certain, but there was nothing he could do about his misgivings except to remain alert and watch for any telltale clues the Dokaalan might offer.

The sound of the doors to his left opening caught Picard's attention, but it was who entered the observation lounge that took the captain by surprise.

"Data?" Riker said as he caught sight of the android.

"Greetings, Captain," Data said to Picard as he entered the room, offering similar respects to the lounge's other occupants. Still unable to walk, he was seated in an engineer's antigravity work sled just like those offered to some of the Dokaalan to assist their moving about in the *Enterprise*'s heavier gravitational field. The captain noted that while Data still could not move his entire body, the android's right hand appeared to be functioning now as it rested on the chair's diminutive control panel. It was a small feat, but an encouraging one nevertheless, indicating that he was making progress in his efforts to repair the damage done to him.

"Commander," Picard said, "I would have thought you would remain in engineering until your repairs were complete."

Maneuvering the work sled toward to the wall-mounted viewscreen, Data replied, "I am continuing to make repairs to my neural net as we speak, sir. However, I have also been devoting part of my attention to other pursuits, particularly the assignment you gave me. I have spent the past several hours researching the terraforming process currently under way on Ijuuka, and I believe I have devised a solution that will allow us to assist the Dokaalan with a minimal amount of intrusion."

"Commander Data," Hjatyn said, "while I am certain that your intentions are honorable, I must reiterate my people's position that we complete the work of transforming Ijuuka into our new home on our own. It is a commitment we have made to the millions of fellow Dokaalan who were not fortunate to survive the death of our homeworld."

Unable to nod, Data simply replied, "It was not my intention to sully that promise, First Minister. I have limited my research to methods that can only assist your own efforts, not supplant them."

"We should at least hear what he has to say, Hjatyn," said Creij, the Dokaalan science minister. She was sitting straighter in her chair now, leaning forward and gazing intently on Data. "Surely there is no harm in that?"

After receiving approval from Picard to proceed, Data said, "Computer, execute program Data Alpha and display it on this viewscreen." There was a pause as the computer carried out the instructions, and when the image on the viewer shifted, the captain saw what he recognized to be a computer model of the planet Ijuuka.

"The terraforming process being employed by the Dokaalan is based on the introduction of several different chemical compounds into the planet's existing atmosphere," Data said as the world represented on the screen, shrouded in what looked to be a dense blanket of brownish gray clouds, rotated slowly on its axis. "According to the computer models in use at the various atmospheric processors around the planet, the project is proceeding without significant incident. As we know, however, it is an endeavor that has been under way for decades and it will take generations to complete at its current pace."

"But you've found a way to speed things up?" Troi asked from where she stood to his right.

"That is essentially correct, Counselor. I believe that by introducing another substance into the atmosphere, one that is not indigenous to either Ijuuka or anywhere else in this system, we may be able to drastically accelerate the transformation process. Instead of requiring decades to complete, only a handful of years would pass with the use of this new strategy, after which Ijuuka would be all but ready for colonization by the Dokaalan."

Leaning forward in his chair, Picard said, "What substance are you referring to, Mr. Data?"

"Phylocite," the android replied.

"I can't say I've ever heard of that one," Riker said.

Data turned his attention to the first officer. "It is an artificially engineered element developed as a means of combating a viral plague that nearly decimated the population of the planet Phylos in the mid twenty-third century."

"Their life-forms share many characteristics with that of plant life, as I recall," Picard added. "I'm familiar with this incident. The plague wreaked havoc on their entire ecosystem and nearly all of the planet life, which in this case also included a large segment of the Phylosian population."

Nodding, Data replied, "That is correct, sir. Though not originally intended as an aid for terraforming, it was later discovered that many of phylocite's characteristics held much in common with what were at that time leading terraforming practices. It was not until the early twenty-fourth century and lessons learned from the Genesis Project and other experiments in the field that the properties of the phylocite element were further refined. Though used with great success in several terraforming projects, in recent years it has been replaced as more advanced techniques have become more commonplace."

From the other side of the conference table, Hjatyn said, "Yet you believe this substance can be useful for our needs here?"

The android replied, "I do, sir. In the computer simulations I have conducted, it has proven to be the one element most capable of safely advancing the chemical conversion process currently under way in Ijuuka's atmosphere. The use of phylocite as an accelerant produced no ill effects in any of the simulations."

"I do not understand," Hjatyn said. "As you have already stated, the transformation process is a lengthy one. Even if this acceleration idea of yours has merit, how do you propose introducing this . . . substance you speak of into the atmosphere?"

By way of reply, Data said, "Computer, display the current program's seventh graphic." A second later, the image on the viewscreen shifted to show dozens of points of blue light moving over the computer-generated model of Ijuuka, assuming what Picard recognized as equidistant positions in high orbit above the planet.

"It is my belief that a synchronized detonation of twenty-six quantum torpedoes will be sufficient. Each can be equipped with a warhead composed of phylocite and delivered to locations plotted to cover as much of the atmosphere as possible while providing an overlapping effect that ensures against gaps in the coverage." On the viewscreen, Picard watched as the group of blue orbs moved closer to the planet and then flashed in unison. An instant later a blue field began to spread outward from each point, expanding until the entire planet was covered by the effect.

"How long will this process take, Commander?" he asked.

Turning his chair until he could look directly at the captain, Data replied, "After detonation, the spread of phylocite throughout the atmosphere will take approximately seven point four days. The initial chemical reactions will begin almost immediately, but the process is intended to continue in concert with the Dokaalan's own terraforming procedures for the next several years. Based on computer projections, the time required for the transformation of the atmosphere into one usable by the Dokaalan people will be reduced by sixty-seven point five percent."

Picard said nothing, instead turning in his chair to study the reactions of the Dokaalan delegation seated around the conference table. Creij, true to her nature as a scientist, seemed both excited and skeptical at the proposal Data had just presented. Conversely, the captain could see that Nidan was taking the appropriate stance as a sworn defender of the Dokaalan's security, his expression doubtful touched with an air of suspicion. Hjatyn, the one to whom the others would be looking for confidence and certainty, was nodding thoughtfully as he studied the viewscreen.

"While I cannot say I am entirely convinced by your findings, Commander," Creij said, "I would welcome the opportunity to discuss it with you in greater detail."

"Certainly, Minister," Data replied. "With Captain Picard's permission, I am at your disposal."

Turning in her seat until she faced Hjatyn, the science minister said, "But if this procedure is sound, we should consider employing it."

"Detonating so many weapons in the planet's atmosphere without any negative effects?" Nidan asked, his voice neutral. "Forgive me, Captain Picard, but I have trouble accepting that."

Picard nodded. "I understand your concerns, Minister Nidan, but the quantum torpedoes Commander Data speaks of are designed to be configured for a variety of uses that are not offensive or destructive in nature. They are routinely used to deliver similar payloads into all manner of stellar phenomena for scientific research. If the decision is made to go forward with this plan, you would all be invited to examine the devices and be present at all phases of the operation." Turning to Data, the captain asked, "Would it be possible to arrange some form of demonstration, Commander?"

"Yes, Captain," the android replied. "It will require time to replicate the necessary quantities of phylocite and load it into the torpedoes, during which time I will have ample opportunity to answer any remaining questions or concerns."

From where he sat at the conference table, Hjatyn nodded slowly before a small smile crept onto his aged features. "Such a remarkable being you are, Commander. Despite your condition, you have still managed to bring this gift to us." Pausing a moment, the elderly leader bowed his head as if in thought before returning his attention to Picard.

"Captain, one of my primary duties since accepting the role of First Minister has been to ensure that the will and vision of my people is preserved as we move forward into this new stage of our society. The remaking of Ijuuka has been fueled by the knowledge that we were creating a monument to those lost as well as a home for those left behind."

Rising from his chair, Hjatyn politely declined the offer of assistance from Picard as he stood up and shuffled his way around the conference table to where Data sat. Placing one hand on the android's shoulder, the Dokaalan said, "I know that I have been most zealous in maintaining that edict in the face of all that you have offered to us, but now I find myself questioning my earlier conviction. One of the greatest obstacles facing the remaking process is the time required. Many who were present when the work began have since passed on, just as many who are involved now will be gone before its completion. It can be discouraging. Your suggestion offers me the option of honoring the spirit of our pledge while still allowing us to complete the labor ourselves." Looking to Data, he added, "Conduct your tests, Commander. I am most interested to see if what you propose is possible."

Picard made no effort to quell the feeling of satisfaction that washed over him at the minister's words. He had suspected that Hjatyn might decline this offer of assistance just as he had all the others, including the option of Federation-aided relocation to a suitable planet for the Dokaalan people. It would have been disappointing to have to accept that decision, but in the end the choice was the Dokaalan's to make, after all.

That Hjatyn had instead accepted this latest idea buoyed the captain's spirits. For the first time since arriving in the Dokaalan system, Picard was finally beginning to feel as though they had a true purpose for being here. So positive was his reaction to this latest development that he even noted Counselor Troi turning in her seat, smiling in his direction as her empathic abilities registered the positive change in his emotional state. Bowing his head formally, he allowed a small smile to play at his lips as he acknowledged her.

Still, he noted that the counselor's own expression was not entirely free of concern. Had her Betazoid senses picked up something else from the Dokaalan leaders during the course of the meeting? She did not seem terribly alarmed, but Picard had long ago become accustomed to even the slightest changes in the body language of his officers. She definitely had something to tell him, he decided, but was waiting for a more appropriate time to bring it to his attention.

Refocusing his attention on the matter at hand, Picard turned to Data. "Make it so, Commander."

"Thank you, sir," Data replied as he began to maneuver his chair toward the exit. He stopped at the sound of the ship's intercom coming to life with the voice of Lieutenant Vale.

"Bridge to Captain Picard," the security chief said. *"Sir, we've received a message from the Dokaalan Security Ministry. They wish to speak to Minister Nidan, but they also inform us that Commander La Forge's shuttlecraft left Ijuuka this morning. They were under the impression that he was returning to the* Enterprise."

The fulfillment Picard felt at the progress made here began to evaporate in the face of Vale's report. If the report from Ijuuka was accurate, the shuttle carrying La Forge, Lieutenant Taurik, and a Dokaalan engineer whose name the captain could not remember just now had been missing for more than ten hours. He was not comforted by the images conjured by this development. Had the shuttle experienced some kind of malfunction? Had they crashed into or onto one of the countless asteroids they would have had to navigate in order to return to the ship?

What if their having gone missing was not an accident at all?

"Number One," he said, turning to Riker, "coordinate a search operation with Lieutenant Vale. Start with the planet and work out from there. I want all of our remaining shuttles out looking for them." With their sensor ability inhibited by the radiation field, they would have to rely on this more rudimentary yet admittedly less effective search measure.

"Aye, sir," Riker said, already rising from his seat and

heading for the bridge with Counselor Troi following after him.

"I am most disturbed by this report," Hjatyn said, returning to his place next to Picard, "and I must admit to feeling somewhat responsible for what has happened. If your people have encountered some difficulty, they have done so while they were our guests. May we assist in your search efforts somehow?"

For a moment Picard considered declining the offer, but to do so might invite suspicion if there was indeed something untoward happening in the shadows here. What if La Forge and Taurik had found something suspicious on Ijuuka? Could it be related to the disaster that had befallen Mining Station Twelve? Would Hjatyn or any of his leaders know about it? Even if none of them were involved, excluding them from any search efforts might alert those actually responsible for the acts of sabotage. Picard decided he could not afford that now, not while he was still lacking so much critical information.

"We welcome any help you are able to provide, First Minister," he replied, forcing his most diplomatic smile onto his face and trying to keep his own misgivings at bay.

As the meeting ended and Hjatyn and his party departed for the docking bay, Picard was left alone in the observation lounge with nothing to do for the moment except wonder about the fate of his wayward officers. It was not the first time an away team had gone missing, of course, but each time it happened it caused a knot of worry to form in his stomach. It would remain there until the fate of La Forge and Taurik was known.

Stopping before the row of viewing ports that formed

the room's back wall, he once again beheld the dense asteroid field surrounding the *Enterprise,* illogically looking for a small, errant shuttlecraft to appear from the debris and put his unease to rest.

Naturally, it did no such thing.

"Damn," Picard said, though there was no one to hear him.

Chapter Nine

ON THE SEVERAL OCCASIONS that he had been taken hostage during his Starfleet career, Geordi La Forge had been thrown into all manner of prison cells, brigs, and various rooms and shipboard compartments converted for such purposes. He therefore considered himself at least somewhat of an informed authority on what it was like to be detained by a hostile party.

Comparatively speaking, the space he and Taurik found themselves in now was an utter pit.

"I see they spared no expense with our accommodations," La Forge said as he paced the length of the room, which he had already measured to be five steps.

From where he sat on one of two makeshift cots provided for the engineers, Taurik said, "From my observations, this room offers little variation from other such areas within this facility."

Unsure as to whether this might be one of the occasions where the Vulcan offered one of his deadpan comments, La Forge nevertheless allowed himself a humorless chuckle. His friend did have a point, in that like every other compartment he had seen on the mining outpost, this one had been built with efficiency rather than comfort in mind. The walls, floor, and ceiling were bare metal plating formed from uniform sections, which the engineer surmised was part of an overall methodology used throughout the colonies. It made sense to construct habitats and other buildings from materials that could in turn be easily employed anywhere else they might be needed with minimal conversion or adaptation requirements.

The room La Forge and Taurik had been confined to was cool though not uncomfortable, with illumination offered by a pair of lighting panels set into the ceiling. Other than the two cots, there were no other furnishings. A small enclosure in the room's far corner, little bigger than a cargo container, housed the room's sparse lavatory.

"Be it ever so humble, I guess," La Forge muttered, returning to his own cot and propping himself up against the wall. The bed's thin mattress did little to protect his body from the cot's metal frame, and a casual feel of the single blanket he had been given added fuel to his suspicions that sleeping here would be anything but pleasant.

It beats being dead.

The bitter reminder pushed to the front of the engineer's thoughts, along with the image of Faeyahr's murder at the hands of the Dokaalan who had captured them on the asteroid. It had been unnecessary, as neither he nor the engineers had posed any threat. Their captors had done it merely to show the *Enterprise* officers that they were willing to go to any lengths in pursuit of their goal, whatever that might be.

Following their capture, the engineers were loaded into the two skiffs and brought to one of the dozens of mining colonies scattered throughout the asteroid field. La Forge had not been able to ascertain their location, or where they were in relation to the Dokaalan's central habitat or the *Enterprise,* despite his best efforts. Upon their arrival here, the Starfleet officers' environmental suits and other equipment had been confiscated, leaving each of them with nothing but their boots and the standard-issue one-piece garment each of them had been wearing underneath his suit.

"I wonder if we got close enough to the ship for them to pick us up on sensors," La Forge wondered aloud as he adjusted his sitting position on the cot in a futile attempt to get more comfortable.

Seated on the edge of his own cot, back straight, both feet flat on the floor and with his hands held clasped before him in what La Forge recognized as a meditative posture, Taurik replied, "I was unable to ascertain their location before we crashed, but the asteroid field's background radiation was interfering with our own sensors as well. The sensors on the *Enterprise* are more powerful, so there is a possibility they may have detected us."

"Even if they didn't," La Forge said, "they'll start wondering where we are in a few hours. I figure the captain will have search parties out looking for us before the next shift change." As he spoke the words, he hoped they sounded more optimistic to Taurik than they did to him.

Trying to ignore the crossbeam from the cot's bed frame that was digging rather rudely into the back of his thigh, he asked, "Any thoughts on why they're keeping us here?" Neither the Dokaalan who had captured them nor those who had taken custody of them upon their arrival here had been forthcoming with any sort of useful information. With what appeared to be plenty of time on his hands, the chief engineer saw no harm in speculating a bit.

Taurik, having not moved from the same sitting position he had assumed nearly half an hour ago, replied, "There are a number of possibilities, Commander. First, there is the perceived value they might place on our engineering skills. We may have also been taken captive for use as leverage should a disagreement develop between Captain Picard and First Minister Hjatyn. I believe humans use the term 'bargaining chip' to describe prisoners placed in similar positions."

"That doesn't sound right," La Forge said. "Hjatyn has been gracious to a fault since we got here. The same for most of his staff." He shook his head. "I don't buy it."

His right eyebrow arching, Taurik said, "Two of the people who participated in our capture did reference the security minister, Nidan."

La Forge continued to vainly squirm for several seconds on the cot before finally giving up and rolling off the oppressive bed, deciding instead to pace the room again. *If nothing else,* he mused, *maybe I'll wear a hole in the deck plating.*

He was almost to his feet when he felt a tug, and looked down to see the material on the leg of his white jumpsuit snagged on the cot's frame. Designed to protect its wearer in survival situations even after the bulkier SEWG was discarded, it was, among other things, tear-resistant, a quality that prevented it from being damaged as it became ensnared on the cot's rough edge. It also kept La Forge from standing up until he could extricate the bit of material from its trap.

"Using his name could have been a ruse," he offered as he freed himself before starting to pace. "And remember, we still haven't found out who's behind the weapons they're using, or that device we found at the processing station." It had become obvious to the chief engineer back on Ijuuka that someone, an outside influence, was working behind the scenes here for some as yet unknown purpose.

The presence of alien weapons, among them outdated Starfleet armaments as well as Klingon and Bajoran disruptors, was evidence enough, but it was Taurik's discovery of the odd contraption connected to one of the processing plant's enormous chemical storage tanks that was the real clincher. With its rodinium outer casing and internal components that were far too sophisticated to have been created with Dokaalan technology.

"That's the big question," he continued. "Who built that thing we found, and why?"

At first looking as though he might reply, Taurik stopped just as he opened his mouth, and La Forge saw his eyes turn toward the door to their room. "Someone is approaching," the Vulcan said as he rose from his cot. La Forge heard nothing, but quickly remembered that his companion's hearing was far better than his own.

True enough, he thought. Several more seconds passed before he heard the telltale sounds of booted feet walking on metal plating, growing louder with each step.

"They're at the door," Taurik said a moment later, after which there was the sound of a locking mechanism being released. The door was pulled open from the outside, revealing two Dokaalan security officers, one shorter than the other. Their pale blue skin contrasted with their single-piece green uniforms, which where highlighted by polished black boots and matching belts. La Forge noted that these were not the two individuals who had captured them on the asteroid.

"Commander La Forge, Lieutenant Taurik," the shorter Dokaalan said, affecting what looked to be a pleasant expression. "My name is Barmiol. I apologize for your being detained, but in time you will understand that it was a necessary action."

Remaining in place, La Forge said, "What I understand is that we were chased and shot at, our friend was killed, and now we've been locked up in this hole. I want to speak to someone in charge, and I want to contact my ship."

Barmiol stepped into the room, his silent companion directly behind him. The affable demeanor did not waver, but when the Dokaalan spoke, some of the geniality was gone from his voice. "That will not be possible for the time being, I'm afraid. Your being allowed to communicate with your superiors would raise many questions we are not prepared to answer just now. I have been instructed to see to it that you are made as comfortable as possible, but I also have orders to kill you should you try to escape or interfere in our operations here in any way." As if to emphasize this last point, the Dokaalan casually rested his right hand on the butt of what looked to be a Klingon disruptor holstered at his waist.

"And what exactly are you doing here?" La Forge challenged. "It's obvious that you've been getting help from an outside source." He pointed to Barmiol's weapon. "Where did you get that, or the others we found?"

Barmiol shook his head. "That is not your concern,

Commander. Instead, you should concentrate on being as cooperative as possible. For example, I have been sent here to determine how much you learned about our activities on Ijuuka. What did you find during your inspections?"

The way the question was phrased told La Forge that Barmiol probably already knew the answer. After all, it had not been until after their discovery of the mysterious device attached to the processing plant's storage tank that they were challenged by anyone. Someone had to have been monitoring the engineers' activities, no doubt waiting to see if they stumbled across something incriminating and then moving to seize control of the situation before either he or Taurik could make contact with the *Enterprise*.

With that in mind, La Forge saw no reason to engage in deceit or some other stalling tactic that would ultimately prove fruitless and perhaps even anger their captors. Still, there was a chance that someone on the *Enterprise* might discover something suspicious going on with the Dokaalan. Therefore, the trick here and now, he decided, was to provide enough truth to placate Barmiol and his companion without letting on precisely how much the engineers knew.

"We found a device down on Ijuuka," he said. "It's designed to interfere in the atmospheric plant's chemical mixing process. Since we didn't have time for a complete investigation, we don't know exactly what it's doing, or why."

Nodding, Barmiol replied, "You also detected variations in the computer systems overseeing the plant's automated processes, yes? The conversation with your friend was overheard by one of our people in the control room."

So much for half-truths, La Forge thought, feeling his

pulse beginning to quicken a bit. Was it his imagination, or had the room grown warmer in the last few minutes?

"Given that the changes we detected were very subtle," Taurik said, "almost undetectable except by someone possessing extensive software programming expertise, it is logical to assume that whatever is happening in the processing facility is taking place without the knowledge or consent of most of the Dokaalan people."

Barmiol actually laughed at that. It was a short, lifeless reaction that grated on La Forge's ears, sounding to him as though the man was anything but amused.

"Lieutenant," the Dokaalan said, "it would be logical to assume that what we are doing is without the knowledge or consent of *any* of these people."

Clasping his hands behind his back, Barmiol began to pace the small room, an action that caused both engineers to move out of his way as he stepped forward. La Forge gave brief thought to trying to overpower the other man, but a glance toward the door showed that Barmiol's companion had placed his hand on his own weapon, ready to draw and fire at the first sign of trouble. He had done nothing else during the entire conversation except to stand silently in the doorway and look intimidating. Definitely a subordinate, the engineer decided, an assistant or perhaps just a low-ranking soldier of some kind.

"Make no mistake," Barmiol continued, "the task the Dokaalan are undertaking here is nothing short of extraordinary, and the planet their efforts will eventually yield will be quite beautiful indeed. However, without several modifications their work is ultimately useless to us."

"Us?" La Forge asked, his brow furrowing in confusion. "Who is 'us'?"

Ignoring the questions, Barmiol continued, "Changes in the composition of the planet's new atmosphere and ecosystem are needed before it will be able to support my people. Fortunately, the reformation processes already put into motion by the Dokaalan have proven to be compatible with our needs, and the changes we must make to complete the process are not drastic. They simply take time and patience in order to prevent detection."

"So, you're not Dokaalan," La Forge said. "You and whoever else is working with you." He stepped closer, but halted as Barmiol's companion started to draw his weapon. Holding his hands out away from his body, he locked eyes with the security officer, studying him but unable to discern any clue as to his real identity. "What are you, some kind of shapeshifters? Changelings?"

During his career, the engineer had come across a handful of races possessing the ability to alter their physical form, from the allasomorphs of Daled IV to the Founders of the Dominion from the Gamma Quadrant to the omnipotent being known simply as Q. Was one of those races up to something out here in the farthest reaches of the explored galaxy? Had Q set into motion another of the maddening games or tests he had inflicted on the *Enterprise* crew in the years since they had first encountered him? La Forge doubted that. After all, it had been years since the annoying entity had made his unwelcome presence known, and the goings-on here did not smack of Q's usual flights of whimsy.

No, he decided. *I'm missing something here, but what?*

"If you require stealth for your activities," Taurik said, his hands clasped behind his back, "then it seems the

Dokaalan would be most displeased to learn of your interference here."

Chuckling in that manner which unnerved La Forge, Barmiol replied, "Considering that the changes we are introducing will leave the planet unusable to them, you would be correct."

"These people have been working for generations to make a new home for themselves," La Forge said, feeling his anger rising, "and you're just going to take it from them? Eventually they're going to find out what you're doing. Do you expect them to sit by and let you ruin their hopes for a future on that planet?"

Making his way back to the door, Barmiol shook his head. "Of course not, and we have plans to deal with that problem when the time comes." He let the sentence hang in the air for several seconds, allowing the true meaning of the words to sink in, and La Forge felt his stomach tighten at the unspoken threat they conveyed. Who was this person, and whom did he represent?

Apparently noting the engineer's increasing ire, Barmiol said, "Now you understand why you must remain our guests for the time being. Cooperate and no harm will come to you." He stepped back into the passageway outside the room along with his still silent companion. When he turned to look back at the Starfleet officers, the smile that had teased his features throughout the conversation was gone. "Any attempt to escape or to cause other disruption will be met with harsh consequences."

With that the door slammed shut, its echo resonating across the room's metal surfaces but not so loud that La Forge failed to hear the sound of the door's locking mechanism clicking back into place.

"Nice guy," the engineer said, listening to the fading footfalls as their visitors walked away. When he could no longer hear any sounds from the corridor beyond their cell, he turned to Taurik. "Well, they're not Dokaalan, so who the hell are they?"

Moving to retake his seated position at the edge of his cot, the Vulcan replied, "As you said yourself, they could be some form of shapechanging life-form, though we do not possess sufficient information to know whether they are of a race we have previously encountered. Is it possible the Dominion has launched a new offensive against the Alpha Quadrant?"

La Forge shook his head. "We're a long way from the wormhole near Deep Space 9." The unique stellar phenomenon, found nearly a decade earlier in the Bajor system shortly after that planet's liberation from the oppressive rule of the Cardassian Union, was a stable conduit that led more than seventy thousand light-years across the galaxy to the Idran system in the Gamma Quadrant.

Starfleet exploration of this newly accessible area of the distant galaxy had begun almost immediately after the wormhole's discovery, an initiative resulting in contact with new races both friendly and hostile. The Dominion had fallen squarely into the latter category, led by a race of shapechanging beings who called themselves the Founders. With their armies of genetically engineered soldiers, the Jem'Hadar, the Founders had nearly succeeded in conquering the Federation and its allies during the Dominion War, which had ended three years ago.

"Even if they *had* found another wormhole or other method to get here from the Gamma Quadrant, which I doubt," the chief engineer continued, "we're weeks away from Federation space even at high warp. Why set up camp all the way out here?"

Nodding, Taurik replied, "It makes no logical sense to do so, at least from a purely military perspective."

"Another thing," La Forge added. "In their natural forms, the Founders can exist in pretty much any planetary environment. They don't need to terraform a planet to a specific set of parameters." He had started to walk the length of the room again as he talked, all five paces of it, with the slight metallic clank of the deck plating beneath his boots almost calming as he tried to think.

Almost.

"Whoever they are," Taurik said, "they are obviously concealing their true appearance in some manner, be they shapeshifters or simply employing a form of disguise. If so, then there is a strong possibility we are dealing with a humanoid species. Their life-support requirements are obviously similar enough to the Dokaalan that they can exist in these mining colonies at least for short periods of time. They may have fashioned other facilities for extended habitation that better suit their own environmental needs."

Running his hand along the surface of their cell's metal door, La Forge nodded. "It all sounds great, but it'd sound better if we could tell someone else." He was only paying partial attention, though, as he examined the door's lock with his ocular implants. It was a formidable mechanism, he decided, and would not be easy to overcome.

"And the only way we're going to do that," he said, "is if we find a way out of here."

Chapter Ten

IN THE YEARS that had passed since he had become a starship captain, Jean-Luc Picard had mastered the art of interpreting a situation by studying its effects on the body language of the men and women under his command. It was a time-tested technique upon which he had come to rely, whether he and his crew were encountering a unique stellar phenomenon for the first time, making contact with a previously unknown alien race, or even preparing for battle. Silent gestures, the way his people held their posture while manning their stations, how they spoke to one another or did not speak—all of that, along with an assortment of other telltale indicators both noticeable and intangible, had long been his guide as he sought to gauge how a given set of circumstances might play out.

Right now, as he sat in his command chair on the bridge of the *Enterprise,* watching the men and women around him see to their respective duties with a vitality that seemed to have gone missing during the past weeks, all of those signs told him that his crew was hopeful. There were no overt clues this time as there had been on other occasions, but Picard was still able to sense an energy playing about the corridors of his ship that had been missing for too long, he decided.

And much of that energy was focused here, in the nerve center of his beloved vessel.

"Mr. Data," he said as he swiveled his chair around to face the science station at the rear of the bridge, "are you ready to commence your experiment?"

Still using the antigravity work sled to move about, the android turned the chair in response to the captain's query. "Yes, sir. I have just finished entering the torpedo firing sequence into the computer and I am making my final adjustments now. Once the sequence is initiated, the computer will direct the launching of all twenty-six quantum torpedoes."

Picard knew that the process would take several minutes, with the ship's colossal computer system overseeing everything about the process, including timing the reloading of the ship's torpedo launchers. Allowing the proper interval to elapse between volleys was just another aspect of this finely timed operation, ensuring that each of the projectiles could pursue their individually plotted courses through Ijuuka's atmosphere to detonate almost simultaneously as the weapons reached equidistant positions around the planet.

Satisfied with the report, Picard said, "Proceed at your discretion, Commander."

Data had overseen every last detail of the operation, from directing the outfitting of the suite of quantum torpedoes with their newly fashioned phylocite warheads to designing the spread pattern they would need to perform as they flew through Ijuuka's atmosphere and even programming the firing sequence necessary to accomplish that goal. Science Minister Creij had assisted him, of course, her knowledge of the planet's environmental composition and the progress of the Dokaalan's own terraforming efforts proving to be nothing short of instrumental. Using information she provided, Data was, he believed, able to determine the proper quantities of phylocite needed for each torpedo in order to balance out the weapons' combined effects as they entered the planet's atmosphere.

What if he's made an error?

The question flashed without prompting through the captain's mind, and for the briefest of instants Picard felt his expression falter in response. It was unlike him to doubt the abilities of his second officer, but it was also unusual for the android to have suffered the type of debilitating injury from which he was still recuperating. In addition to the work he was overseeing here, Data was also devoting a significant portion of his formidable internal faculties toward repairing the damage inflicted upon him.

He had continued to make progress, Picard knew, as he watched Data work at the science station. Though still reliant on the engineer's work sled for mobility, he was now able to move both arms now and turn his head. The physical effects of his impairment were being dealt with, and the captain expected that his friend soon would make a full recovery.

However, what if he had also suffered some form of mental breakdown of which he was not yet aware? Recent events had forcibly reminded Picard that Data was still a machine, and not an invulnerable one at that. Was he still susceptible to further incapacitation? What if his efforts to help the Dokaalan were being hindered by a lingering side effect of the mysterious malady he had endured, something that might not make its presence known until the worst possible time?

No, the captain decided. Based on past experience, he was certain that Data would not place himself in a position where he might threaten the ship or any of the crew if he believed himself to be dangerously impaired.

Would he?

Stop it, Picard chastised himself. *Trust your people.*

"Data," he heard Riker say a moment later, "how long after the torpedoes detonate will we know if we've been successful?"

Still working at the science station, the android turned and replied, "Preliminary indications of the proper chemical reactions should be apparent within three minutes of detonation, sir. As I explained earlier, however, the total impact of the phylocite's introduction will not be complete for approximately twelve point six years, assuming there are no changes in the Dokaalan's own atmospheric processing efforts."

"Do not worry about that, Commander," said Creij, her aged blue face brightening the image of her displayed on one of the science station's monitors as she offered what passed for a Dokaalan smile. *"Your work here has served to renew our commitment to seeing this project through to the end."*

Like Hjatyn and the rest of his delegation, the science minister had elected to remain at the Dokaalan's central colony. The time required for the *Enterprise* to traverse the asteroid field was long enough that Dr. Crusher had recommended against any of their hosts staying aboard the ship. Creij had resisted at first, but the scientist in her saw the logic behind the doctor's request.

"I wish I could be there to witness this momentous occasion firsthand," she said a moment later, *"but it is a small price to pay. Besides, I have plans to walk around on the planet itself, and I have already selected a location upon which to build my new home."*

The sentiment drew pleased reactions from the rest of the bridge crew, Picard noted, only adding to his growing enthusiasm. It had taken little time for word about Data's bold proposal to aid the Dokaalan to spread throughout the ship, relieving much of the regret everyone seemed to share over what had happened with the rescue operation at the mining outpost. The potential to help these people make their dream a reality after so many years of labor and sacrifice, beyond the superhuman efforts they had expended merely to survive, was working to strengthen the crew's blunted and burdened resolve.

The positive emotional change was still somewhat tempered, of course, by the knowledge that two of their fellow crew members remained missing. Though the full complement of the *Enterprise*'s shuttlecraft and shuttlepods had been deployed into the asteroid field in search of Commander La Forge and Lieutenant Taurik or any sign that their own shuttle had crashed into one of the asteroids, so far the effort had yielded no results. Even during its own maneuver through the field in order to position itself in orbit over Ijuuka, the starship's formidable array of sensors had been brought to bear but to no avail. Not even the *Ballard*'s distress beacon had been detected, though Picard knew there was no way to know whether that might be due to radiation interference.

What he did know was that he was dissatisfied with the progress of the search to this point, as well as the apprehension he felt over the implications such failure represented.

Still, he could not allow that anxiety to cloud his emotions now, not while there was still so much to be done.

Turning his attention to Troi, who until now had been observing the proceedings in silence, he asked, "Counselor, have you sensed anything new?"

"Only an anticipation over what's about to happen," the counselor replied. "There seems to be some nervousness, of course, but that's to be expected. Mostly I sense that they're hopeful our plan will work. As Hjatyn said earlier, this seems to have reinvigorated their passion for the terraforming project."

"It's not as if they'd grown complacent or discouraged," Riker said. "Considering they've been at this for more than a hundred years, I don't think anyone can question their dedication."

Picard agreed. From what he had seen, the Dokaalan were anything but an impatient or easily disheartened people. Given their situation, those were indulgences they would not have ever been able to afford.

"Captain," Lieutenant Vale called out from the tactical station, "we're being hailed by First Minister Hjatyn."

"On screen," Picard ordered.

During the journey to reach Ijuuka, the captain had ordered the dispersal of three subspace repeater beacons within the asteroid field at Data's recommendation in order to better facilitate communications between the *Enterprise* and the Dokaalan central habitat. The decision was a wise one, as evidenced by the clarity of the image on the main viewer as it switched to a picture of the elderly leader.

"First Minister," Picard said by way of greeting. "We are almost ready to commence the firing sequence."

Nodding, Hjatyn replied, *"So Creij tells me, Captain. I wanted to wish you good fortune. You carry with you the dreams of all my people."*

"And we will do our utmost to safeguard that, sir," the captain said, bowing his head formally toward the viewscreen. "Please stand by." At his prompting, the image of the Dokaalan leader vanished from the screen, replaced once more with a view of Ijuuka. From the *Enterprise*'s current position, orbiting twenty thousand kilometers above the planet's surface, only its curved edge was visible as it dominated the lower third of the display. Beneath Ijuuka's oppressive, enveloping pale brown cloud cover was a world in waiting, he knew, waiting for science, technology, and sheer force of will to wrestle it from its prison.

Studying the image on the screen, Picard envisioned the planet as it might be a decade hence if all went according to plan, lush and green and vibrant. It would be a paradise from which the Dokaalan would build a new society, using the steadfast community they had already forged here among the asteroids as a foundation.

It will be a prize worthy of these people's indomitable spirit.

Turning his chair to face the science station, Picard asked, "Mr. Data?"

"I have finished my preparations, Captain," the android replied. "We can begin on your order."

As Data gave his report, the captain imagined he felt a

tingle of electricity move across the bridge. Officers at their various stations straightened in their seats and fingers moved a bit faster across consoles. There was no denying his people's anticipation as they waited for the operation to begin. That in itself seemed like a good enough reason to avoid delaying any longer.

"Make it so, Commander."

The first volley of four quantum torpedoes launched ten seconds later, blue-white streaks arcing away from the *Enterprise* and immediately separating to follow their prescribed trajectories toward the far side of the planet. Within moments the next wave was fired, no one on the bridge saying anything as the process repeated itself again and again until all twenty-six weapons were away.

"Shifting to tactical view," Data called out as the final two torpedoes pulled away from the ship, heading directly for their assigned positions over Ijuuka's surface. Then the image on the viewscreen changed to show a three-dimensional computer-generated schematic of the planet. Twenty-six points of blue light now formed a pattern across the graphic, illustrating the independent trajectories now acting to guide the torpedoes to their designated positions.

"Detonation in ten seconds," Data reported, his attention focused on his console. No one else said anything, the only other thing Picard could hear on the bridge being the normal ambient sounds of the various workstations. Watching the torpedoes' final seconds of life, the captain realized he was holding his breath in anticipation. He remembered to exhale just as Data counted down.

"Zero."

Twenty-six eruptions of blue light flared simultaneously on the viewscreen, and from each a yellow sphere began to expand outward, pushing away from each torpedo's detonation point and beginning to canvas a portion of the planet. In his mind's eye Picard saw the phylocite mixing with and commencing the lengthy process of altering the chemical structure of Ijuuka's atmosphere.

"Total atmospheric exposure should be complete within two hours, Captain," Data said as he turned from the science station. "I am already beginning to register minute alterations in the composition of the upper mesosphere."

Picard could not tear his eyes from the viewscreen as the first moments of the operation unfolded just as Data had predicted. Watching the computer's representation of Ijuuka and the changes the torpedoes were affecting on the planet's atmosphere, the captain permitted himself the private luxury of basking in pride at what Data and his team, and by extension the rest of the *Enterprise* crew, were accomplishing here. Until this moment, it had been nothing more than an abstract theory, but now it was happening—an outlandish premise willed into reality by his people's technical acumen, their dedication to duty and to the Starfleet principles of helping others in time of need, and even simply because of their passion to triumph over any obstacle erected before them.

From the report Data had submitted, Picard knew that the process would continue for several weeks. Like a timed-release fertilizer that a gardener might use to nourish the plants and flowers in his care, the terraforming agent Data had introduced here would bond itself at the atomic level to the conglomeration of artificial and Dokaalan-engineered gases currently composing Ijuuka's atmosphere. Then the truly wondrous properties of the phylocite would go to work, laboring to accelerate the process the Dokaalan had already put into motion in a dogged attempt to push the transformation of Ijuuka into high gear and giving even the oldest members of the beleaguered mining community a chance to see the fruits of their labor within their lifetimes.

Having seen flourishing examples of terraforming for himself, it was easy for Picard to envision the end result of what was happening here today. Should the Dokaalan efforts prove successful, the planet that emerged from the process would undoubtedly be the object of study by Federation scientists for years to come. Ijuuka could well take its place alongside Blue Horizon, New Halana, and Venus as landmarks of this most audacious example of living beings challenging nature and their place in it.

"Lieutenant Vale," he said, "open a channel to First Minister Hjatyn. I'm sure he and the rest of the council will be interested in our progress."

The security chief's smile was nearly infectious as she nodded in reply. "My pleasure, Captain."

An insistent beeping alert suddenly filled the air of the bridge, making everyone turn to the science station. Rising from his chair, Picard looked to where Data was already working, his fingers dancing across his console so fast that they seemed almost a blur.

"Mr. Data?" the captain prompted.

Not turning from his workstation, the android replied, "Sensors are picking up deviations in the chemical reactions taking place in the planet's atmosphere. I am attempting to analyze them now."

Silence engulfed the bridge as Data worked, each second that passed adding to Picard's growing dread that something was wrong. On the main viewer, the yellow plumes were continuing to enlarge over the computer graphic of Ijuuka, pushing outward from the torpedoes' original detonation points. Did the picture represent new hope being infused into a dead world, or had the *Enterprise* merely succeeded in pulling a shroud over an already long-dead corpse?

"The introduction of the phylocite into Ijuuka's atmospheric composition is not in line with our computer projections," Data finally said after nearly two minutes of silence. "I am detecting the release of several elements that should not be factors in the terraforming process. Argon molecules are moving to fuse with the existing oxygen and nitrogen, and I am picking up indications of methane and lithium being introduced, as well."

Stepping up from the command area until he stood directly behind Data at the science station, Picard asked, "What are you saying, Commander?"

"The alterations currently under way in the atmosphere are inconsistent with what is required for our acceleration of the terraforming process to be successful, sir." The android's expression remained neutral as he turned from his console, but Picard thought he could see resignation in Data's gold eyes.

"I will need to conduct further scans," Data continued, "but it is possible that we may have damaged or even nullified the changes introduced by the Dokaalan."

Just as he had felt their excitement only minutes earlier, Picard now sensed the energy draining away from everyone on the bridge. Their enthusiasm, and his, had all but evaporated in the face of Data's report.

Simply put, they had failed.

Chapter Eleven

IF THE MOOD on the bridge had been somber, Picard decided, it was now positively dire in the observation lounge, and with good reason, so far as he was concerned.

"I don't understand," Riker said, his expression glum as he sat slump-shouldered with both hands placed palms-down on the polished surface of the conference table. "Everything was plotted and calculated down to the last detail." Looking up to where the android had positioned himself near the room's main viewscreen, he added, "Wasn't it?"

"That is correct, sir, within a certain context," Data replied. "The formulae mixing phylocite into the Ijuukan atmosphere were devised using all the information at my disposal, whether gathered using our own sensor equipment or given to me by Science Minister Creij. I cross-referenced everything she provided against the operational records and design specifications for their processing plants, and compared those findings to the relevant information available to us from Terraform Command. This in turn allowed me to devise the proper ratio of phylocite and other elements that could best interact with the planet's natural atmospheric composition as well as with the changes being made by the Dokaalan's own reformation efforts."

"So what happened?" Riker asked, frustration lacing every word.

To Picard, the android seemed to ponder the question for several seconds before slowly shaking his head. "I do not know, sir. In all seventeen computer simulations I performed, the results were virtually identical, varying only with respect to the rate at which the phylocite began to bond with the other elements comprising Ijuuka's atmosphere. These variations were explained by different patterns I experimented with for spreading the quantum torpedoes around the planet."

"And nothing in any of those tests suggested anything resembling what we're witnessing now?" Picard asked from where he sat at the head of the conference table.

Pausing momentarily, Data actually bowed his head, a gesture that for someone with emotions would almost certainly have been born out of shame. "No, sir. I am at a loss to explain it at this time."

The gesture of concession, real or mimicked, did little to ease the captain's growing anger and frustration. Amid all of that, the questions Picard had earlier raised to himself regarding Data's competence were now clamoring for his attention. Had the android made some sort of colossal error due to a curtailed ability to carry out his duties?

Try as he might, the captain simply could not bring himself to believe that. There had to be some other reason for what had happened, something of which they were not yet aware. What could it be?

"Is the process reversible?" Riker asked. "Is there something else we can do?"

"Further tests and examination of the effects currently taking place in the atmosphere will be necessary to determine that, sir," Data said, "but without additional intervention, I believe the eventual outcome of what is happening now will be an atmosphere incompatible with Dokaalan life-support requirements. I intend to begin my investigation as soon as we are adjourned here."

Replaying the events of the last half hour over in his mind, Picard found himself dwelling instead on the consequences of the failed experiment. How much damage had they inflicted? If he understood the process Data had put into motion, the full ramifications of their actions here today might not be known for years, but the preliminary results were alarming:

The planet would be useless to the Dokaalan.

There were other emotions running rampant, as well, each harassing and threatening to overwhelm him as he struggled with the gravity of this situation. First, there was embarrassment at his and the *Enterprise* crew's apparent inability to aid the Dokaalan after all the promises to the contrary. Sorrow mixed with anger was present, too, of course, at the thought that all of the work these people had performed, more than a century of laboring toward the realization of a dream, might all have been destroyed in a span of minutes.

Overshadowing all of that, Picard realized, was a foreboding sense of déjà vu.

Time had not yet lifted the heaviness weighing on his

heart since the loss of the *U.S.S. Juno* at the hands of the Ontailians. Though he, and the Ontailians, had ultimately been found innocent in the actions that had resulted in that tragedy, the exoneration had not stopped him from repeatedly reexamining the incident in search of some other decision he could have made or some other step he could have taken. Unable to summon any satisfactory answers, Picard knew that the *Juno* disaster would join a relatively short list of events from his life that would forever haunt him.

Right alongside what's happened here today, he mused bitterly as he allowed his gaze to wander beyond the viewports and to the field of asteroids drifting past the ship. *That list seems to be getting longer all the time.*

"Captain?" prompted Counselor Troi, rousing him from his reverie. "Are you all right?"

Aware that she would be sensing the cavalcade of emotions running through him at the moment, Picard knew it was pointless to deflect the question or attempt to offer any false reassurance. "Just considering the enormity of the situation, Counselor." Turning his attention back to Data, he said, "Commander, I assume you're continuing your investigations and attempting to devise possible remedies to this condition?"

"Absolutely, sir," the android replied, nodding excitedly. "I have already begun a full analysis of the . . ."

"Bridge to Captain Picard," said Lieutenant Vale, her voice interrupting the conversation via the intercom. *"First Minister Hjatyn has hailed us and is requesting to speak with you, sir."*

Sighing heavily, Picard exchanged knowing looks with his senior staff. How many more times would he be forced to convey unpleasant news to these people? At each unfortunate card that had been dealt to the Dokaalan since the *Enterprise*'s arrival, Hjatyn and his fellow leaders had shown unwavering forgiveness and understanding. There had to be a limit to their ability to offer absolution, not that he was particularly interested in discovering that threshold.

I'm not interested in hiding from it, either.

"Put him through, Lieutenant," Picard said as he rose from his chair, taking the moment to straighten his uniform jacket before the observation lounge's viewscreen activated and displayed an image of the aged Dokaalan leader.

"Captain Picard," Hjatyn said by way of greeting, and the captain saw that the events of the day were most definitely taking their toll on the first minister. The Dokaalan's eyes seemed heavier and he appeared to stand even more stoop-shouldered than the last time Picard had seen him. In addition to overseeing preparations for the ceremonies and other memorials in honor of those lost in the Mining Station Twelve disaster, no doubt he and the rest of the Zahanzei Council had spent much of the day dealing with the latest developments on Ijuuka and its effects on the rest of the colonies. There would be much in the way of explanations and investigations already under way, to say nothing of trying to assure the people that the situation was not as dire as rumor was sure to have cast it.

But, he wondered silently, *are they lying?*

"First Minister," Picard said, "I have no words that could possibly begin to offer sufficient apology for what we've done."

Hjatyn held up a feeble hand, stopping Picard from saying anything further. *"Captain, did you intend deliberate harm toward my people?"*

His voice was tired, but Picard still picked up the strain behind the words. The captain paused for a moment before answering, realizing as he did so that he had actually allowed his mouth to fall open in surprised response to Hjatyn's blunt question.

Schooling his features to resume his normal, composed expression, Picard said, "Of course not, sir. We were as horrified to learn of the results of the operation as you undoubtedly were."

"I somehow doubt that, Captain," Hjatyn replied, and for the first time Picard thought he sensed bitterness in the aged leader's tone. *"Have you been able to ascertain a cause for what you . . . for what has happened?"*

"No, sir." The words were like daggers in Picard's heart. "Please know that my crew and I will not rest until we have found not only an explanation but also a remedy."

Hjatyn nodded, his expression taking on an almost wistful air. For an odd moment the captain was reminded of a similar mannerism that his father had employed on those frequent occasions when he discovered one of his sons perpetrating some act of mischief. It was a look of understanding, one which often conveyed that Jean-Luc or Robert Picard, or both, had failed once again to outsmart their wizened father.

Dammit, Picard thought. *I don't want to be understood, or forgiven.*

On the viewscreen, Hjatyn said, *"As I am sure you are aware, Captain, today's . . . unfortunate events have caused a significant amount of unrest among my people. Many are calling for an immediate and complete severing of contact with you."* The small, tired smile returned as he added, *"Naturally we have no means of expelling you from our community, or of taking any other form of offensive action against you, but I am being pressured to ask you and your ship to leave.*"

The hesitation was there. Picard could hear it in the Dokaalan's voice, and he also noted how Hjatyn had phrased his statement. He did not agree with those calling for the *Enterprise* to depart Dokaalan space. There was still a chance to salvage something from this situation, to somehow assure the elderly leader that all was not lost and that he and his crew would exhaust every option to help these people.

"If that is your decision, First Minister, then you have my word that we will leave as we came—in peace." He stepped closer to the viewer, holding his hands out in a gesture of supplication. "But I would ask that you consider all of our actions since arriving here before making that decision. Give my people a chance to analyze what's happened on Ijuuka and attempt to find a solution. Let us help you, in whatever way we can."

Picard heard voices blaring through the intercom, their owners somewhere beyond the range of the communication's visual pickup. The words were muddled, but there was no mistaking the sounds of disagreement among members of the chambers of the Zahanzei Council. Hjatyn turned away from the screen, trying to restore order in the room.

"Nothing like being the center of attention," Riker said, softly enough that his voice would not carry across the connection to the Dokaalan.

Ignoring the remark, Picard instead glanced over his shoulder to where Troi was standing. "Counselor?"

"There is a considerable difference of opinion over

whether or not we should be asked to leave," Troi replied, also keeping her voice low so as not to be overheard by anyone on the other end of the communication. The captain noted how her brow knit as she worked to focus her attention on the emotional frenzy apparently unfolding among the Dokaalan leadership. "The council seems divided into factions for and against the idea, with anger, sympathy, even desperation running rampant. First Minister Hjatyn is attempting to maintain his own composure, but he is understandably torn between the two sides." She had more to say, but she stopped as Hjatyn returned his attention to Picard.

"Captain," he said, *"as you can see, tensions are running high. There is much understandable discouragement at the situation on Ijuuka, but already we are learning that there may be some good news. Science Minister Creij tells us that we may be able to adapt our reformation efforts to account for the sudden changes in the atmosphere."* The aged leader actually shrugged at his own words. *"She will need time to investigate her theory, of course, but it would seem that our goal remains attainable even if the challenge has become greater."* He nodded, ostensibly more to himself than to Picard or anyone else, before adding, *"It is a glimmer of hope, but one that we will embrace with the same passion that has allowed us to face other obstacles."*

"If Minister Creij desires or requires anything from us, she has only to ask," Picard pledged, seizing on the sliver of optimism Hjatyn seemed to be offering. Being asked to leave now, without an opportunity to somehow make right what they had done so terribly wrong, would be worse than the failure itself. There was no way he could slink back to Federation space and report to Admiral Nechayev that he had left the Dokaalan in more adverse straits than he had found them. Such a proposition was simply unacceptable to him.

"Do not worry, Captain," Hjatyn said. *"You and your crew have more than proven your sincerity. I believe those who do not currently share my opinion can be swayed, but it will take time."*

The Dokaalan leader stopped as Science Minister Creij stepped into view, bowing her head formally in Picard's direction. *"Captain."*

"Minister Creij," the captain responded. "If you wish to coordinate your research with my people, we can arrange for the necessary personnel and equipment to be transferred to your location. Given the difficulties your people seem to have after spending prolonged periods aboard the *Enterprise,* this seems the better way to go."

Her pale blue features warming as she smiled, Creij said, *"I may well take you up on that offer, Captain, but there is something else that a few of us have been discussing."*

"Creij, wait," Hjatyn said. *"We need to talk more. . . ."*

Placing a withered hand on his shoulder, the science minister offered what Picard took to be a reassuring smile. *"Worry not, old friend."* To the captain, she said, *"There are a handful of us on the council who have been debating the merits of a suggestion you made earlier, Captain, that of relocating us."*

Picard had not been expecting that, and made no attempt to share his look of surprise with Riker and Troi, both of whom wore expressions that mirrored his astonishment. When he had first broached the subject of relocation to the council leaders during one of their first meetings, Hjatyn had expressed polite yet firm opposition to the idea. According to him, a majority of the Dokaalan were driven by the desire to complete the terraforming of Ijuuka, seeking to create both a new home for the colonists and a memorial for the millions of people lost generations ago along with the Dokaalan's home planet.

"It's certainly an option, Minister," the captain replied. "We would be happy to assist you in any way that we are able."

Sighing, Hjatyn said, *"We have given this matter some discussion, Captain, even before the . . . unfortunate incident earlier today. The idea of remaking Ijuuka into a world for us to settle is a grand ambition, and at the time it was first envisioned it was one of a very limited number of options for our long-term survival."* He leaned forward until his withered face nearly filled the viewscreen. *"Your arrival has changed that in ways we scarcely hoped to dream about, even when First Minister Zahanzei himself approved the launch of the drone ships so long ago."*

"There are many worlds where we come from that are ideally suited to your people," Troi said. "You would be welcomed with open arms by any of the races who are members of the Federation, or we can find a world for you to call your own."

"Please understand that this matter is still being debated by the council," Creij said, *"and that we have not yet even posed the question to the populace in order to gauge their opinion. I know that we were rather adamant in declining our earlier offer to relocate us, but there is growing sentiment among our fellow council members that we can forge a new life for ourselves on*

another world, to say nothing of creating a suitable monument to those who perished with Dokaal."

The notion of leaving this existence behind for life on Ijuuka, risking the uncertainty of an artificially engineered planet at the expense of the relative familiarity of the asteroid colonies, would undoubtedly have been a difficult concept to embrace for many Dokaalan. Picard could not help but wonder how they would react when faced with the prospect of traveling across the galaxy, to one of the many stars that had never been anything more than a faraway pinpoint of light. He tried to imagine being faced with the concept for the first time, but found himself ill equipped to envision such a set of circumstances. Though he had spent the majority of his own life traveling among the stars and still believed he possessed an appropriate sense of wonder and awe at doing so, he would never again be able to appreciate the sense of excitement, or trepidation, that came with the idea of journeying to the stars for the first time.

I envy you that, he silently conceded.

As was explained to him during an earlier meeting with Hjatyn and the council, nearly two-thirds of the community had been born on one of the asteroid-based outposts, having never seen the world from which their forebears had come. Many of the younger Dokaalan had not yet been born when the terraforming project began, and many still would not live to see its completion. For them, this was the only life they had ever known. In contrast, Hjatyn himself actually had lived on Dokaal as a much younger man, but he was now approaching the end of even his people's average yet comparatively protracted life span.

"First Minister, the Federation has specialists trained

in handling these types of situations," Riker offered to the Dokaalan leaders. "We've relocated people for all sorts of reasons like war recovery and even natural disasters like what you've endured. It will take time and work, but it can be done, and done well."

On the viewscreen, Hjatyn said, *"Many of our people have looked to your arrival as a gift from Dokaa, Commander. I realize you do not share our religious beliefs, and I confess that I myself am not a spiritual person."* Smiling, he nodded in that genial, paternal manner that undoubtedly reinforced his image as a leader of the Dokaalan people. *"Still, when I see the power and abilities you wield and the generosity with which you employ them, I have to wonder if the more devout among us are right after all. With that in mind, I find myself wondering how best to graciously accept your generous offer so that I may honor Dokaa's wishes."*

"They may not be able to do that."

The voice came from behind Picard, and he turned to see Dr. Crusher standing in the doorway to the observation lounge. So intent was he on the conversation with Hjatyn that he had not even heard the doors open. Having long ago become accustomed to reading her facial expressions and body language, he could tell by the taut line of her jaw that she had brought unpleasant news with her.

"Doctor?" he prompted, the word barely a whisper as he felt his heart beginning to sink.

"We've figured out the problems with the Dokaalan when they stay aboard the ship too long," Crusher replied. "As we suspected, the radiation field does have something to do with it, but that's only part of it."

"I do not understand," Hjatyn said, confusion lacing his words. *"What else could it be?"*

Crusher drew a deep breath before responding. Finally, she shook her head in resignation. "According to our findings, the Dokaalan did this to themselves."

Chapter Twelve

Translated from the personal journal of Hjatyn:

GLANCING BACK THROUGH the pages of this journal, it occurs to me that I have not often received the opportunity to record something positive or uplifting that has happened. Instead, it seems as though I am always writing about one of the many trials that continue to face our people, or even of a grave tragedy that has occurred.

Today is different. A minor victory, yes, but a victory just the same. Given the meager existence we have managed to carve for ourselves in the time since Dokaal's destruction, any success is to be celebrated, and writing about it only serves to heighten my enthusiasm. After all, it is yet another in a string of triumphs our people have forged, all of which I have taken pride in chronicling here. Perhaps one day, we or our descendants will find a way to make a more lasting home somewhere far away from these artificial environs, and someone will read what I have written in these pages and come to know the real story of how the children of Dokaa persevered.

Beeliq contacted me today with information from the Medical Ministry. According to research a group of their doctors have been conducting for some time, we will soon be able to lessen our dependency on the medications everyone must take to combat the radiation that permeates the asteroid field. Additionally, the doctors believe that if this trend continues, we may eventually be able to end the periodic inoculations permanently.

This is wonderful news that everyone will be happy to hear, and my wife is currently working with the first minister and his preparations to address the entire community later this evening about this discovery. It means that yet another of our evening meals together will be sacrificed while she carries out her duties as special assistant to the Zahanzei Council, but we are used to that now. Beeliq has always been consumed by the need to serve others, particularly in government and leadership matters. That did not change following the loss of our homeworld. If anything, that passion only gained a new intensity as those of us left behind found ourselves facing a new and uncertain future.

Even before Dokaal's destruction, as evacuation plans were under way to transfer a pitiful number of fortunate souls to the mining colonies, we confronted the challenge of how exactly to house and support these people. The habitat modules designed to house miners, support personnel, and their families had been intended for temporary use, with workers and dependents being rotated back to Dokaal at the end of their contracted work cycle. As such, these facilities lacked a number of amenities that were commonplace in more permanent residences. With the colonies being pressed into service as long-term homes for those of us who would outlive our planet, the process of converting them for such use required much planning, coordination, and cooperation to complete.

Still, even that task was easy to accomplish when compared with the larger and more daunting task of acclimating those evacuated from Dokaal to the harsh environment created by the asteroid field that forms the foundations for our only remaining home.

The field's ambient radiation raised sizable concerns during the first manned space flights from Dokaal to the other planets in our system. Several of those first travelers to the asteroids suffered debilitating illnesses and slow, agonizing deaths owing to their prolonged exposure. Even beyond the simple tragedy of losing such brave souls, their sacrifice also raised pointed questions about our ability to live and work not only in the asteroid field but also in space altogether.

Despite these setbacks, scientific and industry leaders could not resist the lure of the asteroids as an incomparably rich storehouse of valuable minerals and other raw materials. Powered by that incentive, medicines were soon developed that allowed our people to live in the asteroid field for extended periods, which allowed the construction of permanent habitats and other facilities there. All personnel who contracted to work for the mining operations, be they actual miners or maintenance and administrative personnel as well as those who would support the families of workers, were given a series of inoculations to combat the radiation's effects.

The medicinal regimen, coupled with specialized shielding for our spacecraft and mining colony installations as well as protective garments and suits for workers laboring in the open environment of space itself, succeeded in reducing the instances of radiation-induced illnesses to near zero. To further ensure the safety of the colonists, people were rotated back to Dokaal at the end of individual work contracts that expired well before the medicine's effectiveness faded.

Beeliq's position as assistant to one of the colony administrators would have meant our being separated for far longer than at any other time during our marriage, a prospect neither of us wanted. With that in mind, I opted to seek a position as a teacher at one of the colony schools and subjected myself to the inoculations.

I still remember the waves of nausea I felt after I was given the injections, with my reaction to the medicine lasting for five brutal days. It was an admittedly small price to pay in order to accompany my wife to the colonies, but one I had no intentions of repeating. Our plans were altered irrevocably, of course, with Dokaal's destruction.

Now confronted with permanent residence in the asteroid field, our small cadre of medical specialists was faced with charting a new course for our protection. It was quickly determined that the medicines originally given to us could be modified to allow repeated dosages over time, which permitted those of us already living here to continue benefiting from its effects.

The greater challenge was to those who had been evacuated from Dokaal. Those people had not possessed the luxury of the customary acclimation period between inoculation and transfer to the colonies. Given the vaccines while in transit, the evacuees were required to take additional medication upon their arrival here. Many of those poor souls were unprepared for the faster regimen of injections. Some died while others suffered all manner of allergic reactions and in a few isolated cases failed to respond to the medicine at all. In those tragic instances, death ultimately resulted from radiation exposure.

For those who survived, to say nothing of the rest of us, it meant dependence on the life-sustaining drugs, a situation we all believed we would be saddled with for our entire lives. There were other concerns raised at the time, as well. How would our bodies react after repeated inoculations? What about other side effects that might take longer to become evident, or unknown ramifications that might come about after such prolonged use of the medications? Fortunately, no such consequences ever manifested themselves in the time since the community was forced to undertake the ongoing vaccine.

Considering all of this, today's news from the Medical Ministry is tremendous for a number of reasons. In addition to no longer having to deal with the inoculations and their lingering unpleasant side effects, it also means a reduction in the time and resources necessary to manufacture the medication in the first place. To say that the process is a costly one is an understatement.

Just like a great many other things we had to learn to provide for ourselves, it was necessary to establish and maintain a process to create the medication and see to its proper distribution throughout the colony. On more than one occasion, Beeliq has shown me reports showing the budgetary requirements in terms of personnel and raw materials needed to sustain this program, one we were obviously unable to live without and for which no alternative exists.

Now, though, it finally appears as though we may be able to stop worrying about all of that.

As my wife would say, Dokaa has indeed blessed us.

Chapter Thirteen

As SHE COMPLETED the unpleasant task of offering her sobering report, Beverly Crusher could feel the disappointment washing over her shipmates, to say nothing of the reaction her report had evoked from the Dokaalan leaders on the screen.

"We did it to ourselves," Hjatyn said, finally breaking the silence that threatened to consume the entire room. Studying the Dokaalan leader's image on the viewscreen, Crusher saw him slump visibly, his entire aged frame seeming to shrink into his robes. She watched his eyes drop to regard something out of range of the screen's frame for a moment before he drew what the doctor took to be a restorative breath.

"Our medications," he said. *"Years ago, they were intended to provide short-term protection against the radiation's effects for those who worked in the mines on a rotational basis. When Dokaal was destroyed and we*

were faced with living here permanently, we had to find more enduring solutions."

Pausing a moment before replying, Crusher scanned the faces of her companions, taking some measure of comfort in the supportive gaze of Jean-Luc Picard. Considering all that he had endured just since the *Enterprise*'s arrival in the Dokaalan system only a few days previously, he more than anyone probably understood the feelings threatening to consume her.

"The medicines alone aren't responsible," she said, struggling to keep her voice level. "The radiation itself played as much of a role in what's happened as anything else, but it was the combination of pharmaceuticals used that, over time, enabled a change in Dokaalan physiology at the genetic level."

He leaned forward so that his elbows rested on the polished top of the conference table. "How did you find it?"

"It wasn't obvious until Dr. Tropp and I found records of early genetic tests performed almost three centuries ago, when Dokaalan scientists faced the problem of combating the radiation on a long-term basis. We were able to compare those early samples with DNA taken from several of the patients we treated here on the *Enterprise*. There are genetic sequences that are undeniably the result of mutation based in large part on the original antiradiation treatment regimen."

She saw Captain Picard's brow knit in concern. "And over time, this has had the effect of making the Dokaalan dependent not on the medications they took to combat the radiation's effects, but the radiation itself?"

"Exactly," Crusher replied. "The modified treatment scheme their doctors developed was designed not to counter the radiation." She shook her head, searching for the right words. "Simply put, it enabled Dokaalan physiology to live in harmony with it."

"Is there anything we can do for them now?" Troi asked.

Shrugging, the doctor replied, "Nothing immediately. I'll have to start over from the beginning, studying genetic samples for the effects of prolonged isolation from the radiation. Research like that could take months, or years."

On the viewscreen, Hjatyn said, *"I do not understand. What about Ijuuka? My people have lived and worked on the planet for lengthy periods as part of the reformation project. Why have they suffered no ill effects?"*

Moving to take a seat at the conference table next to Counselor Troi, Crusher said, "Obviously the planet's atmosphere allows enough ambient radiation to pass through, but that's now. What needs to be determined is whether the alterations the processing plants are introducing will interfere with that." She shook her head. "I'm no engineer, though."

From where he sat in his antigrav work sled, Data said, "Dr. Crusher raises a valid point, sir. It is quite possible that the terraforming process might well alter the atmosphere in such a manner that radiation would be unable to pass through at all, or even reduce its influence so that it becomes a detriment to Dokaalan physiology."

"Now that we are aware of the issue," Science Minister Creij said from where she sat next to Hjatyn, *"we can conduct the proper research and study the potential problems."* Looking to Picard, she added, *"Captain, since you have already pledged your people's assistance to remedy the unfortunate setback we have suffered, might we look forward to their help with this new task?"*

"Absolutely, Minister," the captain replied, and Crusher noted the nearly imperceptible tightening of his jaw as he spoke the words. Turning to Data, he said, "Commander, do your best to run some long-range projections on the atmospheric conversion process. Let's find out what we're dealing with."

"Aye, sir," the android acknowledged.

As she watched the exchange, it was obvious to Crusher that the mishap with Data's experiment to help the Dokaalan's terraforming efforts was bothering Picard far more than he had let on to his officers. She knew why, of course. Any failure on this mission, particularly one of such magnitude as they had just suffered, would be weighing on him.

Apparently oblivious of the captain's inner unrest, Hjatyn said, *"Your continued enthusiasm is inspiring, Captain."* There was the hint of a smile on his aged features. *"Your resilience is almost Dokaalan."*

Smiling himself, Picard replied, "I consider that a compliment of the highest order, First Minister. Rest assured that we'll continue to devote our efforts to assist you as long as it's necessary."

"Thank you, Captain." Looking somewhere offscreen for a moment before returning to Picard, Hjatyn said, *"We have another matter that requires our attention."* He bowed his head formally. *"We will speak again soon."*

The connection was severed and the Federation seal replaced the first minister's image on the viewscreen, leaving the *Enterprise* senior staff to sit in silence for several seconds. Crusher found herself feeling the first faint glimmers of new hope.

No doubt picking up her emotional turmoil, Troi said,

"Beverly, there are a number of races who have found ways to overcome the natural obstacles presented by their native habitats."

"She's right," Riker added. "The Benzites, the Medusans, the Elaysians, just to name a few, have all developed methods to live safely outside their homeworlds' unique environmental considerations."

At the head of the table, Picard offered his own encouragement. "If anyone can find a way to add the Dokaalan to that list, Beverly, it's you."

Though buoyed by her companions' support, Crusher still had to wonder: Even if she could find a solution, what would be the price for realizing it?

"Thank heavens for normal gravity."

The emergency diagnostic unit was heavy as she maneuvered it back into its storage container, and Crewman Susan Lomax loved it. She had spent the past several hours jumping back and forth between the *Enterprise*'s regular, Earth-standard conditions and the one-sixth gravity enabled in those areas of cargo bay four that had been set up to treat their Dokaalan patients. She had never liked working or participating in any sports in reduced-gravity conditions, and had never understood those who did.

Once filled with more than a hundred Dokaalan requiring medical treatment, cargo bay four had finally been cleared of its transient population now that the *Enterprise* had arrived at the colonists' central habitat. All that was left was the cleanup and the return of the medical staff's emergency equipment to its proper storage berths. At least Dr. Crusher had made it a bit easier by ordering everything used to create the emergency triage center to remain here in the cargo bay in the event it was needed again.

Taking hold of an antigravity unit, Lomax affixed it to the side of an emergency diagnostic bed. The bed was still awkward to maneuver around the room even with the antigrav to assist her, which she quickly discovered as she began to push the bed toward its storage container.

Maybe I shouldn't have been so quick to say no when Nurse Ogawa offered to help, she thought as she moved the bed across the floor of the bay. *But she seemed so tired, and I didn't want to* . . .

The thought was shattered as the diagnostic bed slammed into its storage berth.

"Nice work, Susan," Lomax said to no one as she examined the situation. The bed itself was undamaged, but she had done an exceptional job of wedging it at an odd angle inside the container.

Of course, if I leave it, she chided herself, *this will be the one Dr. Crusher wants.*

Securing a solid grip on the handle of the antigrav unit, Lomax pulled with all of her strength, but the bed did not move. She tried again, and this time her efforts were rewarded with her losing her grip and tumbling backward to the deck.

"Dammit!" The oath echoed in the cargo bay, and she immediately regretted uttering it. Such a poor lapse in bearing would surely not go . . .

"Hello?" a male voice called out from the other side of the room. "Need some help there?"

Feeling her face flush with embarrassment, Lomax pulled herself to her feet as she heard footsteps coming across the cargo bay from behind her.

"Got yourself in a bit of a jam there, I see," the voice said, and Lomax could hear the humor in behind the words, the speaker no doubt enjoying his intentionally awful joke.

Turning, she recognized Ensign Jarek Maxson from security. He was smiling, but she could tell from the look in his eyes that there was no ridicule or judgment behind the expression. Actually, she thought, in contrast to his somewhat imposing figure it made him look rather coy. She smiled sheepishly in return and backed away from the bed, trying to articulate something that might help salvage some shred of pride. "You'd never guess my father was a freight hauler, would you?"

"Not if he stows cargo like you do," Maxson said, his light tone of voice taking an edge off of the jab. Stepping between her and the bed, the tall, muscled guard took hold of the antigrav unit's handle. Rather than simply coercing the jammed diagnostic bed from the storage container through sheer force of will, he looked over his shoulder at her, smiling again. "What, I have to do this by myself?"

"Oh! Right," Lomax said, and she gripped the edge of the bed. With them working together, even though she imagined that she contributed little to the cause, the bed moved and slid free of its storage berth.

After properly maneuvering the bed back into the storage container, Lomax sighed in triumph. *"Thank you,"* she said.

"No problem," Maxson said, again flashing the smile she admitted was becoming more appealing each time she saw it. "If you like, I can stay and help you stow the rest of these beds. You look kind of worn out."

I look worn out? Great.

"Well, sure," she replied, "if it's not going to make

you late for your next shift or something." Turning from the security guard, she put forth the pretense of absent-mindedly running her fingers through her dirty blond hair, which was in actuality a hasty effort to primp. "There's really not much left to do."

Taking the initiative, Maxson attached the antigrav unit to another bed and began moving it toward its assigned storage container. As he worked, Lomax inventoried an instrument tray before returning it to its medical cabinet.

As she worked, Lomax found herself feeling more self-conscious about the security officer's presence than she anticipated. A relative newcomer to the *Enterprise* medical staff, she had found little time to make more than casual acquaintances among the crew beyond her immediate coworkers. While she recognized Maxson from the dining facility and the ship's gymnasium, she wondered whether he knew who she was at all.

"Hey, uh . . . Nurse?"

I guess that answers that.

Turning to where Maxson was standing next to another of the diagnostic beds, she saw the ensign look in her direction, shock and confusion evident on his features. "I thought these beds were supposed to be, you know, unoccupied?"

Dear God, Lomax thought, horror gripping her. Had someone forgotten one of the patients? Running across the bay, she could now plainly see a humanoid form lying motionless beneath a sheet on the bed. "You've got to be kidding," she said as she stepped up to Maxson. Where the hell had he come from? She was sure all of the diagnostic units had been empty, and that no patients remained in the cargo bay when the rest of the medical staff had departed.

Lomax pulled back the sheet to see the lifeless form of a Dokaalan woman concealed beneath the shroud, her complexion still quite blue despite her having died several hours earlier. Checking the small tag attached to the head of the diagnostic bed, she said, "This woman died of hypothermia, a result of exposure to open space."

Standing silently to one side, Maxson looked down at the deceased Dokaalan and Lomax saw that he appeared to be quite ill at ease. Covering the lifeless woman with the sheet once more, she turned to the ensign. "Maybe you could just move her near the door and I'll move her to the morgue when we're finished here."

"Sure," Maxson said. "I'm just, well, I know this sounds silly coming from a security guy, but I'm not around dead bodies that often."

Fifth-generation Starfleet, Lomax was well versed in the clichéd descriptions put forth by her own family that Starfleet medical officers and, most especially, security officers were awash in bloodshed and corpses as part of their daily routine. In her own experience, however, to find that Maxson had little personal familiarity with death really came as no surprise to her.

Smiling and hoping that a little levity might ease his discomfort, she said, "I'll never forget my first day in the hololabs at medical school. I had to make an incision on this bloated, old Tellarite guy. It was all a simulation, but I still would have hit the deck if not for my lab partner."

Maxson shook his head, holding his hands up in mock surrender. "Tell you what, I'll take this wherever you want it if you keep your lab stories to yourself."

"Deal," Lomax replied, unable to resist the chuckle. "Just move her to the door."

Turning back to sorting equipment in the field medical kit as the ensign began to maneuver the bed away, she allowed herself to smile at the thoughts beginning to swirl in her mind. Maxson seemed closer to her own age, was a friendly sort, and, she reminded herself, was definitely easy on the eyes. Not that she had designs on the guy as dating material, but connecting with someone, especially anyone assigned to another department, would at the very least allow for more than just shoptalk at mealtime, right?

As for whatever else happens, she thought, *well, that might not be so bad, either.*

Lifting the field kit so she could return it to its proper storage box, Lomax stopped at the sound of something falling to the deck elsewhere in the cargo bay.

"Ensign Maxson?" she called out, but received no response. When she repeated his name but encountered the same result, she felt her pulse begin to race. Had he somehow hurt himself moving the heavier equipment? Taking off across the cargo bay, she shouted, "Maxson, are you all right?"

A sharp gagging sound caught her attention, and the hairs on the back of her neck stood up. Maneuvering around a row of storage containers to where she thought the sounds were originating, she lurched to a halt, frozen in place and mouth opening in horrified shock at the sight before her.

Maxson was being held nearly a meter off the deck, one-handed, by the dead Dokaalan female, who had risen from the diagnostic bed and who was now choking the life out of him.

Her voice catching in her throat, Lomax stared at the unreal scene before her as Maxson tried to fight off the attack, swinging and clawing with both hands in a futile effort to loosen the Dokaalan's overwhelming grip. A moment later, the ensign's already fading movements stopped altogether. The Dokaalan woman held his motionless body in that same manner for several more seconds, as if waiting to be sure he was dead, before dropping Maxson unceremoniously to the deck.

Unable and unwilling to speak, Lomax instead stepped slowly back the way she had come, waiting until she was out of sight before turning to run. When she did, she nearly ran into . . .

. . . into herself.

It was as though she were staring into a mirror. The being before her was an exact duplicate of her, right down to the insignia on her collar and the combadge on her left breast.

Not a mirror.

The thought came unbidden, only a single heartbeat before panic set in, and Susan Lomax found her voice. Her scream echoed off the walls of the cargo bay as she turned to run in another direction. Where the hell was the door? If she could just make it into the corridor, there would be someone to help.

Call for help, idiot!

Cursing herself, Lomax reached for her combadge but her hand never made it. Instead it was abruptly grabbed and halted by a larger, meatier hand. Jerking her head to the right, she looked up into the handsome, smiling face of Jarek Maxson.

Lomax tried to scream again, but this time it was cut off as the ensign's other hand closed around her throat.

Mhuic flexed the fingers of his hand and pressed a thumb into his palm, working to relieve the small cramp he had earned while strangling the human woman who now lay in a lifeless heap at his feet. He had anticipated a struggle, but the slight woman had been so shocked that she had been unable to put up any resistance.

He had been studying her from the moment he had been brought aboard the Starfleet vessel, concealed among the injured Dokaalan rescued from the destroyed mining outpost. During his observations, he had determined that her position among the crew was that of a nondescript, menial subordinate, not part of the vessel's leadership caste. Her role was common and yet trusted enough that she could move about the ship freely, but her duties required that she not be anywhere or answerable to anyone of importance for long periods of time. She was a perfect choice for impersonation.

Until the human male had arrived, of course.

Mhuic's head turned at the approach of the other operative who had ended up here as one of the Dokaalan patients but whose form now appeared as that of the human woman. He nodded in greeting.

"It is Alida," his counterpart offered, smiling as she moved to lift the lifeless body of the woman. "Help me," she said, and together they easily moved the dead human to an area of the cargo bay secluded by a grouping of large cargo containers.

"I did not know you were still here," Mhuic said as he

knelt beside the human's body and removed the communicator badge from her uniform tunic.

"I took the chance that the Starfleet people would not notice one more dead Dokaalan," Alida replied. "It was my original intention to take the form of one of their doctors, but that seemed too great a risk."

Mhuic nodded in agreement. "I had planned to assume this human's form but then the human male arrived and opportunity presented itself."

"Fair enough," Alida said, her voice sounding digitized and warbled as her shroud's sonic emitters adjusted the acoustical qualities of her own voice to match the timbre of the human woman's. After a moment she nodded in satisfaction that her transformation was fully in place.

"Do not forget this," Mhuic said as he offered the confiscated combadge.

"Of course," Alida replied, accepting the device and placing it on her own chest. Mhuic watched as her shroud rippled momentarily as it adapted its appearance to the new addition, which he knew carried components imbued with important identification information. To the naked eye, Alida appeared to be Crewman Lomax, but with the communicator and its direct ties to the ship's computer, her impersonation was complete.

"We need to dispose of this," she said after a moment, nodding toward the body before them, "and the other one."

Mhuic replied, "They can be concealed here for a time." Indicating the storage containers that held the portable diagnostic beds, he added, "Unless another medical emergency is declared, this area should remain unused for several hours at least."

He gave brief thought to obtaining a weapon and simply disintegrating the bodies, but just as quickly dismissed the notion. Such an action would be immediately detected by the ship's internal sensors. It was unfortunate, but unavoidable. He did not particularly like killing any subject he was forced to mimic during an assignment, but when required to do so, he much preferred that no evidence of his actions remained to betray him at some later, inconvenient time.

"See to it, then," Alida said, "while I access the computer and determine where our proper duty stations are. The sooner we return to our subjects' regular routines, the better."

Mhuic regarded his fellow operative, making an effort to keep his expression neutral. He knew Alida was his superior, if only by virtue of having completed a few more assignments, but he found himself slightly annoyed at how easily she had assumed the leadership role between them. It was not normal for operatives to work in teams, and it had been a long time since he had taken on any assignment where he had not worked alone. This would definitely take some getting used to, he decided.

"What do we do then?" he asked as he lifted the lifeless woman's body and slung it over his shoulder.

Alida cast a knowing look back at him. "Then, we wait."

Chapter Fourteen

"SOMEONE IS COMING."

Dozing fitfully in his cot, La Forge opened his eyes at the sound of Taurik's voice. According to the Vulcan, it had been nearly two hours since their conversation with Barmiol. What did they want now?

"How many this time?" the engineer asked as he rose to a sitting position.

Listening to sounds La Forge could not yet hear, Taurik replied, "Only one, though he may not even be coming here."

"But if he is, this might be our chance," La Forge said, the first kernels of a plan already forming in his mind. "If we can get the drop on him, can you get us back to the landing bay?"

Upon arriving at this mining colony, the pair of skiffs they had traveled in had made use of a single large compartment constructed on the massive asteroid's surface that already housed two other skiffs. The two engineers had then been marched through the colony's passageways for several minutes before ending up here, and La Forge was sure he would not be able to remember the proper route back to what might be their sole chance at escape.

"I believe so, Commander," Taurik replied. "As for disabling the guard, I do have a suggestion. One of us could feign illness or injury when the guard enters the room. Perhaps the simulated crisis will distract him long enough for the other to overpower him."

La Forge almost groaned audibly at the idea. "Taurik, that's got to be the oldest trick in the book."

Rising to a sitting position on his cot, the Vulcan said, "If you are saying that it is a time-tested tactic, Commander, I would have to agree. In fact, while studying the mission logs of Captain James Kirk at Starfleet Academy, I found that he employed the strategy a number of times. While it was not always successful, he did use it to great effect on . . ."

"We don't have time to discuss this," La Forge snapped, cutting off his companion. He could now clearly hear the guard's footsteps as he drew closer to their cell. "Besides, I can't believe these guys would fall for something like that."

"Perhaps," the Vulcan countered. "Then again, if they are aware of the tactic, then they may well expect us to anticipate that and discard it as a potential course of action. In that case, they would be unprepared for us to actually employ . . ."

"Taurik!" La Forge hissed as he heard the lock on the door being disengaged. In a quiet voice he added, "Just follow my lead, okay?"

There was no time for the junior engineer to answer before the door opened to reveal a Dokaalan security officer carrying a tray. At least, the figure appeared to be Dokaalan. La Forge was still trying to picture what the guard might look like in his real form, if he was in fact employing some kind of disguise or shapechanging ability.

Both La Forge and Taurik remained seated on their cots and the guard stayed in the doorway as he knelt down to place the tray on the deck. "There is water here," he said, pointing to a large bottle. Rising to his feet, his hand came to rest on the butt of the weapon in his holster as he indicated the plate of what La Forge took to be food, oddly shaped and in a variety of colors. "We have determined that these fruits can be eaten by both of your species with no ill effects."

"Sounds delicious," La Forge said, making no effort to keep the sarcasm from his voice. Forcing himself not to make eye contact with Taurik, lest he alert the guard to what was coming, the chief engineer moved to stand up. "What do you call . . . ?"

The question turned into a grunt of surprise as he stepped forward and felt his leg held back, throwing him off balance. Reduced gravity prevented him from flopping face-first to the floor, but La Forge still felt himself beginning a slow fall toward the deck plating.

My damn pants leg. The material of his jumpsuit had snagged on the bed frame. Again.

His unfortunate tumble did have the effect of startling the guard, however. The Dokaalan stepped to his left to avoid becoming entangled as La Forge fell, causing him to move closer to Taurik. He quickly realized his mistake, but not before the Vulcan lunged from his cot.

The guard was smart, and fast, anticipating the assault even as Taurik closed the distance between them. He leapt forward, the one-sixth gravity of the asteroid slowing him somewhat as he pushed forward and into the attack and swung a meaty fist at the engineer's head.

Taurik parried the blow with his left hand, using his body weight to force the guard backward and off balance. The Dokaalan lashed out with his other fist and Taurik ducked to avoid being hit, his right arm sweeping up to force the guard's arm away from his body. Now with an opening, Taurik moved his left hand to his opponent's neck and squeezed. The guard released a quiet moan as his eyes rolled into the back of his head and Taurik caught him as he collapsed.

"Are you all right, Commander?" he asked as he lowered the now unconscious guard to the floor.

With a grunt of frustration, La Forge yanked his leg free of the bedframe joint that had snagged him. "I banged my knee, but I'll be fine."

Reaching for the guard's holster, Taurik removed the Bajoran phaser it held. He said nothing for a moment, and La Forge realized that he was listening for signs that their struggle had been overheard by someone else. Finally the Vulcan nodded, apparently satisfied that their movements had gone unnoticed.

"I must compliment you on a most effective ruse, sir," he said as he checked the phaser's power level. "The guard was taken in completely."

"Uh, yeah," La Forge said. *So was I.* Standing up, he rubbed the sore spot on his right knee where he had landed roughly. *Even in low gravity, that hurts,* he decided. "Those were some nice moves, Taurik. Where'd you learn to fight like that?"

"It is called *suus mahna,*" the junior officer replied, "a fighting art used by my people for thousands of years. It was developed in our ancient past as a technique for close-quarters combat, but over the generations it has evolved into a purely defensive fighting style."

Moving to where the Dokaalan lay unmoving on the floor, La Forge said, "Seems to work pretty good." He checked the guard's pockets for anything that might prove useful.

Taurik nodded, keeping his attention on the doorway and watching out for signs of anyone approaching. "When practiced with meditation, it is a most effective means of focusing the energy of the mind and body."

"Maybe you can teach me sometime," La Forge said, rising to his feet. Other than his weapon, the Dokaalan was carrying nothing of significance. Frowning at a sudden thought, he pointed to the guard's chest. "Hey, if this guy was a shapeshifter, wouldn't he have reverted to his normal form once he fell unconscious?"

"It would be consistent with most of the beings we have encountered with such abilities," Taurik replied. "It seems reasonable to assume that he is employing artificial means to generate his appearance."

"Another thing," La Forge said as he moved to his cot and grabbed its thin blanket. "He said the fruit was chosen because we could eat it. That means that whoever these people are, they know at least something about humans and Vulcans."

Watching as the chief engineer began to tear his blanket into strips, Taurik picked up his own blanket and began to do the same. "An astute observation, Commander. We may be dealing with a race familiar to the Federation. An enemy power, perhaps?"

La Forge shook his head. "We don't have time to figure it out now. We need to get out of here and find a way back to the ship, then we can worry about who our friends are."

After using the strips from their blankets to bind and gag the guard as best they could, the engineers took one more opportunity to ensure that no one else was heading in their direction before stepping out into the passageway. Taurik closed the cell's door and locked it, preserving the image of normality should anyone happen past.

The engineer noted that the lighting level in the passageway was lower than when they had arrived. "You think they reduce power during whatever passes for their nighttime cycle?" he asked, keeping his voice low as they moved down the corridor in the direction Taurik indicated would lead them to the landing bay they had used upon their arrival.

"A distinct possibility," the Vulcan replied, "perhaps as a conservation measure. If that is the case, then there may be fewer people moving about the colony's nonessential areas."

"Somehow I don't think we've got that kind of luck," La Forge countered. "It won't be long before Barmiol or one of his buddies misses that guard."

They stopped at each intersection, Taurik using his superior hearing and La Forge employing the various abilities of his ocular implants to check for the approach of potential enemies. Not knowing how many people were involved in this scheme to undermine the efforts of the

Dokaalan, the engineers could not afford to trust anyone, even if La Forge could determine that they were not employing some kind of disguise.

"How far are we?" La Forge asked as they turned yet another corner in the passageway. Had they taken this many changes in direction the first time they had been marched through these corridors?

"Two more intersections and we should be at the hatch leading to the landing bay," Taurik replied. As he carried their only weapon, he was in front, examining signage and other items fastened to the bulkheads as he retraced their steps.

La Forge had briefly considered trying to find some way to send a message back to the *Enterprise* but opted against that action. There would be plenty of time for that once they had gotten away from the outpost. In fact, it would be a necessity, for a number of reasons. Besides simply alerting Captain Picard to what was happening here, he and Taurik would almost certainly need help just to get back to the ship. Without their shuttlecraft and its sensors and navigational logs, they had no way to make their way back through the asteroid field to the *Enterprise*. He did not know what, if anything, aboard the Dokaalan skiffs aided pilots to successfully traverse the field to their intended destinations, but he doubted it was a method he would have time to learn.

They were coming up on another four-way intersection when Taurik stopped. The action was so abrupt that La Forge nearly ran into him, only just remembering not to say anything loud. Words were not necessary, anyway, as the Vulcan raised his empty hand in a cautionary gesture. He had heard something, or someone, around the corner to the right, which was the direction he had wanted to go. It took only another moment before the chief engineer heard the sounds of footsteps and voices echoing in the corridor and moving toward them.

"No place to hide," La Forge whispered, looking around. The turn in the corridor behind them was too far away to reach before whoever was coming saw them. The images of what might occur in the next few seconds were already playing out in his mind. They had a one-in-three chance that whoever was coming up the passageway would turn left at the corner and run into them. If they kept going straight or turned right at the intersection, then their backs would be to the engineers. With luck, they would be too busy talking with one another to notice that they were not alone in the passageway at this apparently late hour.

Taurik said nothing as he handed La Forge his confiscated Bajoran phaser before pressing himself against the near wall. La Forge followed suit as the footsteps grew louder, and now he was able to make out two distinct voices talking back and forth at one another. He could not understand all of the words, but from their general tone and the occasional laugh, it seemed as though the conversation was a genial one.

Good, he thought. *They're not on alert, or looking for us. Yet.*

They were almost at the intersection. La Forge felt his heart pounding in his chest and blood rushing in his ears. He held his breath as he saw the first shadow begin to darken the floor, and was it his imagination or did he actually feel the deck plate vibrating beneath feet in reaction to the approaching footfalls? Gripping the phaser in his right hand, he realized he was holding the weapon so tightly that it was shaking. He grabbed the phaser's squat barrel with his other hand and held it close to his chest, taking one last look to confirm that it had been set to stun before returning his attention to the corridor ahead of them. The footsteps were loud now, only one or two more seconds before they . . .

Barmiol and another Dokaalan turned left into the intersection and nearly barreled into Taurik.

"What . . .?"

La Forge's first instinct was to shoot the Dokaalan but his aim was blocked by Taurik, who wasted no time lunging at the pair with both hands extended. The Vulcan's right hand closed around the neck and shoulder of the first Dokaalan and he promptly sagged to the deck.

Barmiol was faster. Yelping in surprise, he ducked to his right, knocking the engineer's hand aside as he moved away. His momentum carried him into the center of the intersection and clear of Taurik. La Forge raised the phaser and fired, wincing at the sound of the weapon in the narrow corridors even as its bright orange beam caught Barmiol square in the chest. The echo from the shot continued down the passageways even as the Dokaalan fell to the floor. Though it faded quickly, La Forge knew there was no way it had gone unheard.

"Well, they know we're here now," he said as he regarded their unconscious opponents.

Then he noticed it.

"I'll be damned," he said as he knelt down to more closely inspect the fallen Dokaalan.

"Commander?" Taurik prompted, keeping his attention focused on all four legs of corridor leading away from the intersection.

La Forge pointed to Barmiol. "His body heat is much lower than his friend's. Fifteen point three degrees lower, in fact." He had no idea what Dokaalan body temperature was, of course, but he doubted such a discrepancy from person to person would be considered normal. "I wonder what Dr. Crusher would make of this."

"I would suggest tabling the question until we have found a way out of here, sir," Taurik said, still watching for signs of anyone approaching. "Others will no doubt be on their way here within minutes."

The engineers took off at a run down the corridor. The lower gravity allowed them to lengthen their strides, but the engineers had to be conscious of not launching themselves into the ceiling panels as they ran. No longer concerned with stealth, La Forge ignored the clanking of his boots each time he landed on the metal plating. Only one thought tormented him now: How much farther did they have to go, and who would be waiting for them when they got there?

Pointing ahead of him as they turned another corner in the passageway, Taurik said, "The landing bay should be through that hatch."

La Forge saw that this leg of corridor was short, only a few dozen meters, and ended at what he recognized as a reinforced pressure door. If Taurik was right, this was the hatch leading to the airlock separating the landing bay from the interior of the mining outpost.

They were halfway to the door when it was opened from the inside, revealing a single Dokaalan. While La Forge was certain from the man's heat signature that he was a fake, seeing him raise his weapon in their direction was equally convincing.

"Look out!" the engineer shouted as he ducked to his

left the instant before the Dokaalan fired. Green energy screamed past as La Forge slammed into the bulkhead, his shoulder tingling from the impact. He raised his phaser and returned fire, catching his opponent in the leg. The Dokaalan staggered for a moment from the attack but did not fall. La Forge fired again and it was a better shot, this time hitting the other man in the head.

The Dokaalan fell to one knee, stunned by the attack but not incapacitated. La Forge thumbed the phaser's power level up two settings before taking aim one more time and firing again. The strengthened beam struck the Dokaalan in the chest and La Forge's finger remained on the weapon's firing stud, maintaining the assault until the guard finally collapsed to the deck.

Rushing forward to verify that the Dokaalan was unconscious, Taurik picked up the guard's Klingon disruptor. La Forge moved to join him as the junior engineer aimed his captured weapon through the now open hatch.

"It is clear," the Vulcan said, stepping through the doorway and into the airlock. A similar check revealed that the landing bay also appeared to be deserted.

"It won't take them long to figure out where we've gone," La Forge said as he closed the hatch leading back the way they had come. After ensuring that the door's locking mechanism was engaged, he stepped back, leveled his phaser at the door, and fired, melting the lock.

Observing the chief engineer's work, Taurik said. "That will not contain them for very long, sir."

"It won't have to," La Forge replied. He pointed to one of the three skiffs parked in the small landing bay. "You think you can fly one of those things?"

"I observed my pilot's actions during our flight here

from our crash site," the Vulcan said. "I believe I absorbed enough information to at least launch one of the craft and get us away from here."

La Forge nodded. He was counting on his own observations of the pilot who had brought him here as well as his and Taurik's own abilities to handle small spacecraft to get them out of here. Once they were back in the asteroid field, it was all they would have. "Get one started up and prepare to take off," he said.

As Taurik selected one of the skiffs and climbed into his cockpit, La Forge crossed the deck to what appeared to be a small control room. Its most prominent feature was a large console with a window that offered an unobstructed view of the landing bay.

The console itself was a myriad of buttons, dials, gauges, and status lights. La Forge knew that the bay's outer doors as well as the regulation of internal atmosphere had to be controlled from here, but there was no way he would be able to decipher the odd script that was the Dokaalan written language.

His decision not to try was cemented by the abrupt sounding of a blaring alarm, the klaxon nearly deafening in the confines of the control room. Outside in the landing bay, warning lights began to flash down the length of the chamber, and a voice erupted from a hidden speaker.

"Security to landing bay two. Emergency alert. Security to landing bay two."

Lunging from the control room, La Forge scrambled across the deck toward the trio of skiffs. "Time to go, Taurik!" he called out, shouting to be heard above the alarms.

Rising up from the cockpit of one of the small craft,

Taurik waved. "Commander! What about the outer hatch?"

"Can we use the skiff's drilling laser to cut through?" La Forge asked as he drew closer to the tiny craft.

The Vulcan shook his head. "I do not believe we will have sufficient time for that, sir."

"Then we'll have to speed things up," La Forge replied as he ran forward, checking the power lever on his phaser. There was just enough of a charge left for what he had in mind, he decided.

He did not relish the idea of causing such destruction to the facility and inconveniencing any Dokaalan living here who knew nothing about the deceitful activities taking place in their midst, but that could not be helped now. The chief engineer knew that if he and Taurik were to be captured again, the odds were good that their abductors would simply kill them to avoid further trouble.

It made the choice easy.

Setting the weapon to overload, La Forge heaved the phaser toward the landing bay's outer hatch and ran for the skiff.

"Watch out for debris!" he yelled as he clambered up the small ladder and into the ship's cockpit, feeling its hull vibrating beneath his hands. Taurik had thankfully figured out how to power up the skiff's engines already. Maybe they would get away with this after all.

La Forge was aware of the skiff's cockpit hatch sealing shut before a muffled explosion reverberated through the ship's thin hull. Then he felt the craft lurch as Taurik pushed one lever forward and yanked back on another, lifting the skiff from the deck of the landing bay and maneuvering it toward the chamber's ceiling.

It was a prudent maneuver. As La Forge fell into the skiff's copilot seat he was able to observe the effects of the explosion he had caused. The landing bay's outer hatch now sported a huge, ragged hole, with more pieces of it being ripped away as explosive decompression forced the chamber's contents toward the hatch and out into space. Everything from toolboxes to storage crates to the remaining two skiffs became projectiles as the atmosphere was pulled from the room, and it was taking all of Taurik's piloting skills to keep their own craft from being struck by any flying debris.

The decompression lasted only a few seconds, after which the interior of the landing bay was plunged into vacuum. Now free to maneuver, Taurik pushed the lever in his right hand forward and La Forge felt the increase in the skiff's engine power. The Vulcan touched another control and the craft jumped forward, clearing the bay a moment later and hurtling out into empty space.

Nearly empty, at least. There was still an asteroid field to navigate, after all, and they had no idea which way to go.

"Commander," Taurik said as he adjusted the skiff's course to avoid striking a tumbling rock no bigger than a photon-torpedo tube, "given some time, I may be able to figure out this vessel's onboard navigational aids."

"I'll take care of it," La Forge replied, tightening his seat's safety harness. "You just keep us from crashing into anything." Beyond the tiny vessel's cockpit, even the smallest visible asteroids seemed gigantic.

At least the ride won't be boring.

"Any idea which of these controls works the communications system?" he asked.

Taurik pointed to a small bank of switches set into the

center of the console. "When we were brought to the colony, I observed my skiff's pilot using that component to request clearance for docking."

Watching as the Vulcan demonstrated the proper use of the com system's transmit and receive functions, La Forge reached for the toggle to activate the system and flipped it. He was rewarded with a momentary burst of static filling the cockpit.

"La Forge to *Enterprise*," the chief engineer said, releasing the transmit button to listen for a response. When none came, he repeated the sequence. *"Enterprise, do you read me?"* More static greeted him at first, but then the channel cleared.

"Commander La Forge?" said a faint voice, barely audible through the interference. *"This is Lieutenant Hras aboard the shuttlecraft* Chawla. *We've been looking for you, sir. You're transmitting on a very low audio band. Is your shuttle damaged?"*

Stifling the urge to laugh at the very legitimate question, La Forge instead replied, "It's a long story, Lieutenant."

And it's about time our luck changed.

Chapter Fifteen

PICARD ALLOWED HIMSELF to feel relief at the news of La Forge and Taurik's safe recovery only once the two engineers actually set foot on the *Enterprise*.

While it was a sense of triumph that was much needed after the events of the past two days, it was to be short-lived, quashed within moments of his entering sickbay to greet the engineers.

"Whoever they are, they're not Dokaalan," La Forge said as he sat on the edge of a diagnostic bed. Both La Forge and Taurik had been ordered to report to sickbay so that Dr. Crusher could give them a quick once-over. Picard was encouraged by the sight of both engineers, who appeared unharmed by their experience.

Crusher agreed, decreeing that the worst either man had suffered from their short bout of captivity was mild dehydration and sleep deprivation. She had cleared them for duty on the condition that they got some rest once they were done here before dashing off to continue her research. Working with Dr. Tropp, she still had her hands full trying to find a way to counter the effects of the asteroid field's radiation belt on Dokaalan physiology.

"Shapeshifters?" Riker asked.

Sitting on another of the beds, Taurik shook his head. "It is possible, sir, or perhaps they are merely humanoids employing a form of disguise."

"I discovered a distinct difference in body temperature while examining what I thought were two Dokaalan. Dr. Crusher thinks the variation is too drastic for normal physiological differences within a single species to account for it."

"And you think this means one of those individuals was somehow disguised," Picard said, "but that they're not Founders?"

La Forge shook his head. "Taurik was able to incapacitate a couple of them bare-handed, and none of the people we encountered appeared to possess superior strength or speed we've seen in other Founders. Also, Barmiol didn't strike me as having that attitude of superiority toward non-shapeshifters that the Founders are known for. Besides, from everything we know about them, would they actually need to terraform a planet like Ijuuka?"

It was a logical assessment, Picard decided. If this unknown group of insurgents were not from the Dominion, having found another method of traveling to this part of the galaxy from their homeworld in the Gamma Quadrant, and if he proceeded from the assumption that they were not of another race of shapeshifters, then who were they?

"It is possible they are a form of advance team," Data said from where he sat in his engineer's work sled, "working on behalf of another group that requires the planet."

Hopping down off the diagnostic bed, La Forge frowned at that notion. "That could be. The guy in charge, Barmiol, sounded like he was taking orders from somebody, but I still got the sense that he was invested in what they were doing. It was 'we need this' and 'our plans,' things like that. Whoever he is, I'm pretty sure he has a stake in what's going on down there."

As he paced the length of sickbay, Picard felt his stomach tightening as he considered everything La Forge and Taurik had reported. An unknown alien race, apparently having succeeded in infiltrating the Dokaalan colonies, were now working covertly to undermine the terraforming efforts in order to hijack the project for their own ends? It would have been an outlandish notion a week ago, but if the events of the past few days had shown him anything, it was that nothing happening in this asteroid field could be considered too far-fetched.

His attention wandered to the pair of security guards stationed just inside the entrance to sickbay. On his order, Lieutenant Vale had deployed teams of her people throughout the ship, safeguarding sensitive areas and ensuring that no one entered those sections without the proper authorization. All personnel had been restricted to duty stations and their quarters when off duty until further notice, and everyone had been ordered to move about in pairs. Anyone found alone was to be detained and questioned.

Picard hated enacting extreme measures, but the circumstances, eerily familiar when compared to previous experience, had given him no choice. After all, memories of the Dominion War had not yet faded to the point where they could no longer impart the hard-won lessons that accompanied them.

"Geordi," he said, "did you get a sense of how many of these covert operatives there might be, or how far they may have worked themselves into the Dokaalan community?"

"They didn't give exact numbers or anything," La Forge replied, "but Barmiol seemed pretty confident that they were able to do whatever they wanted. Whoever they are, they know they need the Dokaalan to do most of the heavy work for the terraforming to succeed. They're being very patient and methodical about the changes they're making, by introducing variances in the chemicals being blended together and then released into the atmosphere by the processing plants."

"You mean they're not adding in anything of their own?" Riker asked. "Something they require but the Dokaalan don't?"

Shaking his head, La Forge replied, "Not according to what we found, and what Barmiol told us. It all points to simple rearrangement of the chemical balances to achieve an effect that's different from what the Dokaalan are working toward. The changes are so subtle, and designed to have a cumulative effect over such a long period of time, that they'd be virtually undetectable to anything but the most intensive sensors scans, and only then if you knew what you were looking for." The chief engineer sighed heavily. "They know it will take years, but according to Barmiol they're prepared to wait it out. He even claimed to have a plan in the event the Dokaalan discovered what was happening."

"For them to do all of this," Riker said, "to get themselves into positions to alter or even completely take over what the Dokaalan are doing, that means they've probably assumed the identities of actual people. They may have replaced individuals in key positions, maybe they've even killed those people."

"If what Geordi say is true," Data added, "then it is also possible that these individuals possess the ability to pose as members of the *Enterprise* crew."

It was a chilling notion, Picard knew, made all the more frightening by the fact that it was not a new concept. Ever since first contact with the Dominion, the threat of Founders infiltrating Starfleet, manipulating decisions and war plans from within for their own ends, had been a constant one. Founders had replaced key personnel ranging from the Klingon Empire's chief of staff to a high-ranking member of the Romulan Tal Shiar to the chief medical officer of Deep Space 9. The entire quadrant had been forced to face the idea that anyone, anywhere and at any time, might be a Changeling in disguise.

"If it makes you feel better," La Forge said, offering a tired, humorless grin, "everybody here seems to be themselves. I'm not picking up any odd variations in body temperature from any of you." Moving to where his uniform tunic lay draped across a chair, the chief engineer began donning the garment. "As for these other people, if I heard Barmiol right, then they've been working behind the scenes for years."

"With our arrival," Taurik added, "they would know we might find out what they were doing, otherwise they would not have been watching us and been prepared to take us into custody. Our escape has undoubtedly had an effect on their long-term plans."

"We need to warn the council," Counselor Troi said

from where she stood next to Riker. "First Minister Hjatyn and his fellow leaders may be in danger."

The first officer countered, "That assumes none of them are impostors. What if this group, whoever they are, has managed to infiltrate the Dokaalan leadership?"

"It could explain many of the conflicting emotions I've sensed since the beginning," Troi said. "Several of the Dokaalan leaders have seemed very guarded, especially when in our presence. That would make sense if they were impostors concealing their identities from real Dokaalan."

"What about Hjatyn?" Picard asked.

Shaking her head, the counselor replied, "From what I can tell, he appears to be genuinely grateful for our presence. He regrets what has happened on Ijuuka, but is maintaining a hopeful attitude consistent with a leader in his position."

"If he is the genuine article," Riker said, "then he may be in danger from others posing as council members."

"Actually, Commander," Data said, maneuvering his chair so that he was closer to the rest of the group, "it is very likely that several members of the council as well as others in positions of power have been replaced. That would be a necessary and logical step in order to accomplish a full-scale subversion of the Dokaalan terraforming project."

Picard nodded at the observation. In essence, Data was describing a classic example of clandestine warfare, using limited numbers to coopt an enemy's own resources in order to wage battle from within. This time, however, it did not appear to be about destroying the Dokaalan, but simply incapacitating them in order to loot them of their possessions, which in this case could also mean their very lives.

"Hjatyn said there was disagreement about Ijuuka," he said, not looking up from the sickbay carpeting as he walked the length of the room. "He even believed the second outpost incident was a deliberate act of sabotage."

Riker countered, "But the first one was chalked up to an old, overused power reactor, right?" Then he shared a look with La Forge. "You didn't like the way that one looked, either." The chief engineer had at first suspected that age and negligence had played the key roles in the breakdown and eventual destruction of the immense reactor generating power for the first mining outpost the *Enterprise* had encountered. Examination of certain components of the reactor machinery had given him doubts, however.

"I could never shake the idea that it seemed . . . I don't know, staged somehow," La Forge said, "especially when the reactor blew well before our estimates."

Picard nodded. "If this other group wanted to make sure that the Dokaalan kept up with their work on the planet, they might try to demonstrate that the asteroid colonies were unsafe or vulnerable."

"And by making it look like accidents due to the age of the facilities," Troi added, "people might begin to believe that their best option for long-term survival was the terraforming project."

Continuing to pace the room, Picard tried to let his mind relax, to let the jumble of facts, suspicions, and questions coalesce into a single cohesive line of thinking. Whoever was behind this attempt to seize the Dokaalan's terraforming efforts, the captain reasoned that they could be successful only if the Dokaalan themselves continued the project.

"It all makes sense now," he said a moment later. "The incidents that have occurred since our arrival—the outposts, what you found on Ijuuka—they're all connected. It seems obvious to me now that this mysterious group had been altering their plans in response to our arrival from the moment they learned we were here." He pointed to Data. "Given what we've learned, does anyone really believe Data's calculations were so far off as to all but render the planet unusable to the Dokaalan?"

"If they had placed someone in the Science Ministry," La Forge said, "it's possible they would be able to provide information that would let Data help them without his even knowing it." Looking to his friend, he grimaced as he added, "Sorry, Data, but in your compromised condition, you might very well have been susceptible to something like that."

Moving so that he stood next to Data, Picard placed a hand on the android's shoulder. "And about that, it's apparent to me now that what happened to you was no accident, just as it's clear that what happened on Ijuuka was not a fault of yours." *I'm sorry I doubted you, old friend.*

"I will continue my investigation into finding a way to reverse the affects to Ijuuka's atmosphere, sir."

Shaking his head, Picard said, "That will have to wait, Data. Right now there are larger concerns."

"You think this spy, if there was one, might still be on the ship?" Riker asked.

"It's very possible," Picard replied. From the beginning, he had held doubts that the android's incapacitation was accidental or even due to a freak side effect of the asteroid field's radiation blanket, but he had lacked proof to back up his suspicions. He still had no hard evidence, only circumstantial information that added weight to his instincts. That was good enough, he decided, at least for the moment.

Still, he wanted that proof.

"He may still be here," he continued a moment later, "maybe working alone or with a whole cadre. We have no way of knowing, not yet, anyway." To La Forge, he said, "Commander, work with Dr. Crusher and Mr. Data to find a way to see the presence of these impostors. If you were able to see something different about them with your eyes, it seems reasonable that the ship's sensors can be modified in a similar fashion." Holding up a hand, he added, "But keep this just between us for the time being. I don't want to risk tipping off any spies who might still be among us."

"Aye, sir," the chief engineer said. "We'll get on it right away."

Nodding as La Forge, Taurik, and Data moved for the exit, the captain turned to Riker and Troi. "The Dokaalan have been used, it's as simple as that. Their dreams to forge a better life for themselves have been perverted by a gang of petty thugs, cowards who hide in the shadows and leech off these people's hopes and ambitions." This group of interlopers, whoever they were, needed the planet for themselves, and held no apparent reservations about leaving the Dokaalan in the lurch in order to reach that goal.

The very idea enraged Picard.

"Do we attempt to warn Hjatyn?" Troi asked.

Picard shook his head. "Without proof, we can't afford to reveal our suspicions just yet." The chances were good that someone had been alerted to La Forge and Taurik's escape from captivity by now, which meant that the subversives would already be planning for how to best handle this latest obstacle to their plans.

"We'll find them, sir," Riker vowed.

Trying to draw from the conviction in his first officer's voice, Picard found himself harboring doubts. Would they be able to track down these mysterious invaders? They seemed to be masters of stealth, but there was no way they could hide from the resources available to the *Enterprise* crew, could they?

"I hope you're right, Number One," he said, his voice quiet. "I think we owe the Dokaalan that much, at least."

Chapter Sixteen

READING THE SITUATION REPORT provided to him by one of Nidan's assistants, Daeniq was only just able to maintain his demeanor and avoid arousing suspicion from any of the unwary Dokaalan who surrounded him. It certainly would not be wise for him to do anything out of character for the security minister he was impersonating, after all.

Even though Nidan was among the first Dokaalan to be replaced and Daeniq had played the role from the beginning, experience and training prevented him from leaving anything to chance, especially now when there was still so much at stake. Their mission was far from over, even with the assistance the Starfleet ship had unwittingly given them.

He read the report a second time. The information it contained had not changed, of course.

"It is good news, yes?" the subordinate asked, happiness brightening his blue complexion. "I am happy they were found."

Nodding, Daeniq kept his expression neutral. "Yes, it is good news. That will be all." The lower-ranking security officer returned to his duties, leaving Daeniq with only the report for company.

The Starfleet engineers had been found and returned to their ship. Daeniq had been expecting that, had even warned his superiors of the potential hazard that came with keeping the engineers alive. He had advised killing them when they were first captured but had been overruled. Part of him took satisfaction in having been right, but it was a feeling he would have to keep to himself, at least until such time as those higher up in the chain of command saw the value in having him in charge here.

Even with this new development, Daeniq was fairly certain the Starfleet captain would not act until he had more information. There was no way for him or his crew to know the scope of the new problem they faced. The question now was whether or not Daeniq and his companions would be able to adapt to the rapidly changing situation faster than Captain Picard and his crew.

It was time, Daeniq decided, to put the next phase of the operation into motion.

Leaving the control center, he crossed the floor of the Zahanzei Council chambers and moved to the single door set into the room's rear wall. Like other doors used throughout the central habitat, this one was a simple affair, crafted from the same utilitarian metal sheets used for all manner of construction on all of the colonies. The only thing that differentiated it from the other doors in the council chambers was the seal emblazoned on it, identifying the room beyond as the private office of the first minister.

Without knocking or otherwise announcing his presence, Daeniq opened the door, entering the office in time to see one of his own people standing over the prone body of First Minister Hjatyn.

"Lorakin! What are you doing?" Daeniq asked, his voice nearly a yelp of surprise as he beheld the sight of what appeared to be a dark metallic skeleton bending over the fallen form of the aged Dokaalan leader. He quickly closed the office door, engaging its lock in order to guarantee them a measure of privacy. Turning back toward the center of the room, he was in time to see his companion's mimicking shroud alter and shimmer before taking on the appearance of the first minister.

"He was of no more use to us," Lorakin said once his transformation was complete. "Now that the Starfleet captain knows we are here, I saw no more need to keep Hjatyn in place. We can effect quicker changes if one of us acts in his stead." Lorakin had spent the past months impersonating one of Hjatyn's low-level staff assistants. Perfect for a spy, the position allowed him to keep the Dokaalan leader under near-constant surveillance while at the same time not allowing any significant attention to be drawn to himself.

Now, however, Lorakin had decided that it was time for overt action to replace clandestine observation.

Shaking his head in disapproval, Daeniq regarded the obviously dead Hjatyn lying on the floor of his sparely decorated office. He had hoped to avoid killing the first minister, having grown to admire the elderly Dokaalan. In private moments and when time and circumstances permitted it, Daeniq had even taken the time to peruse Hjatyn's personal journal, a record the first minister had been keeping since before the destruction of his home planet. It was fascinating reading, giving unmatched insight into Hjatyn's prudent and compassionate approach to leadership as well as his unwavering vision of a better future for his people.

Daeniq actually found himself mourning the fact that the journal would now and forever remain incomplete. His training and discipline prevented such emotions from interfering with his mission, but that did not mean he could not pay Hjatyn the respect due him for all he had accomplished here.

He cannot even be remembered or celebrated in death, Daeniq mused—somewhat bitterly, he realized. It was yet another rumination he would have to keep to himself, at least for the time being.

Withdrawing a Klingon disruptor from the folds of his robe, Lorakin adjusted the weapon's power setting before taking aim on Hjatyn's lifeless body and pressing the firing stud. A bolt of vicious orange-red energy spat forth from the disruptor and enveloped the first minister's remains, which flickered and shimmered before disappearing entirely. Not for the first time, Daeniq was thankful that the walls of Hjatyn's office, like his own, were soundproof.

"I did not want to kill him," Lorakin said, noticing the disapproving expression on Daeniq's face. "You of all people should know that. He was beginning to ask questions, particularly about the incident on Mining Station Twelve. It would have been dangerous to leave him in place while trying to deal with the Starfleet ship. You know that the only reason we did not replace him before now was because we needed a defense against the empath."

The Betazoid woman and her ability to sense the emotional state of those she came into contact with had been a threat from the moment they had learned of the Starfleet ship's presence here. With Hjatyn left in place to interact with Captain Picard and members of his crew, his honest emotional reactions of joy and hope had been vital when interacting with Captain Picard and his crew. The empath would pick up on that and it would hopefully be enough to deflect anything she might read from Daeniq and others impersonating various Dokaalan.

"It is troubling enough that anyone from the Federation would travel so far from their home territory to investigate this place," he said. "That it is the *Enterprise* only makes matters worse."

Moving to inspect his appearance in the full-length mirror set into the wall at the back of the office, Lorakin replied, "On the contrary, I find it fitting that they are here, and that it is they who have helped us to achieve our goal. It is the least they can do, considering what they cost us during the war."

"You mean what they cost *you*," Daeniq countered. He was well aware of the reputation of the *Enterprise* and her captain, particularly the footnote they held in the history of the Satarran Confederation.

Turning to look at him with an expression of mild shock, Lorakin replied, "Cost *us,* Daeniq. Picard and his ship cost us dearly. If not for their interference, we would have crushed the Lysians once and for all and been well on our way to rebuilding."

"I *know* the story," Daeniq countered, shaking his head.

Too young for military service at the height of his

people's war with the Lysians, he had nevertheless followed events as they were reported on various news services. Even as a child, he was able to understand that Satarran forces were unable to combat those of their enemy. Losses mounted at a staggering rate, and it soon became evident that, barring a miracle, victory would belong to the Lysians.

He also knew about the various unorthodox schemes developed by the Satarran Military Command, desperate attempts to rally one last time against their enemy. One such ploy was the hijacking of the *U.S.S. Enterprise* and the brainwashing of its crew to make them believe the Federation was at war with the Lysians. The plan had been to use the mighty Starfleet ship's formidable armaments to destroy a vital Lysian command center and render them powerless to resist the Satarrans any longer.

"If you know the story," Lorakin said, "then you know that because of their interference, we were instead left with several more years of war and a world left in ruins."

Daeniq recalled that it was not so simple as his companion believed, even if Lorakin's emotions were not clouded by the fact that his brother had been the operative sent to infiltrate the *Enterprise* and put the daring scheme into motion.

It had involved the use of a specially modified sensor beam, the effects of which were to suppress the crew's memories and make them susceptible to suggestion and direction offered by Lorakin's brother. The plan had worked up to the point where Picard was poised to order the destruction of the Lysian central command, at which time the captain and his people had somehow found a way to counter the beam's effects.

With the failure of that and other similar strategies, it soon became obvious that the Satarrans' defeat at the hand of the Lysians was inevitable. As the war wound down and eventually sputtered out altogether, efforts turned from conflict to reconstruction.

In the case of the Satarrans, Daeniq knew that the war had taken its toll on a number of planets in the confederation, including the homeworld itself. Many parts of it had been rendered uninhabitable and there was a great need to relocate the surviving population, a task made much harder by the fact that very few planets in the galaxy were capable of supporting the Satarran species. He had heard the concept of terraforming put forth on more than one occasion, but the consensus among the scientific community was that even if the technology were available, the process would take far too long to be of any assistance to those awaiting transfer to a new home.

Therefore, it was fortunate happenstance that a Satarran reconnaissance vessel had found the Dokaalan probe. What had begun as a simple investigation of the Dokaalan system in search of anything that could be salvaged for the war effort had instead turned into the best hope for the Satarran people to save what remained of their civilization.

The planet being terraformed by the beleaguered Dokaalan was very similar to the Satarran homeworld. A scientific expedition, conducted in stealth so as to avoid attracting the Dokaalan's attention, had determined that the world would suit their purposes, but only with additional changes in the chemical reactions being made in the atmosphere. The bulk of the work already being performed by the Dokaalan could continue, with the needed alterations being carried out in stealth. It would require subtle changes in both the machinery and computer software overseeing the terraforming process, but technical specialists theorized that such modifications could be made without detection by Dokaalan engineers.

Additionally, the effort would take time. Years would pass before the planet was ready for habitation by the Satarran people, so patience was essential to the success of the operation. By the time the Dokaalan discovered what had happened, it would be too late and the world's atmospheric composition would be well on its way toward conversion for the Satarrans' needs. Daeniq's people would no longer need to live in dilapidated fleets of ships or anywhere else they could find safe harbor. They would once again have a world to call their own.

As for the Dokaalan themselves, part of Daeniq regretted their place in all of this. Such were the misfortunes of war, he knew, even if one was victim to a war in which one did not fight.

Of course, everything he and his people had been working toward had been endangered thanks to the untimely arrival of the *Enterprise*. At least, that had been the original thinking.

Daeniq's attention was drawn to Lorakin as he moved to the simple metal desk that was the office's primary piece of furniture. Reaching for a carafe, his companion poured himself a glass of water.

"I wonder what Picard will say once he finds out he allowed us to reduce our timetable by nearly two-thirds," Lorakin said after taking a sip of the water. "I really must find a way to properly thank him for his assistance. His, and Dr. Geliu's." Holding up the glass in salute, he added, "It was her idea to make use of the android's scheme, after all."

That much was true, of course. Having assumed the identity of Science Minister Creij, Geliu had been in perfect position to examine and comprehend the Starfleet android's plan to deploy a suite of torpedoes to the planet. With each of the weapons carrying an artificially created substance that Federation science had developed for their own terraforming efforts, the transformation of the planet's atmosphere would be accelerated far beyond the capabilities of both Dokaalan and Satarran technology. Acting as the science minister, Geliu had been able to provide the necessary information that allowed the *Enterprise* crew to unwittingly answer the Satarran's needs in one fell swoop.

Still, the mission was not yet complete.

"You look troubled, Daeniq," Lorakin said a moment later.

Sighing heavily, Daeniq replied, "Now that he is aware of our activities here, Captain Picard will exhaust every resource at his disposal to expose us."

"Of course," the senior officer said, nodding. "In fact, I welcome that."

Daeniq did not like the sound of that. "We still have the initiative, but only for a short time. If we do not act now, there may not be time for us to counter any action they put into play. We should end this." Shaking his head, he added, "Order our operatives on the *Enterprise* to destroy the ship."

His face adopting a reproachful expression, Lorakin replied, "The Federation will simply send another ship."

"They are weeks away," Daeniq countered. "By the time they arrive, we will have restored control over the situation and be able to offer any number of explanations for what happened."

Lorakin shook his head. "Not yet. We may still have need of the ship's resources."

Unwilling to believe that, Daeniq fixed his friend and superior officer with a stern gaze. "Do not allow your desire to exact some type of vengeance on Picard to cloud your judgment and compromise the mission."

The interior of the office echoed with Lorakin's laughter. It was a comforting sound, one that had in times past never failed to put Daeniq at ease.

"I would be lying if I said I had not considered that, but do not worry," he said. "Like yours, my training and loyalty is too strong to fall victim to such petty emotions." A sinister smile abruptly curled the corners of his mouth. "At least, not until our work here is complete."

He laughed again, but this time it was a sound Daeniq found most unpleasant.

Chapter Seventeen

"THERE YOU GO," Geordi La Forge said as he watched Data rise to a standing position and hold it for several seconds before lowering his body back to his chair. Once he was finished, a chorus of applause erupted in main engineering, the rest of La Forge's team all smiles at this latest milestone in Data's repair efforts. "Looking good, Data."

Seated in the antigravity work sled, Data raised his left leg until it extended straight out and away from him before testing his knee's range of motion. "I have nearly finished rerouting the neural pathways which oversee my motor functions," he said as he repeated the movements with his right leg. "At my current rate of progress, I anticipate regaining full mobility within two point seven hours."

Though he was certainly happy to see his friend making such excellent progress, La Forge could nevertheless not shake a nagging sense of guilt. "I'm sorry I wasn't here when this happened to you, Data. Who knows if I might have been able to help?" Even as he said the words, he knew they rang hollow. After all, he had already reviewed the diagnostic logs recorded during the android's incapacitation. Whatever had caused the extensive cascading failure in Data's internal processes was unlike anything La Forge had ever seen, far surpassing any similar damage his friend had suffered in all the time the chief engineer had known him.

Holding his left leg extended in front of him again, Data said, "Given the amount of damage, I do not believe you would have been able to effect a swift resolution."

"No, but I might have at least been able to help with the rebuilding," La Forge countered. "Why in the hell did you have to start without me?"

In order to fully recover from the harm done to his neural pathways, Data required a near-total reconstruction of his positronic network. By the time La Forge and Taurik had returned to the *Enterprise,* Data had already managed to affect a temporary solution based in the immense system of software he carried to oversee his numerous functions and abilities. It was not a substitute for the physical repairs needed to permanently overcome the damage he had suffered, but it would, theoretically, allow Data to return to duty until such time as the various current problems involving the Dokaalan were resolved.

"I am sorry, Geordi," Data replied as he lowered his left leg. "There was no way to know when you might return, and Captain Picard had already assigned me to develop a means of assisting the Dokaalan's terraforming efforts. After assessing the situation, it seemed crucial that I return to duty as quickly as possible." He affected a better than fair imitation of a human shrug. "Still, I would have liked for you to have been present during the process. With the obvious exception of myself, you know more about my construction and internal systems better than anyone."

La Forge chose not to argue, even though he knew there were those who would gladly debate the point. An entire department back at Starfleet Command had been formed a few years ago with but a single mission: Study and understand Lieutenant Commander Data. Several high-ranking officials had on several occasions made public their ambitions to duplicate the android, but such efforts had consistently failed. Starfleet science and technology, as advanced as it was, had simply not yet caught up to the talent and skill of Data's creator.

That was fine with La Forge, who had always wavered between disappointment and disgust at Data's treatment by those who saw him as an object of opportunity, especially when those people were in positions of power in the very organization to which he had sworn loyalty. In addition to being a unique and remarkable individual in his own right, Dr. Noonien Soong's crowning achievement had chosen to devote the totality of his functional life to serving Starfleet and the Federation. He deserved better than to be the focus of curiosity and potential exploitation, at least so far as Data was concerned.

There's that motherly instinct of yours acting up again, he mused, knowing there was some truth in the notion. From their earliest days serving together on the *Enterprise*-D, La Forge had been protective of Data in ways that went far beyond his role as the ship's chief engineer. Though he of course had not participated in his friend's creation, he had taken it upon himself to understand everything there was to know about the android, a stance that had helped him to assist Data in recovering from various injuries and other problems he had suffered.

And it was that attitude which made him feel guilty and even angry that he had not been here when his friend had needed him most.

"Well," La Forge said finally, "I'm here now, and we'll get you through this. Then, the first chance we get, we're going to see about reconstructing your neural net the right way." It was a laborious task, and one that he did not relish performing, but in the long run it was the best means to ensure that Data experienced no lasting effects from his incapacitation.

"The measures I have enacted will be more than sufficient for the time being," Data replied. "Until now I was able to divide my attention between my internal diagnostics and continuing my investigation into what happened on Ijuuka. With the progress I have made, I can now also assist you in your efforts."

Nodding in grudging agreement, to say nothing of unfettered admiration at his friend's ability to simultaneously concentrate on several tasks, La Forge sighed heavily. "Well, I can sure use your help." He indicated the workstation display monitor and the series of instructions he had so far devised for modifying the ship's internal sensors. "Without knowing what species we're dealing with, and considering the variety of races that make up the crew, figuring out how to isolate someone using just variances in body temperature isn't enough. Even if we screened out biosigns for the different species represented by the crew, that's still not a guarantee that we'd pick up anything." Shrugging, he added,

"It's worth a shot, anyway, but I think we need something else."

Looking around, he allowed his ocular implants to home in on the heat signatures of the various engineers working throughout the room. None of them seemed out of the ordinary to him, even the body temperatures of the nonhuman members of his staff. Taurik's was warmer than Ensign Leisner, for example, while Ensign Veldon registered as cooler than Lieutenant Diix.

"If we went with the idea that it's a spy using some kind of holography to alter his appearance," La Forge said, "we could reprogram the sensors to register anyone who looked to be carrying a portable power source." As soon as he said the words, though, he shook his head and dismissed the idea even before Data could counter the suggestion.

He did so, anyway.

"The ship's sensors are already configured to detect and report the use of any unauthorized power sources anywhere on board," he said. "If such a source is in operation, it seems reasonable to assume that it is being concealed in some fashion."

"You're probably right," La Forge said, shaking his head. "At least if they *were* Founders, we'd have a few tricks up our sleeves."

During the Dominion War, methods had been developed to identify shapeshifters who had infiltrated Starfleet and the Federation as well as the Klingon Empire and the Cardassian Union, in some cases adopting the personas of individuals possessing much influence and authority within each society. The tactics had been crude, consisting of blood tests of suspected impostors and, in more extreme situations, phaser sweeps of rooms where changelings were believed to be hiding while assuming the forms of other people or even inanimate objects.

Allowing his gaze to wander about the room, La Forge caught site of the two security guards. Ensign Forst, a human male, and Lieutenant Jeloq, a Bolian female, were each armed with a phaser rifle and positioned just inside the main entrance to the engineering section. Teams like this one had been deployed throughout the ship in accordance with Captain Picard's order, a course of action the chief engineer could not remember being put into play since the war.

In engineering, La Forge had taken additional proactive steps, most notably in erecting the forcefield intended to protect the warp core. Even now he could hear the telltale buzz of the active shield, just barely audible over the powerful thrum of the core itself. If indeed a saboteur was aboard the *Enterprise,* the possibility of that individual disabling the ship's main propulsion system or even using it as a weapon to destroy the ship altogether was a very real concern.

Looking once more at the guard, he shook his head in resignation. It had always unsettled him when circumstances required the employment of such martial methods aboard what was supposed to be a ship of peaceful exploration.

How long has it been since we really were that, he asked himself.

Even their current mission, which had started off with such little promise and evolved into an unparalleled opportunity to aid and learn from an alien race never before encountered, had just as quickly deteriorated into a situation with many sinister underpinnings. Still, helping the Dokaalan through a difficult time in their lives and introducing them to the larger interstellar community that would soon become their welcoming neighbors was absolutely in keeping with the very reasons he had joined Starfleet in the first place.

With that in mind, La Forge decided, the unfortunate militaristic aspect of trying to protect their new friends from those who sought to do them harm was worth enduring.

"So," he said a moment later, "you know what kind of luck I'm having. How's your research coming?"

Turning from the workstation he had occupied for the four hours since the last staff meeting, Data said, "Based on all of the information at my disposal, I have so far been unable to find an explanation for the effects of our introducing the phylocite into Ijuuka's atmosphere. I am now proceeding from the theory that Science Minister Creij was somehow able to deceive me with the information she provided."

"You think she's an impostor?" La Forge asked.

"That, or she has also been misled by someone who is," Data replied, "though I confess I do not feel as confident in that theory. Creij was with me during most of the computer simulation testing, and she played a central role in the final calculations and programming of the torpedo launch sequence. Her unmatched knowledge of the Dokaalan's terraforming procedures was also vital in the final determination of how best to spread the phylocite across the planet's atmosphere."

Listening to his friend's recitation, La Forge found himself nodding in agreement. "So, you're thinking that it wouldn't have been easy for someone trying to fool her."

"Precisely," Data said. "Therefore, I am compelled to pursue the hypothesis that it was Creij herself who undermined the experiment."

Though he had been concentrating on discovering a way to detect the presence of the interlopers pretending to be Dokaalan, or perhaps even members of the *Enterprise* crew, La Forge had not given serious thought to just how far into Dokaalan society these people might actually have insinuated themselves. If Data was right, then how many members of the Dokaalan leadership had they replaced? Positioned as they might be, had they in fact caused the disaster at Mining Station Twelve?

Based on what Barmiol had told him, it seemed likely that he and his companions were orchestrating a carefully plotted campaign of manipulation through clever deception and, yes, fear. If left unchecked, this band of impostors would almost certainly succeed in maneuvering the rest of the Dokaalan into doing whatever was needed for them to succeed in their mission. The arrival of the *Enterprise* would have disrupted their plans to some degree, of that the chief engineer was certain, but it seemed obvious that they had already adapted their methods, if his and Taurik's capture and Data's theory about the failed terraforming acceleration were any indication.

The question now was, could he and Data, and the rest of the crew for that matter, adjust in time to stop this rogue group before they did any more damage?

"Commander La Forge?"

He turned to see Lieutenant Taurik standing behind

him and holding a padd. The Vulcan's expression was one of concern. "What is it, Ensign?"

Holding out the padd, Taurik replied, "We've received a report from computer operations, sir. They have noted numerous discrepancies in the primary core's database access logs over the past several days."

"Let me see," La Forge said as he took the proffered padd, frowning at the report it contained. "The autonomous maintenance subprocessors show more traffic than the system master log can account for." Automated and operating outside the boundaries of the ship's vast computer network, the maintenance subroutines tracked the wear on the system's physical components, notifying operations personnel when scheduled cleaning of data-storage facilities and other pieces of equipment was required based on an individual unit's level of usage.

If the report La Forge was reading was correct, several of the core's data-storage units were in need of routine maintenance far ahead of projected schedules, based on a high level of activity that had not been recorded by the system's access logs.

How was that possible?

"Lieutenant Henderson has been going over the logs for the past several hours," Taurik said, "but he reports that he is unable to account for the disparity. He requests that a level-one diagnostic be scheduled for the entire computer system at the earliest oppor . . ."

The Vulcan's abrupt pause made La Forge look up from the padd to see Taurik's attention focused on something just over his shoulder. "What is it?" He turned to see that, still seated at the engineering workstation, Data had turned away from the console and now sat motionless in his chair. His expression had gone completely blank, and for a panicked moment the chief engineer thought his friend had suffered a relapse of his earlier incapacitation.

"Data?"

The android's eyes blinked in response to the query, and he turned his head until he faced La Forge. "Geordi, I have finished the review of my internal diagnostic logs leading up to the point of my deactivation. It was the result of an actuation servo deliberately directed at me."

Confused, La Forge frowned. "Are you sure?"

"I am afraid so," Data replied, "just as I am sure about who was responsible." Looking about the engineering section, he then pointed toward one of the workstations near the warp core. "It was Lieutenant Diix."

The Andorian was facing away from them, concentrating on whatever task he was performing. Despite a detailed examination using all of the visual abilities his ocular implants possessed, La Forge saw nothing untoward about the lieutenant. "How do you know?"

"I remember turning to ask Diix a question. He was holding a tricorder and aiming it at me, and I detected a brief power surge. After that, my internal logs for that period of time end."

La Forge felt his pulse beginning to race as he studied Diix, who still appeared to be carrying out his duties. "Do you think he's an impostor?" he asked.

Data replied, "It is a distinct possibility, though we have no way of knowing. At least, not without detaining him."

"Well, we can see about that," La Forge said, keeping his attention on the Andorian. The chief engineer was uncomfortable with the idea of Diix working so close to the warp core. If Data was right about him, what, if anything, had the lieutenant done as part of potential contingency plans in the event he was discovered?

La Forge's eyes flickered to the main entrance and the two security guards stationed there. They were the best option for attempting to apprehend Diix, he decided. Crossing the floor of the engineering section, he pretended to study the padd in his hand in the event Diix turned to look in his direction. When he drew within earshot of the security officers, he made a point not to look up from the padd as he spoke.

"Jeloq," he said in a soft voice, "I need you to take Lieutenant Diix into custody and remove him from engineering, as quietly as possible."

The Bolian's response was a quizzical look. "Sir?"

"Commander Data thinks he may be an impostor," La Forge said, knowing that Lieutenant Vale had briefed all of her people on the current situation with the Dokaalan and its possible ramifications for the *Enterprise.*

Jeloq nodded in understanding. "Aye, sir. We'll take him to detention," she said, indicating for Forst to follow her. They wasted no time moving across the room to where Diix was still working at his console.

"Lieutenant Diix," she said, her tone quiet yet carrying an unmistakable authority, "we need you to come with us, please."

The Andorian turned from his own console, confusion clouding his features. "I do not understand. What is the meaning of this?"

"Lieutenant Vale has requested your presence for a security briefing," Jeloq replied. "We are expecting another contingent of Dokaalan visitors later in the day, and your name was listed as one of those who had interacted with previous groups. She wants to cover additional security concerns before they arrive." She spoke with confidence, her voice unwavering even to the slightest degree, and La Forge could not help but be impressed at the practiced ease with which she delivered the completely fabricated explanation.

Diix himself appeared convinced, as well, nodding as he did a moment later. "Very well, Lieutenant." Glancing in La Forge's direction, he added, "I will need to inform Commander La Forge that I will be leaving my station."

As his eyes locked with Diix's, the chief engineer watched as the Andorian's own expression seemed to grow flat and cold, and in that instant La Forge knew the ruse was over.

Before he could shout a warning, say or do anything, the situation dissolved into chaos.

Diix's right forearm was a blur as it lashed out and caught Jeloq full in the face, snapping the Bolian's head back and knocking her off her feet. Her phaser rifle dropped from her hands as she fell, with Diix moving even before her body hit the deck. His left leg came up and his foot struck Ensign Forst in the chest, the younger security officer stumbling backward until he struck another workstation mounted to a nearby bulkhead.

Engineers throughout the room had turned to see what was happening as Diix bent to snatch the phaser pistol from the waist holster of the unmoving Lieutenant Jeloq. La Forge felt his blood chill as the Andorian glared at him, but Diix did or said nothing.

Seeing some crew members moving closer, Diix fired several indiscriminate bursts with his confiscated phaser, high enough not to hit anyone but sufficiently low that everyone scattered for cover. At the same time, La Forge saw the lieutenant's free hand move back to his console, fingers moving at a rapid pace over the keyboard.

What was he doing?

"Computer!" La Forge shouted. "Secure main engineering!"

There was no response from the computer as Diix began moving toward the doors leading from engineering. Despite La Forge's order, the chief engineer saw the doors open at Diix's approach. His lockout command had not been accepted by the computer! Tapping his combadge, he yelled "La Forge to security! Intruder alert in main engineering!"

"Vale here," came the security chief's response. *"Teams on their way, sir. I'm activating intruder protocols now."*

Diix heard the call, too, and he pivoted on his heel to aim his phaser at La Forge.

The weapon that fired was not his.

It belonged to Ensign Forst, who had regained his feet and retrieved his phaser rifle. Orange energy hit the Andorian high on his chest and neck. La Forge saw the lieutenant's form shift and shimmer at the point of impact, with something black and metallic clearly visible only for the instant that the phaser beam washed over Diix's body. Then it was gone, with Diix staggering momentarily from the force of the attack but not falling as he should have, stunned by the phaser's effects.

"What the hell . . . ?" was all La Forge could say before he saw Diix turn toward the doorway once more, his free hand reaching out to tap a control pad positioned next to the entrance. Then he stepped through, pulling his communicator badge from his uniform tunic and tossing it back into the engineering room just as the doors closed.

"Engineering sealed," said the feminine voice of the *Enterprise*'s main computer. *"Security lockdown measures are now in effect."*

"Get a medical team down here, now!" La Forge yelled as he dashed across the room to where Lieutenant Jeloq had fallen. She had not moved since the fight had broken out, and even as he reached out to check her for injuries the chief engineer stopped. There was no mistaking the odd bend of the Bolian's neck, or her wide open yet unseeing eyes.

Diix had killed her with a single blow.

"La Forge to security!" he said into his combadge. "Lieutenant Diix is an impostor and he's just escaped engineering. He's killed one security officer and he's armed."

"He has also modified several of the ship's security protocols," Data said from behind him, and the chief engineer turned to see his friend working rapidly at his console, entering requests and instructions into the computer station faster than any living being could hope to duplicate. "Internal sensors are offline, as are security containment fields throughout the ship."

"Smart bastard," La Forge said, noting Diix's discarded communicator badge lying on the deck, "whoever he is." Without the combadge, it would be that much harder to track the Andorian's movements through the ship.

He's not Andorian, the engineer reminded himself.

Turning from his console, Data said, "Geordi, he is a Satarran."

Chapter Eighteen

KLAXONS WAILED in the passageway and alarm indicators positioned at regular intervals along the bulkheads flared crimson red. Kalsha knew that the entire ship would be alerted to the presence of an intruder by now.

The corridor leading from engineering offered several directions in which he could run. Which way should he go? He knew he could not stay in this part of the ship. Security forces would already be converging here, trying to cut off all avenues of escape. He had bought himself a few minutes, at most, with his security lockouts to the main computer as well as the disabling of internal sensors so they could not track him. It had been an afterthought, occurring to him while working to retune the ship's external scanning equipment in accordance with his superiors' directives.

Still, while he was pleased with himself for having taken the extra time to carry out that task, he held no illusions that the android would not be able to circumvent those measures.

I should have destroyed it when I had the chance.

After failing to completely disable Data during his first attempt, Kalsha had requested further instructions from his superiors. Daeniq's belief was that the task should be completed, but Lorakin had overridden him. The android's incapacitation could, for a time at least, be attributed to something other than a deliberate attack, whereas a second attempt to neutralize him would undoubtedly be seen as suspicious.

Kalsha at first believed that the risk was acceptable, given the alternative of having Data remain operational to any significant degree. His concerns gained strength when the android began to repair himself, but then Dr. Geliu had begun working with Data in her guise of the Dokaalan science minister. Effecting changes in the scheme to launch torpedoes carrying a Federation-created synthetic terraforming compound into Ijuuka's atmosphere, subtly altering the chemical formulas without the android's knowledge, was a brilliant strategy, he conceded. The results, if successful, would only serve to accelerate the completion of the reformation project and make the planet habitable for the Satarran people within Kalsha's own lifetime.

And yet, all of that appeared to be in jeopardy now.

Reaching an access panel leading to one of the numerous maintenance conduits crisscrossing the bowels of the ship, Kalsha opened it and crawled inside. Even as he pulled the hatch closed behind him he heard the sounds of approaching footsteps. Security personnel were finally arriving.

He knew that some of them would be sent to try and gain access to engineering, perhaps even using their weapons to cut through the doors he had sealed as part of his security overrides. The others, along with many more scattered throughout the vessel, would be fanning out in search of him. His mimicking shroud, which was still providing the outward appearance of Lieutenant Diix, would protect him from the ship's passive sensors and the portable units carried by the crew, at least until such time as they determined how to penetrate the garment's dampening field.

How long would that take Data and the engineer, La Forge? They were both gifted individuals, Kalsha knew, and now that they had a purpose to focus on, there would be no stopping them until they achieved success. He had to find a way to escape the ship before that happened, but that would also prove a daunting task. Transporters were still offline owing to the effects of the asteroid field's radiation, and the shuttlebays and escape pods would almost certainly be secured by now. He might be able to reroute security protocols so as to gain access to one of the pods, but that would take time he was sure he did not have.

That left one option: acquiring an environmental suit and departing through one of the ship's several docking ports. It was a dangerous avenue, he knew, but it was also the best of his dwindling number of alternatives. In order to exercise that option, of course, he would need to keep moving. As the entire ship had in all likelihood been informed that Lieutenant Diix was an impostor, which meant he would have to change his outward appearance.

Reaching for the control pad concealed beneath his Andorian façade, Kalsha tapped a command sequence. Diix's form stretched and wavered before the veneer was replaced by that of Lieutenant Tyler, the human female engineer he had first impersonated upon boarding the

Enterprise. It was a disguise he knew would not hold up for very long, but he hoped it might allow him to move freely until he could devise another persona.

He paused a moment to recall the technical schematics of the ship that he had earlier memorized. There were two airlocks on this deck, he knew, used by engineers tasked with performing repairs or other work on the exterior of the ship. Kalsha could not afford to be found in either of those locations, as even with his new appearance he would undoubtedly arouse suspicion. No, he decided, he would work his way toward a similar facility two decks up from his present location.

Moving quickly through the maintenance conduit, he found a ladder that would allow him access to other decks. He perceived no signs that anyone else was in the tunnel with him, despite stopping at the intersection and listening for several moments. Satisfied that he was alone, he ascended the ladder, tracing back through the conduit until he found another maintenance hatch. Listening for signs of activity in the corridor beyond, he heard nothing. The shroud's limited sensors also detected no one, so he opened the hatch and stepped into the passageway, taking a moment to get his bearings.

Excellent, he thought. The airlock he sought was less than two sections away. He was not in the clear yet, but there was still a chance for his plan to succeed. Nodding to himself, he started down the corridor.

Turning at the first intersection he came to, he nearly barreled into two *Enterprise* security officers. Both men, one human and the other Bajoran, were carrying phaser rifles and regarding him with caution. The Bajoran in particular seemed to be particularly wary.

"Sorry," Kalsha said, his voice filtered through the mimicking shroud and adopting the pitch and tone of Tyler's thanks to the sample he had recorded from her. He also remembered to affect an air of nervousness and concern as he spoke. "Did you see him? I think he went this way."

"I just saw you in engineering a few minutes ago," the Bajoran said, his brow furrowing. "You were trapped with Commander La Forge and the others when the doors were sealed. How did you get here?"

"It's him," the human said, raising his phaser rifle. "The impostor."

Kalsha was faster, bringing his own weapon up and firing at the human. Orange energy washed over the man's body even as the Bajoran ducked to his left, twisting his phaser rifle around and trying to aim it at Kalsha, who fired again. In seconds, both security officers lay unconscious on the deck.

Now what was he going to do? Surely someone had heard the sounds of the fight, or else the weapons energy discharges had been detected. Someone would be here in moments.

There was one course of action open to him.

He tapped the control pad on his left arm. The mimicking shroud's sensors scanned the body of the Bajoran officer, using that information to alter Kalsha's appearance yet again. Gone was the image of Lieutenant Tyler, replaced with that of the Bajoran. Now secure behind yet another disguise, he looked around and saw another maintenance hatch nearby.

Kill him and disintegrate the body, he ordered himself. *You have no time for mercy.*

He shook the thought away. Too many lives had been needlessly taken already, he decided. Killing the guard in engineering had been an instinctive act born solely from training and experience, one Kalsha would question long after this mission was completed.

Now hearing running footsteps approaching, Kalsha pushed the unconscious Bajoran's body into the maintenance conduit, breathing through his mouth so as to avoid inhaling the man's unpleasant scent. Bajorans, he realized, smelled nearly as bad as humans.

As he closed the access hatch, he knew that it was possible that someone would find the stunned guard, but that was a chance he was willing to take. Either he would be away from the ship before the Bajoran was discovered, or he would be in the custody.

There was just enough time to return to the stunned human, grab the Bajoran's fallen phaser rifle, and kneel down next to the other man before a human woman and a Vulcan male rounded a corner in the passageway. Their own weapons were up and pointed in front of them, searching for threats.

"What happened?" asked the woman, whom Kalsha recognized as the *Enterprise*'s security chief, Lieutenant Christine Vale.

"It was him," Kalsha said. "We caught him crawling out of a maintenance hatch. He stunned my partner and then ran off that way." Playing the role as best he could, he pointed down the corridor in the direction opposite of the airlock that was his destination. "I fired at him, but I missed and he made it around the corner."

Kneeling next to the unconscious human, Vale's companion looked up. "Carlson has been stunned, Lieutenant, but his injuries are not severe." Tapping his combadge, he said, "Sevek to sickbay. We have a casualty on deck fourteen, section seven. Send a medical team along with a security escort."

"Acknowledged," replied a voice Kalsha did not recognize. *"On our way."*

Vale appeared to be satisfied with that, but Kalsha watched her jaw tighten in frustration. To him, he said, "Our guess is that this guy's trying to make his way to one of the shuttlebays or an escape pod. He's cut off internal sensors, but Commander Data and Commander La Forge are working on it. Until then, we have to do this the old-fashioned way." She paused to check the power setting on her weapon before adding, "This guy owes me for killing Lieutenant Jeloq, and I want his head on a pike. Ensign Liryn, you're with us. Let's move out."

Shoot them!

His mind screamed the command at him, but Kalsha opted against it. Tagging along with Lieutenant Vale's team would provide ideal camouflage, at least until such time as his situation presented a better opportunity for escape.

"Aye, sir," he said as he fell in behind the lieutenant. "Let's go find him."

"A Satarran? Are you sure?"

Studying the image of his captain on the small display monitor above Data's workstation, La Forge saw Picard's brow knit in disbelief as he listened to the engineer's report.

"He was wearing Lieutenant Diix's combadge, sir," he replied, "which means that the real Diix is missing. Considering what happened to Jeloq, I'm afraid that doesn't bode well." Shaking his head and trying not to dwell on the likely fate of one of his people, he added, "We checked the logs of our earlier run in with a Satarran, and the description of the holographic mimicking suit he was wearing when we captured him is pretty close to what we saw down here."

Like every other member of the *Enterprise*-D crew, La Forge had also been affected by the mysterious sensor beam used against them by the Satarrans, which had blanked all of their short-term memories. Unable to remember their own names or positions on the ship, they had all been prime targets when an undercover operative was placed among them in the guise of the ship's first officer, a fictitious Starfleet commander named Kieran MacDuff. It had all been part of an elaborate scheme to hijack the *Enterprise* and use it to levy a devastating, war-ending strike on the Satarrans' longtime enemies, the Lysians. It was a plan that had come perilously close to succeeding.

One thing La Forge had taken away from that experience was the unsettling fact that even he, with the enhanced vision provided by the VISOR he had been wearing at that time, had never suspected that the phony Commander MacDuff had been an alien employing a holographic shroud to disguise his appearance.

"The garment is not dissimilar to the isolation suits worn by Starfleet personnel conducting covert surveillance of prewarp cultures," Data offered, "except that it employs holography and sensor-dampening fields to conceal its presence, rather than the cloaking technology used in our suits."

"Now that you know what you're looking for," Picard said, *"can you track his movements?"*

Shaking his head, La Forge replied, "Not yet, sir. We're still working to get internal sensors back online. He managed to plant several lockouts in the main computer system, and did a great job of hiding them." They had not even been able to circumvent the lock the intruder had placed on the doors. Manual override had been useless, as well, forcing security personnel to cut through the doors with their phaser rifles.

"Computer," Data said, "direct all combadge signals transmitting on security frequency alpha-one to this station." Immediately, a schematic of the *Enterprise* appeared on one of the workstation monitors, two images showing both overhead and side views of the ship. La Forge saw dozens of yellow indicators begin to overlay the image; each point represented a member of Vale's security team.

"Good thinking," he offered, nodding in approval at his friend's ingenuity. Even without sensors to help guide the security teams during their search of the ship, it was a simple matter for Data to keep track of every member of the security contingent based on their communicator signals.

"Ensign LaRock to Lieutenant Vale," La Forge heard a voice call out over the intercom. *"We've finished our sweep of deck eight. Moving up to deck seven."*

"Roger that, LaRock," Vale replied. *"Proceed with caution. Remember that our man has a weapon and isn't afraid to use it."*

Despite the progress Data had made so far, they were still operating blind. "We have to get the sensors back online," La Forge said, shaking his head in mounting frustration.

Much to his and Data's surprise, they had learned that the intruder had not used encrypted access codes, a tactic Data could easily defeat, to protect the changes he had introduced to the ship's computer. Instead, the Satarran spy had actually rewritten some of the operating system software, reconfiguring it for his needs and yet still maintaining interface compatibility with the rest of the system.

"The Satarrans are known to be gifted computer technicians," Data added, his attention remaining focused on his console. "I am having to search for programs the intruder wrote and inserted into the active files. He was quite thorough in concealing his activities, as I can find no evidence of recent software updates or additions."

"In other words, Captain," La Forge said, "we don't have any idea what he might have done. The sensor blocks and security overrides he enacted might just be the tip of the iceberg."

On the screen, Picard said, *"I won't hinder your work any longer, Commander. Keep me informed of your progress. Picard out."*

As the monitor went blank, an alert tone sounded from the workstation and La Forge looked down to see Data's fingers moving across the console once more. "What's that?"

"I have made some progress with the internal sensors," Data replied. "Their capabilities are still limited, but I am able to track individual biosignatures."

"Great," La Forge said. "That narrows it down to only a thousand possibilities." Captain Picard had made matters somewhat easier by restricting personnel to their duty stations or their quarters for the duration of the heightened security measures that had been in effect for most of the day. Still, that left a lot of people, most of them part of the security detail, moving about the ship.

Standing up from where he had been leaning over the console, the engineer tried to stretch the kinks out of tired back muscles. Between his temporary incarceration at the hands of their mysterious guests, two separate bumpy shuttle rides through the Dokaalan asteroid field, and the fact that he had not yet had the chance to get any decent rest since returning to the *Enterprise,* his body was beginning to protest the extended abuse.

"Okay," he said, trying to let his mind relax enough to embrace their current problem from a new angle. "Computer, show me any biosigns within fifty meters of any escape pod, the captain's yacht, or either shuttlebay. Eliminate any biosign for crew members not confined to quarters or for anyone not moving toward any of those locations."

Another set of points illuminated on the technical displays of the *Enterprise,* adding to those representing the security force. Adhering to Captain Picard's standing order that no one travel alone, the indicators were arranged in small groups as they moved about the ship.

All of them, except one.

Walking with Lieutenant Vale and her companion and doing his best not to let on that the odor from their bodies was almost too much to bear, Kalsha decided that the time to make his escape was almost at hand.

It was a plan that was bold in its simplicity. Vale was leading them toward the aft shuttlebay, having elected to search this and other comparably sensitive areas of the ship herself. Kalsha reasoned that once there and with their attention focused on conducting their sweep, the security chief and the Vulcan, Ensign Sevek, would present him with a prime opportunity to immobilize them. That done, he would carry out his plan of acquiring an environmental suit and departing the ship, drifting across the relatively short distance separating the *Enterprise* from the Dokaalan's central asteroid colony. By the time anyone realized he had left, it would be too late for them to chase after him.

He conceded that it was a risky course of action, but he also knew that his time to effect an escape was rapidly running out.

Then time expired altogether.

"La Forge to Lieutenant Vale," came the voice of the chief engineer over the ship's intercom. *"We're now able to track combadge signals for everyone on the ship. We've also found one of your people, unconscious and stuffed into a Jefferies tube on deck fourteen. It's Ensign Liryn."*

The communicator badge, Kalsha realized. He had forgotten to take the Bajoran's after subduing him, and the ship's computer had used it to locate the unconscious officer he had replaced.

There was no time to mentally debate his decision not to kill the Bajoran before, to their credit, Vale and Sevek reacted.

Kalsha felt a hand on his shoulder, Sevek's, and knew the Vulcan was attempting to immobilize him with the curious unarmed defensive tactic his race had long ago perfected. Pivoting away from Sevek caused his hand to slide away, and Kalsha used the opportunity to strike out at Vale just as the security chief was bringing her phaser rifle up and around. The kick spoiled her aim, Kalsha's superior strength knocking the weapon out of her hand and forcing her back.

He sensed movement behind him and ducked to his left just as the phaser strike caught him in the back. The familiar jolt washed over him as the mimicking shroud dispersed the weapon's energy across the surface of the garment. At such close range the attack was nearly over-whelming, even though the shroud could withstand such assaults for a short time. The effects on the wearer were somewhat more severe, and Kalsha knew he had to end this quickly if he hoped to escape.

Still on his feet and holding his phaser rifle, he swung the weapon around and fired indiscriminately in what he believed was the Vulcan's direction. The beam went wide as Sevek ducked to his right even as Kalsha brought the weapon around to shoot at Vale, but the security chief was not where she had been mere heartbeats before.

He smelled her before he saw her, her human stench assailing his nostrils. Then she was right in front of him, stepping so close that her left arm was able to sweep the barrel of his weapon up and away from her just as her other hand, the one holding her hand phaser, struck him in the face.

He was totally unprepared for the suddenness or the ferocity of the attack. The butt of the weapon collided with his nose and Kalsha's vision exploded from the force of the impact. His left hand lashed out, a protective strike that hit nothing as another phaser burst punched him in the chest.

Then he was hit again as Sevek fired a second time, orange energy washing over everything for an instant be-fore fading to black.

Chapter Nineteen

EVEN BEFORE THE DOORS to the *Enterprise*'s security detention area opened and allowed him to enter, Riker made sure his expression was schooled so as not to betray any of the anger or frustration he was feeling. He knew that the emotions might very well serve him during the forthcoming interrogation, but only if he controlled them and not vice versa. It would not do to present anything other than a calm, controlled demeanor to the Satarran when he finally met the captured spy face-to-face.

When the doors opened, however, he saw from the look on Deanna Troi's face that his presentation still needed work.

"Will?" she said, her eyes conveying her obvious concern. "Are you sure you'd rather not wait to do this until later? Your emotional state may not be conducive to the interview."

Noting her use of the less confrontational term to describe what was about to occur here, Riker shook his head. "There's no way of knowing what he's been up to without questioning him. We can't afford to put it off."

"I can sense your resentment toward him," Troi warned. "If he detects it as well, he may find a way to turn that against you."

"Of course I'm resentful," Riker countered. "He's killed at least one member of the crew, perhaps two. What else has he done, or what was he planning to do, before we caught him?"

Hearing the edge in his voice, he drew a breath. Troi was right, of course. In order to extract any useful information from the Satarran, he would have to form some bond of trust with the prisoner, something he would not be able to do if he allowed his emotions to control his actions and words during the interrogation. Hopefully, that in turn would provide a means of assessing the spy's character and determining the truth of any answers he offered.

"I'll be fine," he said after a moment, offering a small smile. "Besides, you'll be there to make sure I stay on track, right?"

The counselor seemed to relax, obviously picking up on his attempts to calm himself. "Count on it," she replied, hands on hips and her own smile laced with an air of caution that made her seem like a mother warning a recalcitrant child to behave in front of guests. The humorous image evoked by her words actually succeeded in allowing him to relax, if only to a small degree, which naturally was Troi's goal all along.

You really do know me too well.

Riker motioned to one of the two ensigns seated at the

detention area's control console. "Let's go see our guest," he said.

"Commander Riker," said the ensign, an Indian man who the first officer remembered was named Mansingh. The younger man rose from his chair as Riker turned to face him. "Sir, Lieutenant Vale has requested to be present during questioning. She apologizes for any delay, but she's on her way here now."

Shaking his head, the first officer replied, "Tell her to take her time. I don't want any more people in there right now." To Troi he said, "It'll make him nervous enough with two of us. Any more, and he might clam up for good."

Troi seemed to consider the notion briefly before nodding in agreement. "Her emotions will also be running high from the loss of her lieutenant. I don't want to have to ride herd on both of you." Turning to Mansingh, she added, "Ensign, please tell Lieutenant Vale I'll want to speak with her when we're finished with the prisoner."

"Yes, ma'am," the ensign acknowledged as he returned to his duties at the console.

Led by the other security officer, Ensign Sevek, Riker and Troi walked to the brig's only occupied detention cell, the one farthest from the door. As they drew closer Riker felt an almost electrical tingle playing on his exposed skin, the effect of the active containment field that formed the cell's front wall, the sensation serving to remind him that it had been a very long time since he had ventured down to this part of the ship.

Then they were at the cell, and Riker got his first look at their most unwelcome guest.

The Satarran was a lean, muscular humanoid, dressed in a brown Starfleet-issue one-piece coverall that was standard issue for brig detainees. The drab color of the garment contrasted sharply with his pinkish skin. His face was long and narrow, with long, dark hair swept back from his face and tied at the base of his neck.

His eyes were narrow, bright yellow orbs that peered out from beneath a pronounced brow, and they locked with Riker's own from the instant the first officer had moved into his view. Other than that, he remained motionless, lying down on the cot that was affixed to the cell's rear wall.

"Open it," Riker said, and Ensign Sevek, with one hand on the phaser still in its holster at his waist, used his free hand to key a command sequence to the control pad mounted just to the side of the cell's entrance. Energy crackled as the forcefield deactivated, creating a hole where the cell's front barrier had been just long enough for Riker and Troi to step inside the small compartment. To Riker's surprise, the Satarran said nothing, not even when the forcefield was reestablished.

The cards are dealt, Riker mused as he felt the field's tingling sensation tickling the back of his neck. *Let the games begin.* After studying the prisoner for several seconds and deciding silence had hung in the air long enough, he broached the first nonconfrontational subject that came into his mind.

"Are you well?" he asked. "I know that you were injured during your capture."

"I am," the captive said in a voice that Riker found to be neutral in tone, even friendly. Reaching up to touch his narrow nose, the Satarran added, "Your security chief proved to be a most formidable opponent. Please pass on my compliments. As for the rest, your medical officer healed my injuries, and everyone I have come into contact with has treated me most fairly. Thank you."

"My name is Commander Riker, second-in-command of the *Enterprise,*" he said, "and this is Commander Troi, our ship's counselor."

"I am well aware of your identities," the Satarran replied, his eyes never leaving Riker's. He moved to a sitting position on the cot, and the first officer felt his muscles tense in anticipation of the prisoner launching some sort of attack on him or Troi. Instead, the Satarran merely placed his hands on his knees, his expression remaining passive. "We have spoken at length already," he added, "if you'll remember."

Riker did indeed remember, but saw no reason to concede that fact just yet. "I have some questions for you."

"I should think so," the Satarran said, and Riker noted how the prisoner seemed to be absently stroking his left forearm as he spoke. "Though it would appear that you and your people are well suited to solving any mysteries I represent. I doubt anything I say would be of any use to you."

Shrugging, Riker kept his own expression pleasant. "Let's start with something simple, like your name."

The Satarran smiled. "Simple indeed. Very well. My name is Kalsha."

"And how long have you been aboard the *Enterprise,* Kalsha?"

Apparently mulling over the question, the prisoner paused before responding. "Eight of your weeks."

Riker looked to Troi for clarification, and saw the counselor's brow crease as if she were confused or perhaps even struggling to comprehend a difficult concept. What was wrong?

After a moment, she said, "He's lying." Was it his imagination, or had he heard a hint of uncertainty in her voice? It was almost imperceptible, but he was sure it was there nonetheless.

Regarding the counselor, Kalsha's eyes narrowed and his expression turned to one of appreciation. "I was told a Betazoid was among your crew," he said, and Riker caught him rubbing his forearm again. "Obviously you are that individual, and you are correct. I am lying."

Riker felt his ire rising as the Satarran's wan smile returned. The last thing he wanted was for the interview to deteriorate so quickly. Kalsha was baiting him, obviously. The trick now was for Riker to remember not to fall for it.

"Of course you lied," he said. "You're a professional spy, and that's what spies do. I expected no less from you."

"If that's true, then what is the purpose of this interrogation?" Kalsha asked. "Did you truly expect that I would simply crumble under the pressure of you staring at me?"

"No, I didn't," Riker replied. "But, as a professional, I expected some courtesy, at least."

Kalsha's eyes widened, as did his smile. "Courtesy?" He paused, seeming to weigh the word. "Courtesy, stemming from respect. You have shown me respect, Commander, whereas I have not returned it, though I must admit that I do in fact respect you."

"Really," Riker said, making no effort to hide his skepticism.

Nodding, the Satarran continued, "With that in mind, I have a proposition. No doubt you already have some idea of which questions you might pose that I have no intention of answering. However, I am not interested in weaving a network of lies as we talk. Therefore, I will answer your questions truthfully so long as they remain, as you suggest, courteous of our situations. Is that acceptable?"

Riker looked to Troi, whose own expression was one of surprise. "He's sincere in his proposal," she said.

"Yes," Kalsha said, "let your Betazoid counselor be the arbiter here if you are unsure. What I tell you will be true."

It was an effort for Riker not to cross his arms, stroke his chin, or offer any other physical sign that the Satarran had caught him off guard. This was not at all what he had expected from the captured spy. Kalsha had offered an open, honest dialogue? Riker's gut told him not to squander it.

"It seems," he said a moment later, "that neither of us has anything to lose by that."

Kalsha nodded in apparent approval. "Excellent. So, let us talk."

"I presume," Riker said, "that you are aware we found Ensign Liryn where you left him?" Much to his relief, the Bajoran security officer had been found unconscious but otherwise unharmed inside a Jefferies tube on deck fourteen.

Kalsha sighed heavily at the question. "Of course I am, otherwise I would not be here. Come now, you can do better than that."

Feeling his jaw tighten, Riker forced himself to wait an extra beat before responding. *Poker face,* he reminded himself. Still, he found it easier to sidestep the verbal jab than he had a minute earlier. Obviously, the Satarran was still trying to assert some kind of control over the conversation, even if he had pledged honesty in his answers. "Should we hold out any hope for finding Lieutenant Diix as well?"

He knew the answer as soon as Kalsha's eyes dropped to look at a point on the floor of the cell. He remained that way for a few seconds before slowly shaking his head. "Regrettably," he said, "the Andorian is dead, and I was forced to dispose of his body. For that I sincerely apologize."

"You say that as if his life somehow mattered to you," Riker said, annoyance once again beginning to lace his speech.

Anger flashed in the Satarran's eyes. "It did matter to me. I am not a murderer."

"Forgive me if I think your declaration rings a little hollow," Riker snapped. "By my count, you've killed two of my people."

"Commander," Troi said, her tone one of caution. Though he did not visibly acknowledge her, Riker forced himself to ratchet his emotions down a notch, knowing she would sense the change, or at least the attempt.

"By *my* count, it could have been many more," Kalsha replied, his own voice laced with apparent irritation. He paused, perhaps to collect himself, once more stroking his left forearm before continuing.

What's with that, anyway? For a moment, Riker thought the Satarran might have concealed something beneath his skin, a weapon or communications device of some kind, but he just as quickly dismissed the idea. After all, the prisoner had been thoroughly searched and scanned before being confined to his cell.

"Despite what you may think of me," Kalsha continued, "I do not kill without purpose or reason. I spared the Bajoran man and the human woman before him. Had my mission been to kill all of you, I would have."

"Are you saying your mission doesn't involve killing us?" Troi asked.

The Satarran turned his head to regard the counselor. "That was not my original mission, no." Riker noted how the irritation that had clouded Kalsha's features only a moment ago now seemed replaced with what he might recognize as resignation on the face of a human. "My primary target was the android."

"Disable Data?" Riker asked. "Why?" When no answer seemed to be forthcoming after several seconds, he pressed, "Is that beyond the bounds of our agreement?"

"It should seem obvious to you by now," Kalsha replied. "The android was the one member of your crew who stood the greatest chance of uncovering our operations here. With him neutralized, the threat of discovery was drastically diminished."

"You plotted to kill him," Riker said. "That would seem to go against your supposed credo of sparing life whenever possible."

The Satarran shrugged. "Unlike you, I do not view the android as anything other than what it is: a machine. To me, it was a tool to be used and discarded, and nothing more."

Bracing at the stark admission, Riker leaned forward, his voice taking on a hint of menace. "Data's my friend."

"I meant no insult, Commander," Kalsha said, the cadence and tenor of his voice unchanged. "Understand that our level of technology is far behind yours in a number of areas, particularly with regards to artificial lifeforms. We have not yet had the opportunity to fully appreciate the potential that a . . . that an individual such as Commander Data represents."

Nice save, Riker mused. "Fair enough," he said, allowing a bit of warning to remain in his voice as he spoke the words. "Speaking of technology, let's talk about that suit of yours. Our engineers are having a field day looking it over."

In actuality, La Forge had already reported that there was nothing about the garment which came close to rivaling anything created by Federation science. Only the way in which its network of sensors, holographic emitters, and dampening fields worked together to provide the wearer with the ideal camouflage and ability to mimic nearly any humanoid life-form offered any real interest to the engineer.

Still, it provided a nice way to keep the questioning on track.

"It serves its purpose," Kalsha said. Apparently realizing that the fingers of his right hand had been playing across his left arm, he abruptly ceased the motion. It took Riker several seconds to understand the significance of what he had been witnessing since entering the detention cell.

That's where the control pad was.

The Satarran, no doubt an experienced undercover operative, had probably grown to rely heavily on the metallic exoskeleton and its chameleon-like qualities in the course of carrying out his various assignments. More than likely, the garment had protected him on countless occasions, perhaps even the single thing that had saved his life in some of those situations. For all intents and purposes, it might as well be a second skin for him.

Kalsha smiled again. "I do miss the shroud. It is often

an indispensable tool in my line of work." Indicating his left arm, he added, "It is also possible that I've grown to rely on it too much. Perhaps that is a sign that I have been pursuing my chosen profession for too long."

"They even found the concealed burst transmitter that was activated when the suit was removed from you," Riker said. "What was the purpose of that?"

Kalsha shrugged. "The transmission notifies my superiors that I've been captured. Rest assured that I am considered expendable, Commander. They will make no effort to rescue me."

Glancing to Troi, who after a moment nodded confirmation that the Satarran was being truthful, Riker allowed himself a small smile of his own. "I appreciate your honesty," he said, wondering how far he might be able to push Kalsha's apparent sense of charity in that regard. "With that in mind, I do have some more questions for you. First, how many more of your people are aboard this ship?"

"I have no idea."

The quick answer actually made Riker blink twice before he caught himself and reestablished his bearing. "Excuse me?"

"We operate individually, Commander," Kalsha said. "I was sent here alone to carry out my assignment. If others have been dispatched, it is without my knowledge."

Riker looked to Troi, who seemed to be struggling with her own thoughts yet again. "I'm sensing no deception," she said. "The answers he's given to this point are truthful, so far as I can determine."

The question, he knew, was whether the Satarran was

actually being honest, or if he simply possessed enough experience and savvy to thwart even her abilities.

"Fine," he said after a moment. He turned back to Kalsha. "We already know that you accessed our computer and altered several of the security protocols, deactivated internal sensors and so on. What else have you done?"

"What was required of me, Commander," Kalsha replied, his expression returning to one of unreadable detachment.

Was it Riker's imagination, or had the Satarran's words actually carried a hint of resignation?

I think this interview just became a lot more difficult.

Chapter Twenty

PICARD FELT HIS UNEASE growing with every moment he listened to Riker's report of the interrogation.

"And you're sure he's telling the truth?" he asked as he studied the padd his first officer had given him, which contained the entire transcript of the interview with the captured Satarran.

"Deanna is," Riker replied. "At least, she's fairly certain. After the interview, she said that she had a difficult time reading Kalsha's emotions. It required more effort from her than is usual with most humanoids. She said trying to read him was almost as bad as dealing with a Ferengi."

"Interesting," the captain said. "That would go a long way toward explaining the apparent confusion she experienced during our earlier run in with some of the Dokaalan leadership, assuming those individuals were Satarrans in disguise." He also realized that if the counselor was having trouble reading the emotional state of their adversaries, that might not bode well during any future encounters.

Riker nodded. "That's basically what she said. As for Kalsha, he didn't volunteer a damned thing, but according to her, he didn't lie about anything we asked him, either. We had to pursue lines of questioning if we wanted the complete answer to any particular subject. He's a professional, all right."

"Honest, yet evasive. No doubt an experienced field agent." He dropped the padd onto the pile of other such devices and swiveled his chair away from his desk. "And he's probably correct that his superiors are aware that we've captured him. Given what we know of his people's tactics in situations like this, it's probably safe to assume that he'll be left to his own devices."

When the *Enterprise* crew had captured a Satarran spy operating among them more than a decade ago, they had been surprised to learn that the lone alien had been working completely alone, with no support personnel or facilities anywhere in a position to assist him. Even after his capture, the Satarran government had failed even to acknowledge the spy's existence.

"What I wonder about now," the captain continued, "is just how informed he is of the current situation taking place off the ship. We know from our previous encounter that compartmented security is standard procedure for Satarran intelligence operatives."

"Well, he's got handlers who sent him here," Riker said, "and they've been busy. They've been here for years, working behind the scenes to commandeer the Dokaalan's terraforming project. That includes at least a few of the incidents on some of their mining outposts."

Sighing in evident frustration, he added, "He didn't give specifics, of course, but the general scheme is one intended to manipulate the Dokaalan into supporting the terraforming project on Ijuuka, through fear if necessary."

"Yet he gave no indication of how many of his people were among the Dokaalan?" Picard asked.

Riker shook his head. "He said he didn't know the exact number, but I think it's a safe bet that they've worked their way into positions of power throughout the colony."

The captain was forced to agree. If what Commander La Forge and Lieutenant Taurik had experienced on Ijuuka was any indication, at least a handful of those tasked with overseeing the atmospheric processing centers had been replaced with Satarrans.

"For their plan to be successful in the long term," he said, "it stands to reason that they have at least one person on the leadership council." In fact, Picard was now convinced that Science Minister Creij had to be a plant, using her role to ensure that Data's plan to accelerate the atmospheric conversion process on Ijuuka benefited the Satarrans' needs rather than those of the Dokaalan.

He had no proof to back up that suspicion, of course, but it made perfect sense, serving to illustrate just how far the Satarrans had infiltrated Dokaalan society. Replacing the colony's leading scientific mind would be a logical maneuver, allowing the interlopers to control nearly every aspect of the planetary reformation process, which had ultimately included covert operations aboard the *Enterprise*.

"What I want to know," Riker said, "is how they got here, and how they've been able to worm their way so far into these people's lives and do so much damage." He shook his head. "It's almost too incredible to believe."

Picard was not so sure. Though their level of technology was known to be inferior to that of the Federation in many areas, the Satarrans' ability to compensate for such shortcomings with ingenuity and even guile was well known. The *Enterprise* had been introduced to that adroitness years ago, demonstrated by one lone operative's relatively effortless ability to access the ship's computer, to say nothing of how he had nearly succeeded in brainwashing the entire crew into all but annihilating the Satarrans' sworn enemy, the Lysians.

Now, Picard faced the threat that more of the undercover agents were aboard his ship, moving about in stealth and possibly preparing for . . . what? Sabotage? Murder? There was no way of knowing, even after Riker's lengthy questioning of Kalsha.

And what of the Dokaalan themselves? Were any of them being influenced even more so than by the Satarrans' shadowy operations behind the scenes? So far, there had been no evidence that the Dokaalan had been exploited with the same strange technology the Satarrans had used to suppress the memories of the *Enterprise* crew during that first encounter more than a decade ago, but Picard was unwilling to entirely rule out such a possibility.

Moving away from that disturbing line of thinking, he asked, "What is the progress of the computer cleanup?"

"The techs are still working through the operating system and the bulk of the data storage banks," Riker replied. "They had planned to simply purge the primary computer cores and reload everything from protected archives, but they found signs that Kalsha had infiltrated those areas along with the backup core, too. We can't be sure of anything until a thorough sweep is completed."

It was one thing to be worried about insurgents running about the ship and causing all manner of trouble, Picard knew, but to fear the ship itself? Almost nothing pertaining to the operation of the *Enterprise*'s myriad onboard systems occurred without the influence or even notice of the marvelous feat of engineering that was the main computer. If Kalsha or another as yet undiscovered Satarran agent had subverted it for their own ends, then the safety of the ship and the entire crew was at risk.

"Have Mr. Data assist the computer division," Picard ordered. "Make it his priority to support them until the situation is resolved."

Riker nodded. "Aye, sir."

The captain stopped short of assigning his second officer to take over the department for the duration of the current situation. Such a move would usurp the department head's authority in the eyes of that officer's subordinates. Even tasking a member of the senior staff to play a supporting role was a delicate balancing act of leadership, but there was no arguing Data's specific talents in this regard. If anyone could root out whatever tricks, traps, or pitfalls that lurked within the computer, it was him.

The tone for the ship's intercom beeped for attention, followed by the voice of Counselor Troi. *"Bridge to Captain Picard. Sensors are detecting weapons fire at the Dokaalan colony, sir."*

There was barely enough time for captain and first officer to exchange shocked expressions at the report before Picard bolted from behind his desk. "On my way," he said, the reply coming as the doors to his ready room parted and allowed him and Riker to step onto the bridge.

"Report," he ordered as he moved to stand between the conn and ops stations, taking in the image of the mammoth asteroid and its network of habitation modules centered on the main viewer.

"It just started, sir," Troi said as she vacated the center seat in deference to Picard. "Particle-beam signatures from different types of weapons."

"Where?" Picard asked.

From where she stood at the tactical console, Lieutenant Vale said, "Most of the readings are originating near the colony's central command center and the council chambers, sir."

"Some kind of uprising?" Riker asked as he settled into his own seat and activated the status monitor positioned near his right hand. "Colonists rioting against the council?"

Picard considered the possibility. First Minister Hjatyn had expressed concern that segments of the populace were discontent with the terraforming initiative. Many considered it a hazardous and wasteful use of the limited resources the colonies relied upon to ensure their survival within the makeshift environments they had fashioned for themselves among the asteroids.

No, he decided.

"This has to be the Satarrans," he said, "but why the sudden change in tactics now?" Certainly the insurgents had to know by now that there was little left for Picard and his crew to learn about their operations here, and were probably now wondering when the *Enterprise* would take action against them.

"You're thinking we forced their hand, aren't you?" Riker said, as if reading his captain's thoughts.

Nodding, Picard replied, "Indeed I do, Number One."

To his right, Vale looked up from her station. "Captain, we're receiving an incoming distress call from the colony."

"On screen," the captain ordered, and the image on the main viewer shifted to that of a distressed-looking Dokaalan dressed in the robes worn by members of the Zahanzei Council. Picard could not remember his name, but he realized that he had encountered this particular man during the first meeting with the council only a few days earlier. Fear was evident in the Dokaalan's maroon eyes as he stared out from the screen.

"Captain Picard!" he cried. *"Minister Nidan is leading a revolt. Our own people are turning against us! We need your help!"*

"Nidan," Riker said.

Picard felt his jaw tighten. "The perfect choice for the Satarrans to replace."

"It would explain the feelings of suspicion and anxiety I sensed in him," Troi said.

"What about him?" Picard asked, pointing to the Dokaalan on the screen.

The counselor shook her head. "I sense genuine fear, Captain. He's terrified."

It was obvious to Picard that the Satarrans had given up any remaining efforts to carry out their plan in stealth. If they were taking such rash action now, what else were they willing to do? How far would they push the situation?

"I've had enough of this," Picard said. "Number One, you and Lieutenant Vale prepare security teams to deploy to the colony via shuttlecraft, and a plan to secure the facility as quickly as possible."

"Aye, sir," Riker said as he moved to the tactical station to work with Vale.

Stepping forward until he stood between the two forward bridge stations, he locked eyes with the Dokaalan on the screen. "We're going to help you."

On the screen, the Dokaalan jolted at the sound of something, or someone, pounding on the door to his office. *"Captain,"* he said as turned back to the viewer. *"They're coming for me!"*

That was all he managed to say before the door burst open and Security Minister Nidan, or someone who looked like him, entered the room. He held a weapon that Picard did not recognize, aiming it at the frantic Dokaalan and firing without hesitation. A harsh red bolt of energy struck the other minister and he was thrown from his chair and out of view, falling heavily to the floor.

"Oh my god," Troi breathed.

Having seemingly already forgotten what he had just done, Nidan moved farther into the office until his form nearly filled the viewscreen. He sported an irritated expression, which he levied at Picard.

"I am sorry you had to witness that, Captain," the security minister said. *"Rest assured that Minister Onaec is only stunned. Our work here is far from complete, and he has a role to play."*

"We know all about what you've done to these people," Picard said, allowing the first hint of anger to creep into his voice. "You've used these people and you've manipulated us into helping you hurt them. That ends now."

"I am afraid not."

The voice was not Nidan's, but that of someone else who had entered the room behind him. The security minister stepped aside and Picard watched as Hjatyn entered the office. Unlike the other occasions he had seen the first minister, Hjatyn no longer walked like the aged man he supposedly was. Instead his gait was strong and confident, practically a march as he moved toward the viewer. Even his face appeared younger, dominated as it was by a knowing, arrogant smile.

"Of course," Picard whispered.

"I don't understand, sir," Troi said from behind him. "Even with the difficulties I seem to be having reading Satarrans, I never sensed deception or anything suspicious in our previous meetings with him."

"Where is the real Hjatyn?" Picard asked.

"I regret to say that he is dead," replied the Satarran in disguise. *"It was unavoidable, given our current situation. Perhaps you remember our war with the Lysians, Captain? Do you know that we lost that war?"*

Picard nodded, his throat still somewhat restricted as he reacted to the almost casual dismissal of the genuine Hjatyn's death. "I was informed of that, yes."

As neither the Lysians nor the Satarrans were Federation members, reports of the conflict between the two races had been sketchy, with Starfleet only paying any real attention to the situation after the Satarran attempt to hijack the *Enterprise*-D. Following that incident, Picard had periodically checked with Starfleet Intelligence to receive updates on the war, including the confirmation nearly nine years ago that the fighting had finally ended between the two peoples. The Lysians had emerged the victors, but the homeworlds of both races had borne the brunt of the prolonged conflict and survivors from each planet were faced with rebuilding their societies.

"In the wake of our defeat," the Satarran said, *"we soon learned that the environmental damage done to our world during the war was irreversible, a consequence of the weapons used against us by the Lysians. Our foremost scientists have projected that within my children's lifetime, the planet will be unable to sustain life."* He held out his arms, as if to indicate his surroundings. *"The planet these people have chosen to reform is the closest match to a world with my people's environmental requirements that we have been able to find. It has taken us quite a long time to reach this point, but thanks to your unwitting help, this planet will be able to support Satarran life. My children will be able to live in a world untouched by the scars of war."*

"But no less stained by blood," Picard countered. "You've treated these people little better than slaves, leeching off their hopes and dreams while you destroy everything they've worked toward for generations."

"The Federation pledged assistance to your people and the Lysians when your war ended," Troi said, rising from her chair. "The Lysians accepted it, but your people didn't even acknowledge the offer. Why?"

His expression turning to one of disgust, the Satarran broke eye contact with the captain, his gaze turning as if to look at something in the distance. *"The Lysians are a people without pride and without principle. It was their malicious, cowardly attacks on our shipping industry that started the war in the first place. Even after formal hostilities had been declared, they made no distinction between military and civilian targets. They are animals."*

Turning his attention back to Picard, he added, *"You should have helped us destroy them when my brother gave you the chance."*

"Your brother?" the captain repeated, his blood growing cold at the revelation and the potential it represented.

As if understanding Picard's reaction, the Satarran offered a dismissive wave. *"Do not worry, Captain. He was a soldier who performed his duty, and was defeated by a better opponent. I am not here to extract some manner of vengeance today. There are far greater concerns, after all."*

Picard detected motion from the corner of his eye and glanced over to see Riker standing at the tactical station next to Lieutenant Vale. Out of view of the screen's visual feed, Riker gave the captain a thumbs-up signal, which Picard took to mean that the security teams he had ordered to be prepared for transfer to the Dokaalan colony were now ready.

Good, he thought. *It's time to put an end to this.*

"I'm afraid I can't stand by and allow this to continue," he said. "The Dokaalan have a right to better their lives, as well, perhaps more so than you. They are not yours to control, and I won't stand by and allow you to torture them any longer."

On the screen, the fake Hjatyn's false Dokaalan smile faded. *"Captain, I grant you that your technology surpasses anything we have at our disposal, but we have been here for quite some time, and have prepared for all manner of contingencies. Any attempt to interfere with us will bring harsh consequences."*

Ignoring the threat, Picard replied, "Surrender now, and I'll see to it that this matter is taken to the Federation Council. Your world can be helped, or your people evacuated to another planet, but this action against the Dokaalan cannot proceed. One way or another, it ends today." He looked to Riker. "Number One?"

Moving from the tactical station down into the command well to stand next to Picard, the first officer said, "Security personnel are armed and ready to transfer to the colony, sir. Lieutenant Vale has a plan that will let us secure the command center inside of two minutes from the time they dock."

"I urge you to reconsider that plan, Captain," the Satarran said. *"We have already taken the remainder of the leadership council hostage. Even though the terraforming effort on Ijuuka is well on its way to meeting our needs, we still require the assistance of the Dokaalan people. In some cases, it also requires us to take other steps to ensure their compliance."* He held up a small, rectangular device perhaps half the size of a standard Starfleet tricorder and arrayed with several buttons.

"What is that?" Picard asked.

A look of resignation seemed to grace the Satarran's forged Dokaalan features. *"It is a means of demonstrating that I am sincere in what I say, Captain."*

With that, he pressed one of the small unit's buttons.

"Captain!" Vale called out from tactical. "Sensors are picking up an explosion from the colony."

"What are you doing?" Picard yelled toward the viewer.

His face unreadable now, the Satarran replied, *"I have destroyed the facility that oversees the habitat's magnetic interlock system."*

"He's not lying, Captain," Vale said. "Sensors show

the primary intermagnetic system for the entire colony is offline. Emergency backups are in place and holding."

In his mind, Picard saw the potential for disaster that had been put into motion. The individual asteroids that brought together to form the central colony relied on the intermagnetic locking system to maintain the habitat's structural integrity.

"*I can destroy the backup systems, as well, Captain,*" the Satarran said. "*Additionally, we have placed explosives throughout the colony in such a way that, if detonated, will collapse the entire habitat.*" A small, humorless smile returned to his face as he added, "*I had not considered it until now, but I suppose there would be a sort of poetry to the act if it were forced to occur. The Dokaalan and the world they created for themselves would perish much like their ancestors did, would they not?*"

"You'd be destroying yourselves, as well," Picard offered, knowing even as he spoke the words that pursuing such an angle was useless.

"*A risk we have been prepared to take since the beginning,*" the Satarran replied. "*Despite what happens to us, the planet will still be there for our people.*" He stepped closer until his face filled the viewscreen. "*You will take your ship away from here, Captain, now. If you attempt an assault or otherwise interfere with us, both the colony and your ship will be destroyed.*"

"My ship?" Picard said. "What have you done?"

"*Nothing, yet.*" The Satarran shrugged. "*Perhaps nothing at all, if you obey my commands. Otherwise, your destruction is certain.*" He held up the device in his hand for emphasis. "*Decide, now.*"

"You think he's bluffing?" Riker asked, the worry evident on his own face.

"I don't," Troi said. "There may still be spies aboard the ship, and we still don't know everything Kalsha has done."

Picard weighed the options. If he defied the Satarran, the colony was almost certainly doomed. No doubt the Dokaalan now trapped on the habitat were panicking as initial reports of the explosion began to disseminate. Even if they were not willing to destroy the colony itself, it was obvious that the Satarran leader held little regard for the Dokaalan themselves.

There has to be something I can do, he berated himself, knowing even as the thought asserted itself that he had been outplayed by these renegades, again.

"Helm, set a course," he finally said, nodding his head in defeat. "Take us away from here."

Chapter Twenty-one

SEATED AT THE ENGINEERING STATION situated at the rear of the *Enterprise*'s command center, Mhuic continued his pretense of being engrossed in the array of monitors and computer interface consoles before him. In truth, he could care less about any of the information streaming across the various displays, as they had long since told him everything he needed to know about the operation and capabilities of the massive vessel. In his guise as engineer Lieutenant Pauls, were he asked to carry out a task by any of the officers here, he would be able to do so with as much alacrity as the person he had replaced.

In the meantime, Mhuic watched, and listened.

Were he not currently involved in carrying out his covert assignment, he would find amusement at the seemingly dejected individuals who surrounded him. The mood in the command center was one of defeat and of anger at being bested. The only thing that prevented him from allowing a smile to crease the features of the man he was impersonating was that, apparently, stress made humans smell worse than they did already.

"Captain," he heard the security officer, Lieutenant Vale, call out from her station over his left shoulder, "sensors detect the approach of two Dokaalan skiffs. They're taking up positions aft of us." After a moment, she added, "I'm not picking up any appreciable weapons."

"Escorts?" said Commander Riker, the imposing human first officer. "Making sure we behave on the way out?"

"It would seem so, Number One," said the captain, Picard. "Monitor any communications, Lieutenant. If they communicate with the colony or anyone else, I want to know about it. Helm, maintain course, space-normal speed."

Mhuic heard the annoyance in the man's voice as he uttered the words. It was obvious that Picard was most dissatisfied with the current situation, which made Mhuic wonder why he had acquiesced to Lorakin's demands so easily. He found it hard to believe that the captain had acted with such apparent cowardice merely out of concern for the Dokaalan.

Of course, Lorakin did hold the upper hand, so long as he controlled the fate of the magnetic coupling network that held the Dokaalan habitat's conglomeration of asteroids together. Destroy the interlock system and the colony itself would quickly follow suit. It was a plan elegant in its simplicity, and one that Picard was powerless to act against.

The reports I have read about this human's tactical prowess would seem to have been exaggerated, Mhuic mused.

"Lieutenant Pauls," he heard Picard say, and the disguised Satarran promptly turned his chair until he faced the captain.

"Yes, sir?" he asked, affecting the tone of the nervous junior officer he was supposed to be.

Still standing in front of the chair he normally occupied while in the command center, Picard asked, "Why were our sensors unable to detect the presence of explosives on the colony?"

Mhuic paused for a moment, as if he needed an extra moment to compose the answer he had actually prepared several moments ago. "Commander La Forge and Commander Data have reported some reconfiguration of the software overseeing the scanning systems, sir. It's possible our sensors were programmed so that they would not register them."

The beauty of the answer was that it was in fact the truth. Mhuic had discovered evidence of some covert reprogramming to the sensor control systems by another Satarran operative. He had suspected it to be Kalsha's handiwork even before hearing of his friend's capture only hours ago. Ironically, Kalsha had been taken into custody and his true identity revealed at almost the same time that Mhuic himself had emerged from hiding and seized Lieutenant Pauls.

After he had assumed the form of the other low-ranking officer, Ensign Maxson, it had not taken him long to discover that in order to more effectively gain access to the computer and other sensitive systems, he would have to adopt the guise of someone assigned to one of the ship's technical departments. It had required careful planning and patience to select a candidate and then wait for the individual to be isolated long enough to carry out the replacement.

His opportunity came when Lieutenant Pauls was dispatched to conduct a maintenance task inside one of the ship's numerous maintenance conduits. Forced to kill the human, Mhuic had secreted his body behind one of the conduit's access panels. Still, disposing of the human had given the agent the opportunity he needed to better position himself to take action against the *Enterprise,* should the need arise.

From the looks of things, however, such action would be unnecessary. With the ship making its way out of the asteroid field, its captain and crew retreating like cowed animals, it appeared that all of his efforts, to say nothing of Kalsha's, had been for naught.

Or, had they?

"There has to be a way to beat these people," he heard Riker say, noting the frustration in the large man's voice.

At the tactical station, Lieutenant Vale replied, "What about taking out the explosives themselves with targeted phaser strikes? If we can work out the problems with the sensors, we should be able to find and neutralize them all."

"That'll take time," Riker countered. "Time that Hjatyn, or whoever he is, certainly won't give us."

The first officer was right, Mhuic knew. Lorakin would not hesitate to destroy the colony the instant he realized the *Enterprise* was coming back. As soon as one of the skiff pilots saw the vessel change course, they would call back to him, giving him plenty of time to carry out his threat long before the ship could get close enough to execute such an audacious plan.

"Data to Captain Picard," a new voice said over the ship's intercom. Mhuic recognized it, and the speaker's name, as belonging to the ship's android crew member.

"Sir, I believe I have some information that might prove useful."

His interest piqued, the Satarran operative turned in his seat, though he nearly jerked himself to a halt as he realized he had broken protocol by taking his attention from his station. To his relief, he noted that nearly everyone else in the command center had done so, as well.

"Go ahead, Mr. Data," Picard said.

"I have examined the sensor recordings from your last conversation with the Satarrans," the android replied, *"and I discovered a low-frequency transmission just before the destruction of the primary intermagnetic system. It is logical to assume that the Satarran impersonating First Minister Hjatyn triggered the explosion himself, rather than communicating instructions to subordinates to carry out the action."*

Of course Lorakin would perform the act himself, Mhuic thought. The commander was notorious for his inability to delegate authority, to say nothing of possessing a near-obsessive flair for the dramatic. In this case, the tactic had worked. With the press of a single button, Lorakin had moved the entire Dokaalan colony and its fifty thousand inhabitants to within a single step of total destruction. He was simply incapable of deferring that kind of responsibility to anyone else.

"Data," Picard said, "can such a signal be disabled or jammed?"

The android replied, *"I do not believe it can be disabled completely, but it may be possible to interfere with the signal for a short period of time."*

"How long?" the captain asked.

*"No more than eighty seconds, based on my prelimi-
nary estimates, sir. It could be less."*

Watching Picard consider the information his officers
had given him, Mhuic could see the captain beginning to
put the pieces of together. There was an energy in his
eyes that had not been there mere moments ago, the operative realized.

Turning to Vale, the captain asked, "Lieutenant, based
on what we know of the Dokaalan habitat, would you be
able to make targeting selections within sixty seconds?"

"With the fire-control computer working like it's supposed to?" The security officer nodded with conviction.
"I don't see why not, sir."

"We'd still have to maneuver into position," Riker
said. "What about our escorts?"

The captain replied, "If we're to ensure surprise, they'll
have to be taken out of the equation. Continue to monitor
them and once we're out of their communications range
with the colony, we'll take the necessary action."

Like everyone else, Mhuic found himself nodding in
approval and even satisfaction as he listened to the plan
being laid out before him. It seemed that Picard was
going to make a fight of it. Further, in only a handful of
minutes he had taken the negative emotions threatening
to undermine his subordinates' morale and was chan-
neling it into determination and a course of defined action.

*Perhaps the reports of this human's abilities are accu-
rate, after all.*

"We should exercise caution," said Counselor Troi, the
Betazoid empath. "There may still be Satarran operatives
aboard the ship. If they learn about what we're doing,

they'll certainly try to contact their superiors at the colony."

She was right, of course, more right than she knew, and it was then that Mhuic realized he would have to exercise even greater caution the longer he remained in the command center. It required effort to maintain as close to an emotional detachment as possible while carrying out his charade here, with the constant threat that the Betazoid might somehow become aware of his presence.

From what he had reviewed of the previous occasion where a Satarran operative had infiltrated the *Enterprise* crew, the empath had been unable to sense the agent's deception while impersonating a human officer. The details of that mission report had not revealed whether her failure to recognize the impostor was due to how well the operative had performed his tasks or because of some lingering effect of the sensor probe used to wipe the crew's short-term memory.

Even with the complications the Betazoid had expressed regarding her ability to comprehend the emotions of his people, Mhuic was taking no chances. He would avoid direct contact with the counselor if at all possible, especially now, when it appeared that he would have need to find a way of communicating with his superiors.

"Lieutenant Vale," Picard said, "Enable security lockouts on the com system. All communications from the ship are restricted until further notice, unless cleared beforehand through myself or Commander Riker." Turning to his first officer, he added, "That should make things at least a bit difficult for any uninvited guests."

Indeed it would, Mhuic agreed, just as he silently conceded that there was little, if anything, that he could do about it. Attempting to circumvent any such restrictions without raising notice to his efforts would prove challenging, if not impossible. The time required to carry out such an exercise in stealth would also be considerable, he judged, but necessary.

Necessary if notifying his superiors was the primary goal, that is.

As an experienced covert operative, Mhuic had long since grown accustomed to working without direction for extended periods of time. Being out of contact with those who dispatched him on an assignment was of no particular concern to him. Even without their direction, there was still much he could do here, especially if Picard and his crew were making plans to defy Lorakin and stage some daring raid to rescue the Dokaalan.

Turning back to the engineering console and once more taking up the act of monitoring the array of information being directed to his station, Mhuic requested direct access to the computer's data-storage facility. Scattered throughout the vast collection of software, many of Kalsha's surreptitious additions still waited. Several of them were precautions, intended for use only if Kalsha's own situation deteriorated to the point that drastic action was required.

It would seem, Mhuic mused as he began to familiarize himself more thoroughly with a few of the protocols, *that we have reached that point.*

Ensconced in her office with her eyes focused on her computer terminal, Beverly Crusher reached blindly for the half-eaten lettuce and tomato sandwich sitting on a plate next to her right arm and took another bite without tasting it. The food was fuel, little more than a distraction as she reviewed her latest Dokaalan DNA test results on the terminal's display.

Face it, Beverly, she thought, *there aren't going to be any quick answers this time.*

With a sigh of fatigue and resignation, Crusher leaned back in her chair. Unraveling the delicate chains of nucleotides and using that information to develop a new medicinal regimen with a chance of reversing the Dokaalan's dependence on the asteroid field's ambient radiation was by nature a laborious effort, her rational self offered a reminder. No one expected her to suddenly burst from her office with a miracle cure. The hard part, she admitted, was not expecting that of herself, and pushing herself too hard as she fought to realize an elusive and possibly unobtainable goal.

"Dr. Crusher?"

Only when she heard the voice did the doctor realize she had allowed her eyes to close as she took a moment to relax. She opened them to see one of her nurses, Susan Lomax, standing in the doorway to the office. "Yes?"

Lomax, as always, seemed a bit nervous when confronting someone in authority, shifting her weight from one foot to the other as she replied, "I've finished assisting Dr. Tropp and I was thinking about running some calibrations on the diagnostic monitors in the patient recovery section. I need to spend some time on those units for my certification, anyway, and since we're on our way out of the asteroid field it seems like we'll have some time on our hands."

Nodding in appreciation of the nurse's initiative, Crusher offered an encouraging smile. "It'll take a while to clear the radiation as it is, and as much as I hate to say it, we might need the beds before we're out." Her smile faded as she thought of the possibility that Satarran agents might still be running around loose on the ship. "Anyway, I don't see any reason to do the recalibrations twice."

"You're probably right," Lomax replied. As she turned to head out of the office she abruptly leaned forward to catch a look at Crusher's computer terminal. "The Dokaalan DNA studies?"

"That's right," the doctor said. "The proverbial haystack, as it were."

Frowning, Lomax shook her head. "It's a shame that all of your efforts to help them are going to go to waste."

Her eyebrows rising at that, Crusher replied, "I wouldn't call any research a waste. The information we've gathered here may end up being useful down the road for who knows what we might encounter." Shrugging, she added, "Besides, I'm not so sure we've seen the last of the Dokaalan."

"You think we'll be back someday?" the nurse asked.

Offering Lomax a knowing look, Crusher said, "I think it'll be a lot sooner than that. I know you're new on the *Enterprise,* but Captain Picard's not in the habit of just turning tail and running, at least, not unless he's got something else up his sleeve. Don't think this is over. It's not, not by a long shot."

"I suppose not," the younger woman replied after a moment. "After all, Captain Picard's reputation is one of the reasons I wanted to serve on this ship."

"If that's the case," Crusher said as she reached for her sandwich once more, "then he won't disappoint you."

The sandwich never made it to her mouth before the

ship's intercom system blared to life with the voice of Lieutenant Vale. *"Security to sickbay."*

"Sickbay," Crusher answered. "What is it, Christine?"

"We've got a situation in cargo bay four, Doctor," the security chief replied. *"A maintenance team has discovered the bodies of two crew members. It appears they've been strangled."*

Crusher felt her body gripped by an involuntary shiver as Vale relayed the news. She saw the troubled look on Lomax's face and understood what the young woman was probably feeling. It was one thing to deal with the deaths of so many Dokaalan patients as she and the rest of the *Enterprise* medical staff during the past several days, but this was different. These were members of the crew, perhaps even people the nurse or even Crusher herself knew.

"Have you identified them, Christine?" she asked, struggling to keep her voice level and professional.

"Yes," Vale replied. *"Ensign Maxson from security and, I'm sorry to have to tell you this, Doctor, but the other victim was Nurse Lomax."*

Crusher's first reaction was to frown in confusion. "What? That's impossible."

Then time seemed to slow to a standstill in the office, with Crusher looking up to lock eyes with the woman standing before her.

Nurse Lomax, the impostor.

"Intruder alert in sickbay!" the doctor suddenly yelled, and even the woman who looked so much like Lomax started in reaction to the abrupt command. She recovered herself quickly, though, turning and rushing from the office as she sprinted across the medical ward.

"Security teams are on the way, Doctor!" Crusher

heard Vale say as she bolted from behind her desk in time to see the other woman nearly run into the doors leading to sickbay. The doors had closed and locked in response to enhanced anti-intruder protocols put in place by Lieutenant Vale, and the Lomax impersonator turned, her young features now clouded with an expression of frustration at having been trapped inside the room.

"What's going on?" she heard a voice ask, and looked to the far end of the room to see Dr. Tropp emerge from the small laboratory, his hands tucked into the pockets of his blue medical smock.

Holding up a hand, Crusher said, "Just stay there, Doctor." To Lomax, she said, "Security's on the way here right now. There's nowhere for you to go, so let's just keep it easy, okay?"

"I take it she's a Satarran in disguise?" Tropp asked, his eyes wide with the naturally curious expression that seemed to characterize all Denobulans.

"It seems that way," Crusher replied.

The Lomax look-alike said nothing, her attention obviously focused on finding some way out of her current situation. Wary of an attack, Crusher moved to her right so that a diagnostic bed separated her from the other woman.

"Vale to Dr. Crusher," the voice of the security chief said over the intercom. *"We're at the entrance to sickbay. Where's the intruder?"*

"Don't open the door, Christine," Crusher warned. "She's standing just inside."

Lomax turned to face her. "Not wise advice, Doctor," she said as she took a step forward. "They cannot save you if they are trapped outside." Then she stopped, looked at what she was doing, and when she smiled

Crusher was struck once more by how perfectly the Satarran had re-created Susan Lomax. "It seems we have a stalemate. So long as I stay near the door, they cannot open it."

"Then perhaps you should move," Tropp said just as Crusher saw bright orange energy cross the room. The beam washed over the Satarran's torso and the doctor saw black as part of the alien's mimicking suit was revealed, and Crusher was surprised to see the Satarran still on her feet.

The Satarran turned to face Tropp, who Crusher saw held a phaser in both hands, having obviously secreted the weapon in his coat pocket. He fired again as the alien charged, this time catching her in the chest. This time Tropp kept his finger pressed down on the phaser's firing control, its beam of energy continuing to disrupt the illusion of Lomax her suit was projecting. Then the alien cried out in pain as she finally succumbed to the attack, falling to the deck in a crumpled heap. As she collapsed, the image of Lomax faded completely, leaving behind only the metallic exoskeleton of the Satarran's mimicking suit.

"Open the doors, Christine!" Crusher called out as she stepped toward the fallen intruder. Retrieving the medical tricorder from the pocket of her smock, she knelt beside the unmoving alien and scanned it.

The doors to sickbay opened and Lieutenant Vale rushed in, a phaser rifle in her hands and aimed ahead of her as she entered the room. A quartet of security officers followed her in, separating and spreading out around the room to cover the alien from all sides. Vale leveled the muzzle of the weapon on the Satarran as she stepped forward. "Are you all right, Doctor?"

"We're fine," Crusher replied as she scanned the Satarran. "She's unconscious, but otherwise unharmed, so far as I can see." Looking over to Tropp, she said, "Good thing you were here, Doctor."

"Indeed," the Denobulan replied. "I'm certainly glad you sounded the alarm, or I never would have armed myself." Holding up the phaser he still carried, he added, "I'm hardly the combative type."

"Could've fooled me, Doc," Vale said, smiling grimly. Stepping closer to inspect the unconscious alien, she shook her head. "I was afraid of this happening. We've no way of knowing how many of them are running around the ship."

"One's more than enough," Crusher said, motioning for two of Vale's security officers to lift the Satarran onto a nearby diagnostic bed.

Somehow, she doubted the Satarrans would agree with her.

Chapter Twenty-two

"I'D LOVE TO BE A NASAT right about now," La Forge said, more to himself than anyone else as he moved back and forth between three different workstations in engineering. "I could use the extra hands."

He did, in truth have several extra sets of hands, as well as extra minds, with members of the computer support staff and his engineering teams deployed throughout the ship to monitor key areas for any signs of possible sabotage or other tampering by Satarran agents. That left La Forge himself, with the assistance of Data and a few others both here and in the main computer centers, to scour the ship's network of integrated systems in search of any booby traps the captured Satarran spy or any friends of his might have planted.

Easier said than done, he mused. The Satarran agent who had infiltrated engineering and taken on the persona of Lieutenant Diix was obviously a talented computer expert. Data's efforts to weed out alterations the spy might have made to any of the key components in the computer's immense software library had proven to be anything but simple.

The task La Forge had assigned himself, that of safeguarding the ship's warp drive, was no less difficult. As he moved between the workstations situated near the mammoth warp core, most of his attention was devoted to the consoles and their array of status monitors. Despite that, the engineer realized he was repeatedly casting glances at the core itself. The reaction of matter and antimatter within the reaction chamber was a visual frenzy when viewed through his ocular implants, and on any other occasion La Forge would have found this, the veritable heartbeat of the *Enterprise*'s propulsion system, soothing.

Instead he found himself searching for any signs of fluctuation in the chamber, or any other visual clue that something might be wrong. Part of him wanted to believe that he might be able to spot potential danger this way, perhaps even keep the ship safe through his ability to see what others could not. The engineer in him knew better, reminding him that even if he did see something, his reaction time would never be a match for the plethora of safety systems overseen by the ship's computer.

"Forcefield is in place and holding," said Lieutenant Taurik from an adjacent workstation to La Forge's right. "All systems continue to read well within acceptable parameters, sir."

Nodding, the chief engineer replied, "Yeah, I know, but this is way too tempting a target to pass up. If I were a lone spy and needed to cause trouble, this is the first place I'd look." Word was rapidly spreading about the Satarran agent who had been found impersonating one of the medical staff. La Forge knew that this latest development would do little to improve the morale of the crew, who were already looking for threats around every corner.

Taurik considered that for a moment before saying, "Agreed, but perhaps he has considered the option and discarded it, precisely because it is a tactic we would anticipate."

"Maybe," La Forge said, "but then again, if he's decided that he's run out of time or options, he might just decide to take a shot regardless of the consequences."

The thought of spies running around the ship, disguised as any member of the crew and perhaps even killing the people they replaced, was chilling enough. That one of those agents might come charging into engineering, carrying some kind of explosive tucked under one arm or strapped to his chest and hell-bent on detonating it here, caused an involuntary shiver to run down his spine.

"Geordi."

Turning at the sound of the voice, La Forge saw Data making his way, on foot, across the engineering room. The android had completed the repairs to his neural net less than an hour ago and had wasted no time putting his restored mobility to use. There was no fighting the smile that forced its way onto the engineer's face at the sight of his friend moving under his own power again.

"What is it, Data?"

Holding up a padd he carried in his right hand, the android replied, "I have isolated what I believe to be common programming artifacts in several different application modules throughout the computer network. Using the information gathered during my investigation, I have created a search protocol that should prove effective in isolating and neutralizing unauthorized software alterations."

"Hallelujah," said La Forge, though even he noted how tired he sounded as he spoke the words. "Is it ready to go? If we can get it up and running, who knows how much time it might sa . . ."

He was cut off by the sudden blare of an alarm klaxon echoing through the engineering room, followed by the impassive voice of the ship's computer. *"Warning. Intruder alert."*

In accordance with the additional security protocols put in place by Lieutenant Vale, the main doorway to the engineering deck slid shut and locked into place. La Forge knew that the same thing was happening with hatches leading to sensitive areas throughout the ship.

"Where's the intruder supposed to be?" he asked after a moment. "The computer didn't specify a location."

To his right, Taurik was already at work examining one of the status monitors overseeing the ship's internal sensors. "I am seeing no indications of an intruder anywhere on the ship, Commander."

At another station, Data entered a series of commands to his console and, after studying the results his query generated, turned to La Forge. "The alert appears to have been a false alarm. I have found indications that the software for the internal sensor system has been accessed and updated within the hour."

"Cancel the alarm," La Forge said to Taurik, shaking his head in irritation as he tapped his combadge. "La Forge to bridge. Captain, Data has determined that the alert was a hoax, most likely as a result of someone tampering inside the main computer again."

"That's our assessment as well, Commander," the captain's voice replied. *"Can you prevent it from happening again?"*

Data nodded to him as he continued to work and La Forge said, "Affirmative. Data's handling that right now." Noting one status indicator on the monitor before him, he added, "And we should have the lockdown protocols rescinded in a minute, sir."

A moment later, he heard the sound of magnetic locks releasing and turned to see the large pressure doors that formed the entrance to engineering begin to slide open again, revealing the empty corridor beyond.

"If only everything else could be so easy," he said.

Turning away from his workstation, Data replied, "It was surprisingly easy to find where the infiltration had occurred." He pointed to the computer screen and the lines of computer programming code displayed upon it, several of which were highlighted. "The areas I have highlighted indicate recent additions to the software. Very little was done to conceal the modifications, leading me to believe that stealth was not a primary concern."

"So what was?" La Forge asked. "Simple disruption? Cause confusion, maybe even panic?"

Data nodded. "That is certainly a possibility." He tapped another series of keystrokes to the console. "I have now activated my new search protocol. It will begin its interrogation of suspected software updates immediately, automatically isolating those modifications and, where necessary, restoring programs to their unchanged state from the computer's protected archives."

"Excellent work, Mr. Data," Picard said. *"How long will this process take?"*

"At least several hours, sir," the android replied. "I have instructed the new protocol to make a comprehensive sweep of the entire primary computer core."

"Very well." There was a pause before the captain added, *"Now that we know we have other spies on board, what can we do to find them?"*

Frowning, La Forge said, "Assuming they're wearing the same kind of suits as the Satarran we captured, that won't be easy, Captain. We'd have to modify the internal sensors to identify the dampened energy signature the garment's stealth features emit, and that's sure to be something they anticipated when they set up their alterations to the computer."

As he turned to head back toward his console positioned before the warp core, the chief engineer froze in midstride as his gaze fell upon the reaction chamber. What had he just seen? For an instant, he was sure something had been different within the kaleidoscopic swirl of colliding energies. It was not there now, of that he was certain. Had he simply imagined it?

"Taurik," he said, his voice low and quiet. "What are the current readings on the warp core?"

Taking a moment to study his own set of status monitors, the Vulcan replied, "I am reading nothing unusual, sir. There was a minute dip in antimatter levels, but it was well with operational specifications. Nevertheless, I did perform the appropriate adjustments."

"Something's not right," La Forge countered as he returned to his station, his fingers playing across the computer console. "I'm increasing the plasma infusion stream by point zero zero eight. See it now?"

Taurik's right eyebrow arched. "Indeed." He then pointed to another monitor. "Antimatter levels have dropped again."

"Geordi," Data said, working at another console. "I have initiated a level-one diagnostic on the antimatter flow sensors." La Forge and Taurik watched the monitor as, within seconds, the true nature of what was happening abruptly revealed itself.

"The antimatter containment pod is failing!" La Forge said, rushing back to his workstation. His fingers danced over the console, racing against his brain as he struggled to fit the pieces of this barely believable puzzle together. "The regulation subroutines have been bypassed. At the rate we were injecting new plasma, we would have blown ourselves up." It was a scenario that should have been impossible given the number and variety of redundant safety protocols built into the warp-drive systems. "Our saboteur is even craftier than I thought."

At his station, Taurik said, "We are able to vent excess plasma, Commander." The Vulcan's voice remained neutral despite the escalating situation unfolding around him.

La Forge nodded. "Do that now. I'm taking the pod offline until we can balance this out."

"Is there anything I can do?" Data asked.

"Yeah," the chief engineer replied, keeping his attention focused on his console. "I'm betting the same guy who tripped the intruder alert did this, too. Maybe he did the same sloppy job covering his tracks. Go find him."

Data nodded. "I will begin at once."

As his friend resumed his own work, La Forge finally

saw the results of his own efforts beginning to bear fruit. "Antimatter containment pod is offline, which means we're without warp power for the time being."

"Plasma venting is under way," Taurik reported. "Levels should be returned to normal in twenty-six seconds."

"Great," La Forge said, sighing in relief. Whoever was sneaking around inside the *Enterprise*'s computer, the engineer decided, he was good. What else did he have up his sleeve?

And how long before he triggered something that neither La Forge nor anyone else on the ship could counteract?

Chapter Twenty-three

"CAPTAIN," LIEUTENANT VALE CALLED out from the tactical station, "my security team reports that the skiff pilots are in custody and have been transferred to the brig."

"Excellent," Picard said from where he sat in his command chair, demonstrating the very epitome of calm and control as his crew worked around him.

Seated at the engineering station, Mhuic nodded to himself in approval. The captain had left nothing to chance, waiting until the ship and its escort of two Dokaalan mining skiffs had moved beyond the communications range of the smaller craft before taking action. With the skiffs unable to send word back to the colony, Lorakin would never see the *Enterprise*'s attack coming until it was too late.

There was nothing Mhuic could do about that, of course. All he could do was continue to carry out his assumed duties in his guise of Lieutenant Pauls.

"Captain," he said as a status message appeared on

one of his station's monitors, "Commander La Forge reports that the drive-plasma imbalance has been corrected."

Picard nodded. "Thank you, Lieutenant."

Mhuic almost found the situation amusing. Working here in the ship's command center, he was in the perfect position to keep apprised of the various initiatives currently under way. He knew about the android's comprehensive computer sweep, and had even managed to forge himself an access code that enabled him to review the newly created software protocol. It was effective, he conceded, and would almost certainly uncover most if not all of the alterations Kalsha had entered while posing as an *Enterprise* crew member.

Mhuic had given serious consideration to interfering with the new program's operation, but had abandoned the idea when he found the tracer algorithm embedded within the protocol's complex string of instructions. Any attempt to sabotage the program would alert both engineering and security not only of the action, but also the computer interface terminal where the directive originated.

The android is even more resourceful than I gave it credit for.

What concerned Mhuic more than the new security program was the undercurrent of confidence and determination he was sensing among the officers here in the ship's command center. With a strategy of action for returning to the colony in play, Picard and the key members of his staff were now fully immersed in their final planning. At the center of their preparations was the captain, who Mhuic had come to realize had never resigned himself to defeat at the hands of Lorakin.

"Captain," Vale said, "I've finished reviewing the sensor logs we recorded of the Dokaalan colony, and I've pinpointed thirty-two concentrations of diburnium alloy at various points around the asteroid."

"Let me guess," Commander Riker said as the captain swiveled his chair to face the security officer. "Diburnium isn't an element native to this system."

Nodding, Vale smiled. "Not a hint of it in any of our scans, sir. I don't have enough information to figure out what they might have used for explosives, though. We'll need to conduct a more intensive scan for that."

"I assume you have enough data to plot your firing pattern?" Picard asked.

"Not a problem, sir," the lieutenant said. "If the jamming signal Data came up with can give me sixty seconds, that should be plenty of time to lock on and destroy all thirty-two targets."

"Excellent," Picard said. Turning to face the two officers seated at the command center's forward stations, he ordered, "Helm, bring us about, and lay in a course back to the colony."

"Aye, sir," replied Lieutenant Perim, the Trill currently seated at the helm station.

Mhuic knew he should have foreseen this happening from the moment Picard had given an order that on its face had seemed innocuous. However, the instruction to the helm officer to proceed out of the asteroid field at a pace slower than the fastest speed obtainable by the Dokaalan mining skiffs had been the captain's way of stalling for time. He was able to present the appearance of obeying Lorakin's demands while also providing time for his people to prepare his response to Lorakin. When Picard ordered the ship turned around to head back for the colony, it would be with one mission in mind: to oust the Satarrans.

Realizing well before now that there was precious little he could do to interfere with the pursuit of that goal, Mhuic had instead turned his energies toward the one meaningful action remaining to him. He had to find a way to alert Lorakin of the pending attack, a task made much more difficult by Picard's order locking out the communications system so that no messages could be transmitted beyond the ship.

Still seated at his engineering station, Mhuic had accessed the computer and called up the new security protocols Vale had enabled to comply with the captain's instructions. With time, he might be able to create a program to circumvent the lockouts and give him access to communications, but would he be able to do so before the *Enterprise* turned back toward the colony?

"Data to Captain Picard," said the voice of the android over the intercom once again. *"I believe I have found a way to reveal the presence of Satarran operatives on board the ship."*

The simple statement, delivered with the android's usual lack of urgency or other emotion, nevertheless had the immediate impact of causing everyone in the command center to turn toward the captain, who Mhuic saw was exchanging with his second-in-command what the agent interpreted was an expression of surprise.

"Go ahead, Commander," Picard said.

"I have examined the suit we confiscated from the Satarran we captured," Data replied, *"particularly the network of holographic and sensor emitters it uses to scan its environment and deploy its false image of an imper-*

*sonated individual. I believe that by broadcasting a hy-
personic signal through the ship's communications system, we can in effect create a type of overload that
would disable the embedded systems of such a garment."*

"That doesn't sound like it'd be very pleasant for anyone wearing the thing, either," Counselor Troi said from
where she sat next to Picard.

The android replied, *"That is correct, Counselor."*

"How soon can you be ready to broadcast the signal,
Mr. Data?" Picard asked.

*"I am making my final preparations now, and should
be ready in a moment."*

Panic flashed through Mhuic's mind at the report, and
he began to consider courses of action. He could not leave
the command center, at least not without an escort, thanks
to Picard's order that no one move about the ship alone.
Besides, simply doing so might draw attention to himself
even before the android's plan was put into action.

He gave brief thought to attacking Picard. Killing the
captain might have the effect of disrupting the ship's chain
of command, after all. The idea was just as quickly discarded. Mhuic was unarmed, but Lieutenant Vale was carrying a phaser and he was certain she would not hesitate to
use the weapon, especially if she felt Picard was in danger.

The only thing for him to do, he realized, was to remain at the engineering station and continue his attempts
to warn Lorakin. However, planting a covert instruction
to override the lockouts to the communications system
and transmitting the alert signal he had already composed would be too time-consuming. Data would almost
certainly be ready to put his own plan into motion before
Mhuic could complete his task.

There is no more time for stealth, he reminded himself. *You have a single chance. Do not waste it.*

He entered instructions to his console, reviewing the program he had created and trying to identify and correct any lingering errors. There had been no time to test the new protocol. If he executed it now, there was still a distinct possibility it would fail before carrying out its set of instructions.

That does not matter now. Either it will work, or it will not, but you are almost out of time.

"Captain," he heard Counselor Troi say from behind him, "I'm sensing something odd."

"Odd?" the captain repeated.

Mhuic did not stop what he was doing, did not look up from his console.

"Powerful emotions. Panic, anger, determination. It just seemed to come out of nowhere, sir."

"Captain," he heard Data's voice say. *"I am ready."*

Though Mhuic did not turn to look at Picard, he noticed the momentary pause after the android's report. Was the captain still trying to interpret what the empath had told him?

She can sense you, he told himself. *You're sacrificing your emotional control, and she can detect that.*

He continued to work.

"Make it so, Commander," Picard said.

Mhuic recorded his final changes to the new program. It needed to be moved to the proper area of the ship's main computer core before it could be executed.

"Captain!" Troi said, and Mhuic heard her rise from her chair. "There's someone here."

"A Satarran?" Riker asked. There was no mistaking the mood of warning in the command center now.

"Lieutenant Pauls," Vale said, her voice hard and echoing with authority, "step away from that console, now." Mhuic did not have to turn to know that the security chief had drawn her weapon and was almost certainly aiming at him.

The program was in place. His hand moved toward the console key that would execute it.

Then Mhuic's world exploded.

Picard flinched as Lieutenant Pauls shrieked in apparent pain, his entire body spasming as if enveloped by an immense electrical charge.

The engineer lunged from his chair but could do nothing but stagger about the rear of the bridge, his body writhing and, to Picard's shock, beginning to flicker in and out of existence. In the next instant his uniform and features faded away to reveal the now familiar black and silver exoskeleton of a Satarran mimicking suit. With his true form now revealed, he continued to twitch in obvious discomfort for another several seconds before collapsing to the deck.

Her phaser drawn and leveled at the now unmoving Satarran, Vale tapped her combadge. "Security team to the bridge." She probed the Satarran with the toe of her boot but the intruder remained motionless. "I guess Commander Data's dog whistle worked," she said, and Picard saw the knowing smirk on the lieutenant's face.

"Captain," Riker said, his attention on the status monitor situated next to his chair, "we're getting reports from across the ship. So far, six Satarrans have been found, all of them reacted to Data's signal like . . ." He paused as he looked over his shoulder at the fallen Satarran. "Like Lieutenant Pauls."

Six? Picard could only wonder which of his officers and crew members had been replaced with operatives lying in wait to betray and kill them all.

"Engineering to Captain Picard," Data said over the intercom. *"Sir, I have detected an unauthorized computer access originating from the engineering station on the bridge."*

The captain frowned as he looked to where the Satarran agent had been setting mere seconds earlier. What had the spy managed to do before being caught?

His answer came in the form of an alert signal blaring to life from the tactical station.

"What the hell is that?" Riker asked.

Handing her phaser to the first officer so that he could keep watch on the unconscious Satarran, Vale rushed back to the tactical station. After several seconds of intense scrutiny, she looked to Picard. "He enabled some kind of invasive program to circumvent the security lockouts I put in place."

"What's it doing?" the captain asked.

"Captain," Data said, *"the program is working to bypass the protective measures Lieutenant Vale deployed to secure various shipboard systems."*

"He's right," Vale said from the tactical station. "I'm registering simultaneous assaults on fourteen separate systems, including environmental control, communications, the warp propulsion oversight systems, and even central computer operations itself."

"Can't you stop the program?" Troi asked. "Or purge it from the computer?"

"No, Counselor," the android replied. *"It is designed to self-replicate as many times as necessary in order to complete its instructions."*

Vale said, "This thing is corrupting other software as it worms through the system. We'll have to restore several subsystems from protected backups when all this is done."

"How long before it breaks through the lockouts?" Picard asked.

"I am endeavoring to ascertain that now, sir."

Feeling even his legendary self-control beginning to falter, Picard silently cursed this latest obstacle thrown into their path by the rogue Satarran operative. Even a last ditch action borne of desperation in the waning seconds before his inevitable capture had been enough to cause them strife.

"Captain," Vale said a moment later, "Commander Data has stopped the infiltration of the environmental systems."

There was a collective sigh of relief at the lieutenant's announcement. At least the crew would not have to worry about suffocating or having to cope with any other radical changes the Satarran's sabotage might have inflicted upon them.

From the intercom, Data said, *"Captain, I believe I have circumvented the program's attempt to take control of central computer operations."*

"Whatever he did," Riker said as he stepped aside and allowed two of Vale's security officers to take the stunned Satarran agent into custody, "it doesn't look as though he did a good job of it."

"Small favors, Number One," Picard said, his brow furrowing in concentration as he regarded the unconscious operative.

Noting his captain's expression, Riker asked, "Something wrong, sir?"

Picard said nothing for a moment as he watched Vale's team remove the operative from the bridge. Despite the apparent ease with which Data was handling whatever the Satarran had inflicted upon the *Enterprise*'s computer system, the agent's modifications were still requiring a great deal of attention in order to remove its influence.

The Satarran had been working feverishly up to the point that Data's hypersonic signal had incapacitated him. Had his actions truly been a final frantic attempt to inflict chaos on the ship and the crew?

"Our friend and his companions were quite effective at infiltrating the computer system and maintaining their secrecy," Picard said as his gaze came to rest on the engineering station where the Satarran impersonating Lieutenant Pauls had sat. "I find it hard to believe that even when faced with imminent capture, he would suddenly take leave of his training and abilities."

The thoughts were a jumble in his mind, and the captain fought to bring order to them. What was he saying? That the Satarran had deliberately set up problems that his crew could solve with only moderate effort? Why?

Then the questions were pushed aside, and the only thing Picard saw was the answer.

To direct our attention elsewhere.

"Mr. Data," he said suddenly, "what systems are not yet secure from the program's effects?"

The android's reply was immediate. *"Warp drive, weapons, communications, deflector shield control, sensor. . . ."*

"Communications," the captain interrupted. "That's it. Data, concentrate your efforts there."

Instead of a response from Data, Picard instead heard another alert tone from the tactical station. Turning to Vale, he asked, "What now?"

Her expression a mask of frustration, the lieutenant said, "The program's broken through the security lockout on the comm system, sir." Tapping controls on her console, after several seconds she shook her head. "The instant it broke through it opened a channel and sent a burst transmission."

"Where?" Troi asked.

Picard already knew the answer. "The colony."

Vale nodded. "Yes, sir."

"Are we far enough away that the radiation field could disrupt the signal?" Troi asked, stepping closer to Picard.

The security chief entered another string of commands to her station. "It looks like the radiation did degrade the transmission, but I'm not sure it was enough to totally garble the message."

"Which means that Lorakin probably knows we captured his agents," Riker said.

Picard nodded in agreement. If that were the case, how long would it take for Lorakin to carry out his threat and detonate the explosives dispersed throughout the Dokaalan central habitat?

Another tone sounded from Vale's console, and after a moment she looked up and added, "Captain, the attacks on the other subsystems have stopped. It's as if the program just quit working."

"Of course," Picard said, his voice barely a whisper. The Satarran's use of misdirection had been an elegantly simple tactic, launching the simultaneous attacks on the ship's various critical systems and occupying Data just long enough to accomplish his true goal of alerting his superior to Picard's actions.

Turning back to face the viewscreen, he said, "Helm, increase speed to full impulse." He saw the young woman's shoulders tense up as she heard the order, and understood her pang of anxiety. Maneuvering through the asteroid field at such speed was a difficult, and dangerous, proposition, perhaps even for Data.

Her reaction was momentary, though, passing almost as quickly as it had appeared before Perim's hands began to move over her console. "Full impulse. Aye, sir."

Apparently noting the lieutenant's possible unease with what had been asked of her, Riker stepped down into the command well and tapped the ensign seated at the ops station on the shoulder. "Let me take over for a bit, Mr. Basore," he said, and the younger officer vacated the chair so he could sit down. "This could get tricky," he offered to Perim, casting a supportive smile in her direction. "I'll keep an eye on the navigational sensors, and you just get us there. Deal?"

"Deal, sir," Perim replied, keeping her attention focused on her instruments, but Picard saw the Trill officer sitting a bit straighter in her chair as she continued to work.

"Time to arrival?" Picard asked.

Not looking up from her station, Perim replied, "Two minutes, twelve seconds, sir."

The captain turned to Vale. "Any indication of detonations on the asteroid?"

Consulting her sensor displays, the lieutenant said, "No, sir."

Did that mean that Lorakin had not received the message sent by the agent now in *Enterprise* custody? Picard considered that wishful thinking. Regardless, he knew there was nothing he could do about the Satarran leader, not from out here. Therefore, the only course of action remaining to him was to carry out his plan to seize the colony and wrest it from the grip of the Satarrans.

That, and hope his luck held out just a bit longer.

Lorakin was worried.

He did not allow his anxiety to show, of course, not to his subordinates or to any of the sixteen Dokaalan currently occupying the chambers of the Zahanzei Council. To them he presented the outward appearance of a leader in total control, an image that was necessary given their current situation.

"What have you done with Hjatyn?" asked one of the colonists, a member of the staff who had been working in the command center when Lorakin ordered the room secured. "And how long are you going to defile his image?"

Pacing the room slowly, hands clasped behind his back, Lorakin regarded the faces of the Dokaalan staring back at him, including the colonist who had just challenged him, and understood their confusion and their contempt. He still maintained his persona of Hjatyn, which was no doubt upsetting to the colonists now that they realized he was not their beloved leader.

The first minister was respected by all of Dokaalan society, he reminded himself. For them to see Hjatyn's image portrayed by someone who was treating them as Lorakin and the other Satarrans were had to be upsetting, of not outright offensive to the Dokaalan gathered here.

"Until I have need to appear as something else," Lorakin replied, allowing his expression to harden as he glared at the outspoken Dokaalan. "That will most likely occur at the same moment I decide that I no longer have any reason to keep you alive."

The obvious warning had the desired effect of cowing the colonist, and he returned to his place among his companions. Lorakin maintained his menacing expression until his pacing caused him to reverse direction and proceed back across the room, not even looking over at the rest of the Dokaalan as he walked past them.

In truth, he had no desire to kill any of these people, just as he had regretted every person who had been killed in order to protect the secrecy of what he and his team were doing here. Since the Satarrans had arrived here several years ago and begun insinuating themselves into Dokaalan society, Lorakin had issued strict instructions to avoid killing anyone unless failing to do so threatened to reveal their presence here. With a joint colony of tens of thousands of people in which to blend, he had not seen the need for murder without such dire conditions to justify the action. His order had been broken a handful of times, and even though the reasons had been legitimate and had saved their operation from being exposed, Lorakin still regretted what circumstances had forced upon him.

And what about now? Their efforts to take control of the Dokaalan's terraforming of Ijuuka had been uncovered, and would surely be hampered once the balance of the Dokaalan population learned how they had been manipulated and used and how everything a large segment of their society had worked toward for generations had been taken from them. The reformation of the planet had not progressed to a point where Dokaalan involvement was no longer needed, but Lorakin did not see how that assistance could be assured without some sort of threat held over their heads. It therefore fell to him to decide the fate of an entire society.

That was assuming Picard allowed him to do so, of course.

The human captain had left far too easily for Lorakin's comfort. Based on the reputation Picard had garnered, it made no sense for him to so readily accept defeat, which was why Lorakin had taken the precaution of dispatching escort ships to make sure the starship left the Dokaalan system. There were also several independent operatives still hiding among the vessel's crew, with orders to act in defense of the mission here should Picard decide to return to the colony. Lorakin believed the captain would make that decision, and when that happened the agents' mission would be to ensure the *Enterprise*'s destruction.

"How long are you going to keep us here?"

The question startled him from his reverie, but Lorakin was able to retain his composure before turning back to the collection of Dokaalan. He saw that it was Minister Myjerol who had stepped forward to speak this time. Lorakin remembered from previous encounters that the council member usually had a tendency to be soft-spoken, but that did not seem to be the case now. He appeared to carry himself with a newfound confidence. Lorakin suspected that the sudden change in the minister's personality was due in no small part to the fact that with the removal of Hjatyn, Nidan, and Creij, he was now the senior member of the Zahanzei Council.

"Are you required to be elsewhere?" the Satarran asked, maintaining a neutral expression as he spoke. To his credit, Myjerol did not waver, did not even blink in response to the blunt query.

"You have taken us hostage," he said, "and used us as leverage to force Captain Picard and his vessel away. This, after your uncounted cycles of using us for your own ends. How much longer is this to go on?"

"As long as it is necessary," Lorakin replied, allowing the warning to creep back into his voice once more.

Myjerol shook his head. "No. It will go on no longer. There are far more of us than there are of you, and we will resist you with all of our strength."

The minister's words were already having an effect on the other colonists, Lorakin noted. Even his own men, Daeniq and five other Satarrans all projecting the appearance of various Dokaalan, were beginning to look to him for direction. If allowed to continue, Myjerol could very well incite a small riot here in the council chambers. The Dokaalan would almost certainly all die in the attempt, of course, but possibly not before one or more of Lorakin's own people were injured or killed.

He had to regain total control of this situation, now.

Making a show of drawing the disruptor from the holster at his waist, he said, "I do not need to kill very many of you, Minister. A few well-publicized executions should be enough to keep the rest of your people in line."

Incredulously, Myjerol countered, "I can see the uncertainty in your eyes." He shook his head. "You do not want to kill me."

Lorakin raised the disruptor and leveled it at the Dokaalan's chest. "Do not test me," he said, but to his own shock, he heard his voice quaver as he spoke.

He was distracted by the sound of the doors to the command center opening. Turning to look in that direction, Lorakin saw Daeniq, still impersonating the Dokaalan security minister, Nidan, enter the room. There was no mistaking the look of concern on his friend's face.

"Lorakin," he said, holding up his communications device, "we have just received an incoming transmission. It was badly distorted and took several moments to decipher, but our technicians were able to filter out most of the interference so that we might decode it."

He tapped a control on the device, and Lorakin heard a momentary burst of static followed by a shrill alert tone. Then he heard an alternating series of low and high beats. It was an easily recognizable pattern, mostly due to the fact that it was Daeniq who had created it. His eyes widened in shock as the signal repeated itself over and over again.

Uttering a particularly vulgar Satarran profanity, Lorakin looked to his friend. "Our agents on the *Enterprise* have failed." Daeniq had created the encoded signal to have but a single meaning: the ship was on its way back here.

What had happened? Had all of the operatives covertly dispatched to the Starfleet vessel been captured? That was the most likely scenario, given the alert he had just received. That it had been sent at all meant that whoever had sent it was most likely dead or in custody.

As for Picard, what was his plan?

Lorakin's thoughts were interrupted as he felt the deck plating shudder beneath his feet. The vibrations translated to the bulkheads and even to the pieces of decorative artwork hanging on the walls, which quivered noticeably.

"What was that?" Daeniq asked just as another tremor shook the room, only this time the sensation was more pronounced.

Before he could answer, the doors leading to the command center burst open and Geliu ran into the room, still posing as Science Minister Creij. There was no mistaking the look of worry clouding her features.

"All systems in the control room have just gone inoperative," she said. "Everything is being jammed."

"It's the *Enterprise*," Daeniq said. "We are under attack!"

The room trembled yet again. This time Lorakin reached out as he felt the deck plating sway beneath his boots. "Not on the colony," he said as he righted himself, "but on the explosives we set." Reaching for his communications device, he activated the unit.

"What are you doing?" Geliu asked.

Lorakin shook his head. "Telling Picard about the mistake he has just made." He pressed the com unit's transmit key and was rewarded by a burst of static. Frowning, he attempted to establish a connection again and received the same response. "Communications are also jammed," he said as another tremor rattled the room.

Commotion from behind him made Lorakin turn to see the Dokaalan colonists growing restless and even panicked as the room continued to shake around them. Several of his subordinates had already drawn their weapons and were moving to retain order in the council chamber as Daeniq crossed the floor to meet him.

"They will be coming," he said, pulling his own disruptor from its holster.

Lorakin nodded in grim agreement. Whatever Picard had done, he had done it well. The Satarran leader could feel his jaw clenching at the realization that he had grossly underestimated the captain, not only the man's abilities but also his determination.

"Perhaps we should consider surrendering," Geliu offered.

Anger flared in Lorakin's vision at the sound of the words. He could not simply give up, not now. Too many people were depending on him and his team to accomplish what they had been sent here to do. Nothing less than total success was an acceptable option.

"No," he said, his voice heavy with resignation. "Prepare our people, Daeniq," he said. "We are not finished yet."

Chapter Twenty-four

THOUGH THEY MAY HAVE THOUGHT themselves capable of repelling a boarding party, it was obvious to Riker that the Satarrans were no match for fifty trained *Enterprise* security personnel.

"This is Lieutenant Vale," he heard over his combadge as he proceeded down an empty corridor leading from the airlock he and his five-person away team had passed through after departing their shuttlecraft. *"Encountering minimal resistance. One enemy down, another is retreating. We've suffered no casualties and are proceeding in."*

"Acknowledged," the first officer said, keeping his phaser rifle and his own attention directed toward searching for threats within the passageway ahead of him. The security teams had entered the colony at six different points, with only three of them encountering immediate resistance from the Satarrans. Unlike Vale, Riker and his team had seen no one since entering the colony. "They may be pulling back for a last stand. Be careful."

"Understood, Commander," the security chief replied. *"Vale out."* After she signed off, Riker could still hear her giving orders to her own away team, as he had given orders to keep communications open throughout the assault.

Continuing his advance, he studied the sterile, utilitarian corridor fabricated from the same general-purpose metal plating that had come to typify Dokaalan construction techniques. The air here was cool and tasted vaguely metallic, just as it had been during his first visit to the central habitat.

All the more reason to want to move to a planet, he mused. *Any planet.*

They came upon a door set into the left-side bulkhead, and Riker swung the muzzle of his phaser rifle to cover it. He glanced over his shoulder to Lieutenant Danilov, the security officer walking just behind him. "Anybody home?"

Holding his phaser rifle in his right hand while carrying a tricorder in his left, Danilov aimed the scanning device toward the door and shook his head after a few seconds. "No life signs, sir."

Riker sighed. "Where the hell is everybody?"

This part of the colony housed more machinery and storage facilities than anything else, with the majority of the Dokaalan colonists located elsewhere in the complex. Sensor readings from the *Enterprise* revealed that living quarters and other areas where the people might congregate had been sealed off from the sections immediately surrounding the command center. The readings also showed thirty-four Dokaalan scattered in small groups throughout this portion of the colony, leading

Vale to surmise that they were being held as hostages by Satarrans as a last-ditch defensive effort.

It would make sense, Riker realized. With their primary threat to the Dokaalan colony neutralized and the central habitat in no danger of being destroyed, the Satarrans' options had been drastically narrowed. Certainly aware that there was no way for them to escape, they could very well resort to using the Dokaalan as shields, or they might offer themselves up as part of radical suicide attacks. If Riker had learned anything about the Satarrans, during either the *Enterprise*'s initial encounter or just what had transpired over the past few days, it was that these people were capable of anything.

Splitting his focus between his tricorder and the passageway ahead of them, Danilov paused to wipe away some of the perspiration that had matted his blond hair and was now running down the side of his face. "I'm picking up seven Dokaalan life-forms approximately forty meters ahead of us, in a room off this corridor. No sign of any Satarrans, though." He shrugged. "Not that that's news."

"No kidding," Riker agreed, cursing once more the Satarrans' ability to blend in with the colonists. Their mimicking shrouds allowed them to register as Dokaalan, which meant that any or all of the seven life signs Danilov had detected could be enemies in disguise.

Naturally, the use of the hypersonic signal that Data had devised to expose the enemy agents aboard the *Enterprise* had been considered as a tactic against those Satarrans still scattered throughout the Dokaalan central habitat. Unfortunately, that strategy had been almost as quickly discarded when Data explained that the signal could only be sent on a frequency that was far outside the range of the Dokaalans' own communications network, or even the capabilities of the portable devices employed by the Satarrans themselves.

With that in mind, Captain Picard had decided to send boarding parties to seize control of the central habitat. Riker and every other member of the assault force realized they had lost the element of surprise, but that could not be helped now. The first officer knew that the only thing to do if they were to end the Satarrans' oppression of the Dokaalan was to keep pressing forward.

He waited as one of the ensigns on Danilov's team fused the lock on the door, a precaution in the event the Satarrans had devised another method of fooling tricorder scans. Now reasonably sure that no one would come out of the room beyond the hatch in an attempt so sneak up on them, Riker ordered the group forward with a hand signal.

No one said anything else as they proceeded down the passageway, Riker's eyes wary for the signs of any potential danger despite the reassurance of Danilov's tricorder that nothing was lying in wait for them. They passed three more doors during their advance, the sections leading from which offered no signs of life, and Riker ordered the procedure to secure them repeated for each one.

"Almost there," Danilov said a few moments later as they turned a corner, and the first officer saw the lone door fifteen meters in front of them. It looked no different from any of the other doors they had passed on the way here.

"Any signs of weapons?" Riker asked.

Danilov shook his head. "Not that I can see."

Feeling his pulse beginning to race in anticipation of their first run-in with anyone since their arrival, Riker drew a calming breath before taking up position to the left of the door. Danilov put himself on the opposite side and the two officers exchanged nods before Riker reached for the door's control panel.

Seven surprised faces turned to see the six Starfleet officers storm the room. Riker lunged through the door, phaser rifle up and aiming ahead of him as he moved to his left, searching the storage containers and worktables lining the room for potential threats. Danilov mirrored his actions as he stepped to his right, both officers searching for threats as the rest of the away team entered the chamber.

"We're from the *Enterprise*," Riker called out to the group of anxious-looking Dokaalan, all of whom had raised their hands to show they were unarmed the moment he had come into the room. "We've come to take you out of here."

"Dokaa has not forsaken us," one of the colonists said, relief evident on his pale blue features, "even if our leaders have. Why are they turning against us?"

Stepping forward, Riker allowed the muzzle of his weapon to drop so that it no longer aimed directly at the colonists. "I'm afraid it's a long story, and there'll be plenty of time to tell it later. Right now we have to get you out of here." Indicating Danilov, he added, "If you'll follow this man, he'll lead you to a safer location."

He sensed the movement first, a flickering motion coming from one of the Dokaalan at the rear of the group. The colonist's right hand had moved to touch his chest, and Riker saw the hand disappear through the fabric of the coveralls he wore, as if passing through . . .

"Look out!" he shouted, raising his phaser rifle.

The Dokaalan was faster, his hand reappearing and

now holding a Klingon disruptor. He snapped off a shot and the rest of the group scattered, with Riker dodging the energy bolt that screamed over his left shoulder and tore into the metal bulkhead behind him.

Phaser energy whined to Riker's right as Danilov fired. The orange beam struck the Dokaalan in the chest and the first officer saw the colonist's form shimmer and distort from the onslaught, the black and silver exoskeleton of a Satarran mimicking shroud visible for an instant before the assailant crumpled under the force of the phaser beam.

"There's another one!" Danilov yelled as a second Dokaalan, having sought cover behind a large metal storage container, poked his head up along with the stout, short-barreled weapon in his left hand.

He never had the chance to fire before two members of the away team caught him in a crossfire, the pair of phaser strikes more than sufficient to send the Dokaalan careering backward to slam into the room's far bulkhead before falling to the deck.

Disruptor fire howled in the room once more and Riker saw green energy wash over one of the security team, a female ensign whose name he could not remember. Without thinking, he swung his phaser rifle in the direction from which the attack had come and fired, his own shot striking yet another of the colonists in the leg. The Dokaalan fell to one knee, still holding his weapon, and Riker fired again. This time the beam washed over the attacker and he collapsed in an unconscious heap.

"Nobody move!" Riker shouted, aiming his rifle at the remaining four Dokaalan, all of whom froze in place with empty hands held over their heads. Glancing over his shoulder, he saw Danilov already moving to tend to the fallen ensign. "Is she all right?"

Kneeling beside the prone officer, Danilov reached to her neck to check her pulse. "She's alive, but she's got a nasty disruptor burn to her chest." Even as he spoke he was motioning to one of his men to help him prepare to move the ensign.

"Get her back to the ship," Riker said. Keeping his attention focused on the rest of the colonists, he tapped his combadge. "This is Riker. We've encountered moderate resistance and taken one casualty."

"Three Satarrans are in custody. They're blending in with the Dokaalan, and their shrouds can conceal weapons from tricorder scans."

Picard heard only part of Riker's report over his own combadge, the rest drowned out by weapons fire as he fired his phaser rifle at a retreating Dokaalan. He missed, and his adversary fired a badly aimed shot in the captain's direction before disappearing around a corner in the passageway.

"Devious, aren't they?" he said to no one in particular, feeling his jaw tighten in mounting irritation.

Vale heard him nonetheless, and nodded in agreement. "But you already knew that from past experience, sir. I went over all of the reports of your first run-in with the Satarrans. Interesting reading, to say the least."

Picard said nothing, though silently he commended the lieutenant on her diligence. Simply finding the time during the events of the past days to review the sheer number of log entries and follow-up reports filed in the wake of the *Enterprise*'s initial encounter with the Satarrans was an amazing feat.

The hair on the back of his neck stood up as Picard and Vale, along with her four-person security detail, moved through the large chamber that served as a general-purpose gathering place for the colonists. Wherever he looked the muzzle of his weapon followed, searching for threats that did not reveal themselves.

Riker had expressed his customary disapproval at his captain's decision to lead one of the away teams, but Picard had noted that there seemed to be a hollowness in the objection. Starfleet regulations required first officers to voice such concerns whenever their commanders opted to put themselves in such potentially dangerous situations, and throughout his tenure on the *Enterprise* Riker had unfailingly carried out that duty.

While Picard had routinely allowed his second-in-command to handle away team duties during their years together, he had overridden him on those occasions where he honestly felt his involvement was absolutely essential to the success of a mission.

Is this one of those times?

The question had repeatedly asked itself since boarding the shuttlecraft to make the transfer to the colony, but he had ignored it. In truth, the answer was no, and he knew that, so why had he exercised command prerogative? Was it simply because he wanted Hjatyn, or rather the Satarran currently impersonating him, captured and made to answer for what he had done to the Dokaalan people?

While that sounded good to him, at least on the surface, Picard knew it was little more than a rationalization.

The events of the past days, and yes, the past weeks, had made him question his ability to lead. He believed he had redeemed himself, at least somewhat, in circumstances that required him to demonstrate his control from the bridge of the *Enterprise,* but what about elsewhere, where the situations could become much more chaotic?

Part of him needed to know that he could still command out here, where the people putting their lives at risk looked to him for leadership. Starfleet regulations might not like it, but after more than forty years as a starship captain, Picard felt the regulations owed him this one.

His momentary reverie was broken by Vale, walking to his left and studying her tricorder. "Our guy's heading toward the council chambers."

A wise tactical move, Picard conceded. According to the security chief's previous scans, there was little of value or what might provide concealment between the away team's present location and the section of the central habitat housing the command center as well as the council's offices and meeting area.

They encountered no further resistance as they made their way through the complex, finally arriving at the large hatch leading to the command center. As Picard expected, the door itself was closed, without even a single sentry posted outside for security.

"I'm picking up twenty-three life signs inside," Vale said as she studied her tricorder. "At least seven are armed, not counting anyone pulling that trick Commander Riker pointed out."

"And there's only one other way out of that section?" Picard asked.

Vale nodded. "Yes, sir. Commander Riker and Lieutenant Danilov should have that route covered any time now."

Frowning, the captain sighed. "They're cornered, which makes them even more dangerous." With nearly twenty hostages, there was no telling what the Satarrans would do if they felt their time was running out. If Picard ordered an assault on the command center, there was a good chance that the Satarrans would kill their captives before he and his people could secure the area.

He tapped his combadge. "Picard to *Enterprise*. Patch me through to Hjatyn." Grimacing at the words, he added, "Or whatever the hell his name is." There was a momentary delay as the communication link was established.

"This is Lorakin, Captain," said Hjatyn's voice through Picard's combadge, though the captain now noted a hint of agitation that had not been there previously. The Satarran leader had even given his real name, apparently, perhaps a sign that he was beginning to feel the stresses of his deteriorating situation. *"We seem to have reached an impasse."*

"This can still end well for everyone involved, Lorakin," Picard said, remembering only at the last instant to call the Satarran by his actual name. "There is nowhere for you to go now. Surrender and you have my word you will be treated fairly."

"Captain, you know this is not about my personal situation," the Satarran replied. *"It is about the future for all of my people. I am pledged to see this reformation project to completion."*

"You know I can't allow that to happen," Picard countered, "not at the expense of the Dokaalan."

"Then you are forcing me toward extreme measures,

Captain," Lorakin said. *"Believe me when I tell you that I will kill everyone in this room if you attempt to enter."*

Shaking his head, the captain cursed the futility and desperation that seemed to be all that remained to drive the Satarran leader. After everything the *Enterprise* crew had done to this point to defeat this group of interlopers and what they had done to sabotage the Dokaalan's life-long efforts, there still remained the very real possibility that this final confrontation could end in tragedy.

Not while I have anything to say about it.

Tapping his combadge with a free hand, Picard motioned for Vale to move closer. "Pinpoint the location of everyone in that room."

The security chief studied her tricorder for several seconds before handing the device to him. "It looks like everyone is in the main council chamber. The seven with weapons have placed the remaining sixteen Dokaalan between them and the doors leading from he council chamber to the surrounding sections."

Simple, yet effective, Picard noted. If his team, or Riker's, attempted to enter the room, their adversaries would have several seconds to fire indiscriminately into the crowd of Dokaalan hostages providing unwilling cover for the Satarrans in disguise.

There had to be another way.

Tapping his combadge again, the captain said, "Picard to *Enterprise*. What's the status of the transporters?"

Counselor Troi replied, *"Still questionable, Captain. Engineering has had some success transporting test cylinders, but they're still not satisfied with computer simulations on living beings."*

The memory of the last time he had ordered the use of transporters, during the *Enterprise*'s first rescue mission after arriving in the Dokaalan system, was still fresh and painful in Picard's mind. Twenty-seven lives had been lost to that order, and though logic argued that those people had been doomed even before his actions, their deaths still weighed on him.

Was this time any different? The safety of the people in the next room was hardly guaranteed, after all. They could very well die whether he attempted to save them or allowed Lorakin to dictate the terms of the situation to him. Picard was therefore faced with taking action or standing by and waiting for events to be determined for him.

That's no choice, he chided himself, falling back on the maxim that had guided him throughout his career.

"*Enterprise,* notify transporter room one to lock on to my signal." Entering commands to the tricorder's diminutive keypad until he found the information he wanted, he transmitted the unit's data to the ship. "I want you to put me inside the first minister's office."

"*Captain,*" the voice of Geordi La Forge replied, "*the transporters haven't been certified for humanoids.*" The worry was evident in his words. "*I can't guarantee the thing will work, sir.*"

Checking the setting on his phaser rifle, Picard replied, "I understand the risks, Mr. La Forge. Proceed on my responsibility."

Too arrogant, too old, and too careless?

The words he had spoken to Beverly Crusher one night over dinner echoed in his mind. Even before Starfleet had thrown him onto the professional and psychological examination table in the wake of the *Juno*'s loss, he had questioned not only his own fitness for command, but also his desire to continue in the role he had made his own for two-thirds of his life. The answer then was the same as it was now.

I think I'll stay on the job, anyway.

His attention was drawn to the voice of Commander Riker coming from his combadge. *"Request permission to accompany you, sir."*

"Negative, Number One," Picard replied. "Once I get inside, I'll draw their attention so you and Lieutenant Vale will bring your teams in through the doors. Besides, if I'm wrong, I'll need you here."

There was a noticeable pause before the first officer replied, *"Understood, sir."*

"Captain," Vale said, walking up to him with her phaser rifle cradled in both arms, "with seven of them in there, you'll need another hand."

Shaking his head, Picard replied, "Given the risks, I can't allow that, Lieutenant."

"Sir," the security chief said, "Starfleet general orders require starship captains to be accompanied by an armed escort when entering a hazardous situation."

Regarding her warily, the captain replied, "As I recall, that regulation only applies to officers of flag rank."

Her eyebrow rising in almost Vulcan-like fashion as the hint of a smile teased the corner of her mouth, Vale's voice nevertheless maintained a composed tenor. "Perhaps you're right, sir. I'll make it a point to review the manual when we're finished here."

There was no resisting the small smile creeping onto his own face. "Very well, Lieutenant. Let's go to work."

* * *

No sooner did the transporter beam release him than Picard exchange relieved looks with Vale, and he even made a show of patting himself down to ensure that nothing was missing.

"I seem to be in one piece," he offered, remembering to keep his voice low so as not to attract the notice of anyone outside the office. Tapping his combadge, he said, "Picard to *Enterprise*. Excellent work, Mr. La Forge. Stand by for the next stage."

"Good to hear your voice, Captain," the chief engineer replied. *"Standing by."*

"Vale to Commander Riker," the security chief said into her own combadge, "We're getting ready to move in, sir."

"Understood," Riker replied, and Picard noted the unfettered relief in the first officer's voice.

Always the mother hen, the captain mused silently as he moved across the office of the first minister. The door leading to the council meeting chambers was closed, thankfully, offering the two Starfleet officers some small measure of concealment.

Picard could not keep himself from looking over the empty office, suddenly struck by the tragedy of its occupant's loss. Hjatyn, by all accounts, had been a remarkable leader who had triumphed in the face of unimaginable strife. The legacy he had forged would live on for generations, especially if Picard himself had anything to say about it.

He felt his pulse quickening and his muscles tensing in anticipation, adrenaline beginning to fuel his body for the coming action. There was no reason to delay any longer, he decided. Taking a final look at the tricorder

Vale had given him to pinpoint his first target, he nodded to the lieutenant.

"On three," he whispered, then began to count and when he reached three he said, "Now, Mr. La Forge."

At the same time Vale pulled the door open and Picard pushed out of the office, phaser rifle up and sighting in on the first Dokaalan he saw holding a weapon. His peripheral vision registered the telltale signs of transporter beams as sixteen columns of energy dissolved and disappeared, but he gave it no further thought as he fired without hesitation, the power level on his phaser set high enough that a single shot was more than enough to incapacitate his target.

Even as the first opponent fell he was firing at a second, and then he sensed Vale moving to his right and taking aim on another of the disguised Satarrans.

Then the room erupted into chaos as both sets of doors leading from the council chambers burst open and the *Enterprise* away teams flooded into the room. They began to spread out as they entered, weapons leveled on the five remaining Dokaalan. All five froze in place, obviously stunned at the sudden overwhelming nature of the assault.

"No!" Picard heard a voice yell, the one he now knew belonged to Lorakin, and the captain swung his phaser until the disguised Satarran, still presenting the image of First Minister Hjatyn, was centered in his sights.

"Enough!" he yelled, his finger beginning to depress the weapon's firing stud, but it was obvious that Lorakin had been caught completely off guard by the swift and decisive raid. Defeat and anguish were clearly visible even in the artificially created Dokaalan maroon eyes as he raised his hands in surrender, allowing his own disruptor to slip from his fingers and clatter uselessly to the deck.

Taking a moment to regain some degree of composure, Lorakin nodded slowly. "Excellently played, Captain. We were under the clearly mistaken impression that your transporter systems were inoperative." He motioned to his left forearm, which Picard knew was where the control pad for the Satarran's mimicking shroud was located.

Picard nodded in assent and Lorakin touched his forearm. Immediately the façade of Hjatyn disappeared and was replaced by the now familiar black and silver exoskeleton. The Satarran next reached for his neck and pulled back the garment's hood and mask to reveal his natural pinkish complexion. Narrow, golden eyes filled with pain and sorrow looked back at him.

"I will order my people to surrender immediately and without condition, Captain," Lorakin said.

"And I will see to it that they are treated properly," Picard replied. With members of Vale's security team now flanking the Satarran leader, the captain lowered his own phaser rifle. To Vale and Riker he said, "Number One, please see to the rest of the operation. Alert Dr. Crusher of any injuries requiring her attention. Lieutenant, have the Satarrans transferred to detention on the ship. Since they're going to be our guests until we get back to Federation space, make whatever long-term arrangements for their security and comfort you see fit."

As the officers acknowledged their orders and set about their assigned tasks, Lorakin looked to Picard once more. "What will happen to us now, Captain?"

"I honestly don't know," Picard replied. As neither race was a Federation member, if the Dokaalan wished to hold the Satarrans and try them under their own system of justice, the captain was obligated to respect that decision.

Of course, considering the undeniable disruption to their leadership cadre caused by the Satarrans, they could well decide that restoring order to their own society took precedence over dealing with this band of criminals. Should that be the case, Picard would then remand the Satarran renegades to the nearest Federation starbase and let the Starfleet legal experts sort things out.

"And my people?" he asked. "What becomes of them?"

Stepping closer, Picard said, "As I said to you before, the Federation will almost certainly offer whatever assistance they are able, be it working to solve your homeworld's environmental issues or relocating your people to another planet suitable for your species."

Lorakin shook his head. "You would do all of that, despite what has happened here?"

As he signaled for the security officers to take the Satarran out of the council chambers and to one of the shuttlecraft for the transfer back to the *Enterprise*, Picard offered Lorakin a tired, humorless, saddened smile.

"Yes," the captain said, "we will do all of that, because that is what we do."

Chapter Twenty-five

"WELL, DATA," LA FORGE SAID as he unhooked the optical cabling from the side of his friend's head and closed the small access panel located beneath his hairline, "it's official. Your neural net is completely repaired. Welcome back."

"My own internal sensors would seem to agree with that assessment," Data replied as he stepped out of his diagnostic alcove. "Thank you for your assistance."

Coiling the optical cable so he could return it to his toolkit, the chief engineer smiled. "You know I couldn't resist taking a look for myself." In truth, Data's own repair efforts, as laborious as they had been, had actually required little in the way of improvements. The android's positronic network was now operating at its normal efficiency, and La Forge had found no signs of fault in any of the rerouting Data had done. His friend was as good as new.

"I have been meaning to ask," Data said abruptly, "are you . . . all right?"

The question caught the engineer off guard. "What?"

"I know that you were held captive by the Dokaalan and were forced to devise your own escape," Data said, "but I have not yet inquired as to your condition. I am doing so now."

"Wow," La Forge said. "I mean, yeah, I'm fine, Data. Thanks for asking."

Though he did not say so, he was relieved that his friend had posed the question. When they had begun their mission to the Dokaalan sector, he had been burdened with worries that without his emotion chip, Data would remain cold and uninterested in connecting with the crew on a personal level.

Not just the crew, La Forge admitted, but with *me.*

During his tenure on the *Enterprise,* he had developed many close friendships, many of which would endure long after his time on this vessel had passed. None of them, however, resonated with him as much as did the bond he shared with Data. With the removal of Data's emotion chip, La Forge had worried that its sudden absence, after having been integrated with the android's sophisticated network of software and positronic network for years, would have some sort of debilitating effect as his friend worked to adjust to life or, rather, functionality without the chip.

One of the most immediately noticeable aftereffects of the chip's removal had been Data's apparent loss of interest in many of the hobbies he had acquired over the years. By his own admission, the android no longer needed such diversions, opting instead to devote time once spent in pursuit of those activities to his regular duties.

Also noticeable was a lack of attachment to any personal recollections of past experiences. Data possessed memories of those instances, of course, but without the emotion chip he was now only able to recall them much like one would access information from a computer. Where was the camaraderie they had shared over the years? Was it gone forever, or at least until such time as Starfleet saw fit to return the chip to Data?

With but a single question, however, Data had alleviated some of that concern. Even if some parts of it would have to be re-created, La Forge was relieved to know that their friendship seemed to have remained intact.

"During the reconfiguration of my neural net," Data said, recalling the engineer from his reverie, "I reviewed my internal archives, concentrating on the missions and experiences we have shared together."

"Remembering the good old days?" La Forge asked, offering a smile as he spoke.

"That is an accurate analogy, yes," the android replied. "I found that my review generated a sense of . . . familiarity. It is a response that seems to recur whenever we converse or perform our duties together. I wanted to acknowledge that to you."

"Thanks, Data," La Forge said, patting his friend's shoulder as he dropped the optical cable back into his toolkit. "I like you, too."

Cocking his head slightly to the left in that manner he employed when he was curious about something, Data asked, "Do you believe it is a result of low-level software modifications resulting from my prolonged use of the emotion chip?"

Pausing to consider the idea, La Forge finally shrugged after a moment. "I wouldn't rule it out. It's like I said before. There's no reason to believe that the chip didn't affect your entire positronic network while you were using it. When everything is said and done, it really isn't anything more than hardware and software enhancement. Some residual effects to the overall system are likely, even after a single component's removal."

Data nodded in agreement. "I would like to test that theory by continuing to engage in activities of mutual interest. Perhaps after your evening meal, you would care to accompany me to the holodeck? I had intended to resume my review of the latest additions to the program database."

"Sounds like a plan," La Forge said, a mischievous smile teasing the corners of his mouth. "Once more unto the breach, and all that?"

"Shakespeare," Data replied as the pair began crossing the floor of engineering on their way to the exit. "But, Geordi, the program for *Henry V* has been on file since Stardate 43462.5. That is hardly new."

There was no way for La Forge to resist laughing at his friend's response. "Data, emotion chip or not, you're still the best straight man I've ever known."

"Thank you," Data replied. "I think."

Resilience.

The single word continued to resonate in Picard's mind as he, Riker, and Troi stood in the chambers of the Zahanzei Council. All around him, the business of governing the Dokaalan colony was under way as those entrusted with the mantle of leadership forged ahead with the process of returning their society to something approaching normalcy.

Standing alone in the rear of the council chamber, Picard was content to wait for Myjerol, who had been appointed temporary first minister until such time as a new round of democratic elections could be held to replace the council members lost to the Satarrans. The captain could see that the Dokaalan was already quite busy even in his provisional role as the leader of his people. As he watched the procedures of governmental rule unfold around him, however, Picard became aware of someone moving to stand next to him. Glancing to his right, he saw the smiling face of Dr. Crusher.

"Credit for your thoughts," she said.

Keeping his voice low, the captain replied, "I'm just standing here thinking that I'm leaving these people in a worse state than we found them."

"You don't really believe that, do you?" Crusher asked, and Picard noted the shocked tone in her quiet voice. "If not for us, the Satarrans would still be using these people, for who knows how long before they finally decided the Dokaalan were of no more use to them. You saved this colony from monstrous treachery, Jean-Luc, and you've provided them with assistance that will help them realize their dreams generations ahead of schedule. That's pretty good for one mission, if you ask me."

"I did all of that?" he said, though his tone was teasing.

Crusher nodded. "You're damned right. Not to mention the fact that you introduced them to a huge, wonderfully diverse universe surrounding them and, most of all, you proved that universe to be welcoming. You restored their hope, and it was wonderful to see."

"I only hope Starfleet Command shares your confidence," Picard said. He had not yet transmitted his report back to Earth, opting instead to wait until they had departed the colony and the *Enterprise* was free of the asteroid field. The corner of his mouth curled upward in a wan smile as he added, "It would be interesting to be there when Admiral Nechayev reads it. I'm sure she has several people already in mind with whom to share it."

"To hell with Starfleet," Crusher snapped, "and to hell with anyone who can't see what you've done here. If that includes Nechayev, then so be it. I know the truth, and so does everyone on that ship and in this colony."

She placed a hand on his arm and, in a reaction that was uncharacteristic of him, he allowed the gesture of affection to remain. A smile warmed his features as his gaze met hers, once again comforted by the compassion and support of this, one of his oldest and closest friends.

Perhaps, he decided, it was time to start allowing himself to be uplifted by such encouragement from the people he cared most about, rather than letting himself wallow in the shame and self-doubt that had come at the hands of bureaucrats and diplomats thousands of light-years away. Everything he needed to be certain of his decisions and actions was here now, with him.

"Thank you, Beverly," he said, reaching over to pat her hand with his own.

Looking up, he saw Riker and Troi approaching. His first officer nodded to him. "The last shuttle just departed the colony, sir," he said. "We're the last ones."

"Excellent," Picard replied. "All that remains is to take our leave of the Dokaalan." He indicated the council members and their various staff assistants milling about the large conference table. "I imagine they're more than ready to return to something resembling their normal lives."

Looking to the far side of the conference table, the captain watched as Minister Myjerol reviewed a report of some kind brought to him by one of his assistants. Once he was finished, he handed the report back to the other Dokaalan and turned to cross the chamber floor toward the Starfleet officers.

"As you can see," the minister said, "we have much work ahead of us, but eventually all will be as it was."

Nodding, Picard replied, "The Federation stands ready to assist you in any way possible, Minister. I have already contacted Starfleet and they have dispatched a team of engineering specialists who will help you see to any repairs required of the colony, as well as constructing more permanent facilities to see your people through until the terraforming process is complete." The *U.S.S. Musgrave*, carrying a team from the Starfleet Corps of Engineers, would not be here for several more weeks, but when they arrived Picard knew that the group of engineering specialists would be more than able to see to the Dokaalan's needs.

"I have also spoken with Healer Nentafa," Dr. Crusher said. "He has provided me with all of the relevant medical information that will allow us to continue the research we've begun here. Perhaps one day, we will develop a medicine that will allow you to travel outside your system. I know the Federation would greet you with open arms."

Myjerol smiled at that. "Nentafa has informed me of that, as well. He has even said that he already has volunteers to test any treatment you devise. Apparently, there are many who are willing to take such risk in order to see what lies beyond our own world." Reaching out to take the doctor's hand in his own, he added, "However, should that prove impossible, I would ask that you not consider it a failure on your part. Even if Dokaa decides that we are meant to remain here, your efforts on our behalf will not be forgotten."

Her eyes welling up at the words, Crusher nodded respectfully. "Thank you, Minister."

"You'll also be happy to know that Terraform Command is sending out a team of experts," Riker said after a moment. "Their mission will be to help ensure that the changes Ijuuka has been put through aren't permanent or damaging, and they'll continue what Data and your people have started."

Picard added, "According to the preliminary reports we've already received from them, they're confident the alterations made by the Satarrans can be reversed and Data's original idea can be implemented."

Data, working with the remaining members of Science Minister Creij's team and in coordination with Terraform Command, had developed a theory to counteract the changes introduced by the Satarrans, as well as to ensure that the planet's atmosphere would allow for the same life-sustaining effects as the radiation provided by the asteroid field. It would require a strategy not unlike the android's original plan, and the ultimate results would take several more years to realize, but all parties were confident that the effort would be successful.

"If it is anything like the vision offered by Hjatyn and Creij," Myjerol offered, "we will one day live in a world of beauty perhaps unparalleled even by Dokaal itself."

Then his expression sobered a bit. "Of course, only they would be able to tell us for certain. They will be missed by everyone in our community."

"Ijuuka will provide a lasting monument to them and to all they contributed to your society, Minister," Troi offered. "I can think of no better way to honor them."

Nodding, the Dokaalan's blue features seemed to brighten as he considered the counselor's words. After a moment, he returned his attention to Picard. "As for the Satarrans, what will become of them?"

"They will be remanded to Federation authorities once we reach our nearest starbase," Picard replied. "After that, I honestly don't know what will happen." With no treaties between the Federation and the Satarrans and neither they nor the Dokaalan being a member world, the captain was not sure that anything could be done, at least from a legal standpoint, except to transfer the Satarran renegades into the custody of their own authorities. Picard knew that such an action was equivalent to releasing them altogether, but there was little he could do about that.

"I do not consider them evil for what they did," Myjerol said. "I understand that they were acting on behalf of their people, just as we have been. While I find tremendous fault with their methods, I can do nothing but empathize with their situation and wish them good fortune in the days ahead. I only wish that there was something we could do to help them."

Remarkable, Picard thought. Despite everything the Satarrans had put them through, the Dokaalan leader still found a way to be merciful and benevolent toward their would-be oppressors. After all that had happened here, it was a sign of wisdom and maturity that the captain found particularly comforting.

Smiling in approval, he said, "We have extended another offer to assist them, as well, though Starfleet tells me the Satarran government has not yet responded." With any luck, they would, perhaps avoiding another situation such as the one they had created here.

"Well, then perhaps Dokaa will smile upon them, as well," Myjerol replied.

As one of the ministers approached him, carrying what appeared to be a large parcel, Picard's attention was drawn to the signal of his combadge. Tapping the unit, he said, "Picard here."

"Lieutenant Vale, sir," said the voice of the *Enterprise's* security chief, whom Picard had left in command of the bridge while he was off ship. *"Just informing you that all shuttlecraft and personnel have returned to the ship, and engineering reports we can get under way at any time."*

"Thank you, Lieutenant," Picard replied. "We're almost finished here and should be departing shortly."

"Take your time, sir," Vale said, and the captain noted a somewhat lighter tone in her voice. *"I think I might just be getting used to sitting in this chair. Enterprise out."*

As the connection was severed, Riker made no effort to conceal a teasing grin. "Sounds like she might be after your job, sir."

Without batting an eye, the captain replied, "Or yours, Number One."

He turned back to Myjerol as the Dokaalan accepted the bulky item from his assistant. Picard now saw that it was unmistakably a large book, composed of hundreds of pages and bound within a sheath of some heavy woven material that the captain did not recognize.

"A parting gift, if you will allow me, Captain," the minister said, offering the book to Picard. "I solicited the services of your Commander Data to translate it into your language, but I thought it important for it to be represented in the form closest to what the First Minister intended."

Taking the tome gingerly in his hands, Picard studied the simple cover, which bore only a single word: *Hjatyn.*

"What is it?" he asked.

"His journal," Myjerol replied. "Hjatyn kept a chronicle of everything he experienced, from the days before Dokaal's destruction up until the final entry, recorded just days before his death." Reverently placing one hand on the book, he added, "There is nothing like it in our society, and we would be honored if you carried it with you and allowed it to serve as the formal introduction of our people to yours."

Stroking the cover with the tips of his fingers, Picard found himself awestruck by this gesture. The entire epic history of these people, as recorded by someone who had witnessed it all firsthand, was a tremendous gift and a marvelous means of telling others the remarkable story of the Dokaalan.

"The honor is mine, Minister Myjerol," Picard said, his voice heavy with emotion. He reached out to take the Dokaalan's hand. "Good luck to you and your people, sir."

"We wish you and your crew a safe journey, Captain," the Dokaalan replied, "and hope that you will one day return to see the fruits of our combined labors."

Buoyed by Myjerol's unfettered compassion and gratitude, Picard realized he now felt more alive and confident than he had in weeks, more so than even a few moments ago when Beverly had offered her heartening words.

In fact, even if his next mission was destined to be as unglamorous as this one was supposed to have been, that did not matter. For the first time since the encounter with the demon ship, he allowed himself to believe that his future, and that of the rest of the *Enterprise* crew, had finally begun to burn a bit brighter.

For the last time, Picard bowed his head formally to the Dokaalan leader. "Minister Myjerol, I for one will most certainly look forward to that day."

About the Authors

DAYTON WARD has been a fan of *Star Trek* since conception (his, not the show's). After serving for eleven years in the U.S. Marine Corps, he discovered the private sector and the piles of cash to be made there as a software engineer. He got his start in professional writing by having stories selected for each of Pocket Books' first three *Star Trek: Strange New Worlds* anthologies. In addition to his various writing projects with Kevin Dilmore, Dayton is the author of the *Star Trek* novel *In the Name of Honor* and the science fiction novel *The Last World War.* Though he currently lives in Kansas City with his wife, Michi, Dayton is a Florida native and still maintains a torrid long-distance romance with his beloved Tampa Bay Buccaneers. Readers interested in contacting Dayton or learning more about his writing are encouraged to venture to his Internet cobweb collection at www.daytonward.com.

* * *

After 15 years as a newspaper reporter and editor, **KEVIN DILMORE** turned his full attention to his free-lance writing career in 2003. Since 1997, he has been a contributing writer to *Star Trek Communicator,* writing news stories and personality profiles for the bimonthly publication of the Official *Star Trek* Fan Club. Look for Kevin's interviews with some of *Star Trek*'s most popular authors in volumes of the *Star Trek* Signature Editions. On the fictional side of things, his story "The Road to Edos" was published last year in the *Star Trek: New Frontier* anthology *No Limits.* With Dayton Ward, he has also written a story for the anthology *Star Trek: Tales of the Dominion War* and seven installments of the continuing e-book series *Star Trek: S.C.E.* with more to come. A graduate of the University of Kansas, Kevin lives in Prairie Village, Kansas, with his wife, Michelle, and their three daughters.

The saga continues in June 2004 with

STAR TREK®

A TIME TO LOVE

by
Robert Greenberger

Turn the page for an electrifying
preview of *A Time to Love*. . . .

Picard's dark thoughts were abruptly banished by a chime coming from the right arm of his chair. A flashing light indicated a communication from Starfleet Command, so by the time Christine Vale announced a message was coming in, Picard was already out of his chair. He crossed the bridge and headed for his ready room, his pace increasing with every step.

Once at his desk, he adjusted the angle of the desktop viewer and activated the screen. The blue field with the Starfleet symbol was quickly replaced by the visage of Admiral Upton, a balding, gruff officer Picard could barely remember. Quickly, he mentally sifted through the organizational chart and remembered that Upton was with cultural affairs.

"Picard," Upton said by way of greeting.

"Admiral Upton, good to see you," Picard said, a professional smile playing on his face.

"Are you familiar with Delta Sigma IV?"

"Yes, sir," Picard responded, unfazed by the lack of pleasantries. "It's a few parsecs from our position. I believe they're celebrating their centennial as a successful colony world." That was all he recalled, and that only because it was mentioned on one of the newsfeeds he had read during recent downtime between missions.

"Well, they've just experienced their first murder in a century, and it's our fault," Upton said, his expression grim. His bushy, gray-streaked eyebrows looked like storm clouds over his blue eyes.

Picard frowned as the admiral elaborated on the nature of the mission. It was important, to be sure, but it would be personally trying as well, for one member of his crew in particular.

"You do realize the position this puts Commander Riker in," Picard said, when he finally could get a word in.

"I'm not worried about Riker. His issues have been considered," was all Upton would say.

Knowing it would be unwise to press the point, Picard changed the subject. "This is a higher profile mission than the last few," he noted. "Are we being unleashed?"

Upton paused before replying. *"Actually, this is a lousy mission. We're going to look bad regardless of how it turns out. Just how bad we look is in your hands."*

"Very well, Admiral," Picard replied neutrally. "We'll lay in a course immediately."

"Starfleet out," was the only reply, and the screen shifted back to its standby image. Picard sat back for a moment and let everything sink in. He reached for his viewer, entered in a few quick commands, and then rose.

Moving to the replicator for a cup of Earl Grey tea, Picard tapped his combadge. "Picard to Data."

Instantly, the android responded.

"Mr. Data, I've just routed our latest mission packet to you. Please prepare to give senior staff a presentation in thirty minutes."

"Acknowledged."

That accomplished, the captain once again tapped his badge and summoned Riker to the ready room. This was not a conversation he was looking forward to, but one that he wanted to handle in private, before the rest of the crew learned of the new mission. Seating himself on the couch near a tome of his beloved Shakespeare, Picard sipped the hot liquid and tried to figure how much time had elapsed since he last longed for a new mission. Certainly less than thirty minutes, and he was reminded once more that one needed to be careful about what one wished for.

Upton left his office and took the turbolift to the floor housing a private room. Only admirals were given access to the space, filled with antique furniture salvaged from around the globe. The gleaming wood and brass always had a faint smell of polish, and voices were muted by the plush carpet found nowhere else in the headquarters building. It was a refuge away from staff, from cadets, even from captains light-years away.

The room was capable of holding only two dozen people at most, and usually had less than half that at any one time. However, it was a much desired refuge, and during the worst of times, it was where admirals could be found collecting their thoughts or just grabbing a quick nap when time permitted. The tradition began over a hundred years earlier when the building was repaired after an alien probe nearly destroyed the planet.

He entered the sanctuary and moved with practiced ease past three other admirals seated in a semicircle. He went straight to a sideboard, where he poured a generous amount of amber liquid into a cut crystal glass and then swirled it around three times. Traditional Scotch, there was nothing like it, as his father always used to say.

He took one small sip, let it rest in his mouth for a full ten seconds, and then swallowed. The ritual complete, he turned to face the others, who were debating some point of legislation that had just been passed by the Federation Council. Upton lowered himself into a comfortable wing chair and sipped in silence. The others—Admirals Janeway, Nechayev, and Stek—continued their discussion, with mere nods of their heads in acknowledgment of Upton's presence.

Finally, Stek, a senior Vulcan responsible for technological development, asked Upton, "How was the mission received?"

"Picard's a career man. He knows better than to complain."

"It's a pretty bad assignment. I wouldn't want it," Janeway admitted.

Upton smiled coldly at her. "That's about what he deserves right now."

"So, if he didn't complain, what did he say?" asked Nechayev, the smallest of the four, but the one with perhaps the most forceful personality.

"What do you think? He brought up Riker's issues."

"I'm sorry, I don't follow," said Janeway, newly promoted after successfully returning the *U.S.S. Voyager,* which had been lost in the Delta Quadrant for seven years. She was by far the youngest admiral in attendance.

"With Kyle Riker missing, there are questions we need answered, and Will Riker is his son."

Janeway's look of surprise amused the older admiral. He took another small sip of the aged Scotch and enjoyed feeling it travel down to his stomach.

"Do you know Riker?"

"Actually, Alynna, we had one date at the Academy," Janeway admitted, shifting uncomfortably in her chair. "Nothing came of it, and we never stayed in touch."

"Well," Alynna Nechayev added, "there's little love lost between those two. They've barely spoken over the years, from what I understand."

"But I do know Will helped his dad once years ago," Janeway added. "When the father was suspected of some crime."

"The reunion was brief and of little consequence, it seems," the Vulcan noted. "However, personal conflicts aside, Riker has proven to be a capable man. I do not fully understand why he has refused command."

"Never felt ready, or didn't want something less prestigious than the *Enterprise,*" Nechayev guessed.

"Well, now Picard's holding him back. Maybe we need to force his hand," Upton said. He ignored Nechayev's look and admired the light reflecting off the crystal glass in his hand.

"If you feel that strongly, Jack, should the *Enterprise* be the one for this mission?"

"Kathryn, I know you've taken Picard's side in this," Upton said, "but trust me, any officer who has been through what he has, needs to be watched. But yes, he's closest, and he's come through for us repeatedly on these diplomatic fiascos. He just needs to know we're watching closely to make sure he doesn't get himself into trouble. Again."

Upton stifled the urge to roll his eyes at the disapproving glares that greeted his comments. Was he the only one there who could face the truth?

"All command officers get thoroughly evaluated," Stek said. "Those found underperforming get reassigned."

Et tu, Stek? Upton thought with disgust. Oh for Pity's sake, the man is reckless. Look how he lost *Stargazer* and crashed the *Enterprise.*"

"Actually," Nechayev interrupted, "he's always put the Federation first. We might disagree with how he has handled his assignments—I certainly have—but in the end, he and his crew uphold our ideals. Better than most."

"Good as Picard has been in the past," Upton said unhappily, "right now we have to face the fact that he's a liability. Member worlds have raised concerns with the Council and it's damaged our ability to function. At the first sign of trouble, we need to act decisively. I already have Braddock readying a squadron, just in case."

"With or without all the facts," Janeway noted archly.

"We let the facts speak for themselves," Upton replied.

"Yet, you let him keep the *Enterprise,*" Janeway said, her voice deepening. "You kept his senior crew intact, and you've given him this diplomatic assignment. If the Council has concerns, why give him this? Especially with Kyle Riker in the mix?"

"Ever meet Riker the elder?"

"Yes, briefly, during my Academy days," she said.

"Stubborn and pigheaded," Upton said. "A man of such virtue as Picard should be the one to rein him in. It's also a chance to see if Picard's learned anything these last few months."

He purposely ignored the frown that marred Janeway's features.

Don't miss

STAR TREK
A TIME TO LOVE

**Available June 2004 wherever paperback
books are sold!**

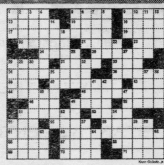